MW00325865

MAYHEM

(AND HERRING)

(A European Voyage Cozy Mystery —Book Six)

BLAKE PIERCE

Blake Pierce

Blake Pierce is the USA Today bestselling author of the RILEY PAGE mystery series, which includes seventeen books. Blake Pierce is also the author of the MACKENZIE WHITE mystery series, comprising fourteen books; of the AVERY BLACK mystery series, comprising six books; of the KERI LOCKE mystery series, comprising five books; of the MAKING OF RILEY PAIGE mystery series, comprising six books; of the KATE WISE mystery series, comprising seven books; of the CHLOE FINE psychological suspense mystery, comprising six books; of the JESSE HUNT psychological suspense thriller series, comprising nineteen books; of the AU PAIR psychological suspense thriller series, comprising three books; of the ZOE PRIME mystery series, comprising six books; of the ADELE SHARP mystery series, comprising thirteen books, of the EUROPEAN VOYAGE cozy mystery series, comprising four books; of the new LAURA FROST FBI suspense thriller, comprising six books (and counting); of the new ELLA DARK FBI suspense thriller, comprising nine books (and counting); of the A YEAR IN EUROPE cozy mystery series, comprising nine books, of the AVA GOLD mystery series, comprising six books (and counting); and of the RACHEL GIFT mystery series, comprising six books (and counting).

An avid reader and lifelong fan of the mystery and thriller genres, Blake loves to hear from you, so please feel free to visit www.blakepierceauthor.com to learn more and stay in touch.

Copyright © 2021 by Blake Pierce. All rights reserved. Except as permitted under the U.S. Copyright Act of 1976, no part of this publication may be reproduced, distributed or transmitted in any form or by any means, or stored in a database or retrieval system, without the prior permission of the author. This ebook is licensed for your personal enjoyment only. This ebook may not be re-sold or given away to other people. If you would like to share this book with another person, please purchase an additional copy for each recipient. If you're reading this book and did not purchase it, or it was not purchased for your use only, then please return it and purchase your own copy. Thank you for respecting the hard work of this author. This is a work of fiction. Names, characters, businesses, organizations, places, events, and incidents either are the product of the author's imagination or are used fictionally. Any resemblance to actual persons, living or dead, is entirely coincidental. Jacket image Copyright Harsh Gada, used under license from Shutterstock.com.
ISBN: 978-1-0943-7585-4

BOOKS BY BLAKE PIERCE

RACHEL GIFT MYSTERY SERIES
HER LAST WISH (Book #1)
HER LAST CHANCE (Book #2)
HER LAST HOPE (Book #3)
HER LAST FEAR (Book #4)
HER LAST CHOICE (Book #5)
HER LAST BREATH (Book #6)

AVA GOLD MYSTERY SERIES
CITY OF PREY (Book #1)
CITY OF FEAR (Book #2)
CITY OF BONES (Book #3)
CITY OF GHOSTS (Book #4)
CITY OF DEATH (Book #5)
CITY OF VICE (Book #6)

A YEAR IN EUROPE
A MURDER IN PARIS (Book #1)
DEATH IN FLORENCE (Book #2)
VENGEANCE IN VIENNA (Book #3)
A FATALITY IN SPAIN (Book #4)

ELLA DARK FBI SUSPENSE THRILLER
GIRL, ALONE (Book #1)
GIRL, TAKEN (Book #2)
GIRL, HUNTED (Book #3)
GIRL, SILENCED (Book #4)
GIRL, VANISHED (Book 5)
GIRL ERASED (Book #6)
GIRL, FORSAKEN (Book #7)
GIRL, TRAPPED (Book #8)
GIRL, EXPENDABLE (Book #9)

LAURA FROST FBI SUSPENSE THRILLER
ALREADY GONE (Book #1)

ALREADY SEEN (Book #2)
ALREADY TRAPPED (Book #3)
ALREADY MISSING (Book #4)
ALREADY DEAD (Book #5)
ALREADY TAKEN (Book #6)

EUROPEAN VOYAGE COZY MYSTERY SERIES
MURDER (AND BAKLAVA) (Book #1)
DEATH (AND APPLE STRUDEL) (Book #2)
CRIME (AND LAGER) (Book #3)
MISFORTUNE (AND GOUDA) (Book #4)
CALAMITY (AND A DANISH) (Book #5)
MAYHEM (AND HERRING) (Book #6)

ADELE SHARP MYSTERY SERIES
LEFT TO DIE (Book #1)
LEFT TO RUN (Book #2)
LEFT TO HIDE (Book #3)
LEFT TO KILL (Book #4)
LEFT TO MURDER (Book #5)
LEFT TO ENVY (Book #6)
LEFT TO LAPSE (Book #7)
LEFT TO VANISH (Book #8)
LEFT TO HUNT (Book #9)
LEFT TO FEAR (Book #10)
LEFT TO PREY (Book #11)
LEFT TO LURE (Book #12)
LEFT TO CRAVE (Book #13)

THE AU PAIR SERIES
ALMOST GONE (Book#1)
ALMOST LOST (Book #2)
ALMOST DEAD (Book #3)

ZOE PRIME MYSTERY SERIES
FACE OF DEATH (Book#1)
FACE OF MURDER (Book #2)
FACE OF FEAR (Book #3)
FACE OF MADNESS (Book #4)
FACE OF FURY (Book #5)

FACE OF DARKNESS (Book #6)

A JESSIE HUNT PSYCHOLOGICAL SUSPENSE SERIES
THE PERFECT WIFE (Book #1)
THE PERFECT BLOCK (Book #2)
THE PERFECT HOUSE (Book #3)
THE PERFECT SMILE (Book #4)
THE PERFECT LIE (Book #5)
THE PERFECT LOOK (Book #6)
THE PERFECT AFFAIR (Book #7)
THE PERFECT ALIBI (Book #8)
THE PERFECT NEIGHBOR (Book #9)
THE PERFECT DISGUISE (Book #10)
THE PERFECT SECRET (Book #11)
THE PERFECT FAÇADE (Book #12)
THE PERFECT IMPRESSION (Book #13)
THE PERFECT DECEIT (Book #14)
THE PERFECT MISTRESS (Book #15)
THE PERFECT IMAGE (Book #16)
THE PERFECT VEIL (Book #17)
THE PERFECT INDISCRETION (Book #18)
THE PERFECT RUMOR (Book #19)

CHLOE FINE PSYCHOLOGICAL SUSPENSE SERIES
NEXT DOOR (Book #1)
A NEIGHBOR'S LIE (Book #2)
CUL DE SAC (Book #3)
SILENT NEIGHBOR (Book #4)
HOMECOMING (Book #5)
TINTED WINDOWS (Book #6)

KATE WISE MYSTERY SERIES
IF SHE KNEW (Book #1)
IF SHE SAW (Book #2)
IF SHE RAN (Book #3)
IF SHE HID (Book #4)
IF SHE FLED (Book #5)
IF SHE FEARED (Book #6)
IF SHE HEARD (Book #7)

BEFORE HE STALKS (Book #13)
BEFORE HE HARMS (Book #14)

AVERY BLACK MYSTERY SERIES
CAUSE TO KILL (Book #1)
CAUSE TO RUN (Book #2)
CAUSE TO HIDE (Book #3)
CAUSE TO FEAR (Book #4)
CAUSE TO SAVE (Book #5)
CAUSE TO DREAD (Book #6)

KERI LOCKE MYSTERY SERIES
A TRACE OF DEATH (Book #1)
A TRACE OF MURDER (Book #2)
A TRACE OF VICE (Book #3)
A TRACE OF CRIME (Book #4)
A TRACE OF HOPE (Book #5)

CHAPTER ONE

For a stunned moment, London Rose felt as though she might faint. *Keep it together,* she told herself. *Now is no time to fall apart.*

But how could she even be sure that what was happening was real? *Is this another dream?* she wondered.

She had dreamed about this very thing happening plenty of times.

But no, this didn't seem at all like a dream. Besides, the woman she'd seen in her dreams still had bright red hair. The wavy, shoulder-length hair of the woman just ahead of her was snow-white.

Even so, there was no mistaking this woman's blue-eyed, smiling face

It certainly seems real, London thought.

Facing her some six feet away on a wooden dock on a small Swedish island was someone London hadn't seen for about 20 years.

"Mom?" London said.

"Yes, I believe you said that before, London," the woman said with an impish grin that London remembered from childhood. "It's been a long time, hasn't it? So are we going to hug or what?"

London hesitated. She wasn't sure why. Whenever she'd tried to imagine this reunion, a hug had always seemed pretty much automatic, even perfectly natural. But right now, hugging suddenly seemed almost like a weird thing to do.

Of course, the circumstances themselves were pretty weird.

In spite of her confusion and the garbled thoughts running through her mind, London took a few more steps forward, and so did Mom.

They wrapped their arms around each other.

They hugged, pulling each other close a bit clumsily and not especially warmly, as if they didn't quite know how to go about this whole hugging business.

It certainly feels odd, London thought.

For one thing, she was startled that Mom seemed smaller than she'd remembered. It made sense, of course. After all, London had barely been a teenager the last time she had gotten a hug from her mother.

At the sound of a sharp yapping bark, they broke off the hug and

1

each stepped back a little.

Mom looked down at the little Yorkshire Terrier there on the dock, wagging his tail and staring up at her.

"Oh, my!" Mom said to London. "Does this adorable little beastie belong to you?"

London nodded and said, "His name is Sir Reggie."

Mom bent down and picked up the little animal. She rubbed her nose against his, and the little dog actually looked like he was smiling.

"*Sir* Reggie, eh?" she said with a giggle. "So he's actually been knighted! It's an honor to meet you, Sir Reggie!"

Sir Reggie snuggled up comfortably as Mom held him in her arms.

I guess hugging doesn't feel weird to him, London thought, with maybe a trace of jealousy.

But then, Sir Reggie didn't have the same troubled history with Mom that London did. To him, Barbara Rose was just another friendly stranger who was eager to give him attention.

Mom smiled at London and said, "You do look surprised to see me, dear. No wonder about that, I'm sure."

London almost choked at Mom's words.

That's like the world's biggest understatement, she thought, as a flurry of possible rejoinders occurred to her — *Oh, it's just been most of my lifetime ... A little bit unexpected after all these years ... We had all wondered ...*

She stopped herself from spitting out, *I didn't even know if you were still alive.*

Instead, she asked simply, "Aren't *you* surprised?"

"Well, a little, I guess," Mom said with a shrug. "I mean, I hadn't expected you to drop in right here in Lillberg this fine morning, at least not until a little while ago. The last I heard, you were on your way to Oslo."

London's chin dropped a little.

"How did you know ... ?" she began.

"That you were on your way to Oslo?" Mom laughed. "Oh, you'd be surprised at the things I know. I like to think of myself as very well-informed. I've kept track of your ship all during its voyage. But let's go find someplace to sit down and have a snack or some coffee or something."

Mom set Sir Reggie down, and London and her dog followed her along the dock toward the shore.

While she walked, London mentally replayed the events of the last

2

hour or so, trying to bring the present moment into sharper focus.

The cruise ship she'd been working aboard, the *Nachtmusik,* had left Copenhagen just yesterday. This morning the ship had been sailing smoothly along the Kattegat Sea between Denmark and Sweden. And just as Mom somehow knew, their next destination had been Oslo, Norway.

But a dozing pilot in a small boat had accidently rammed the *Nachtmusik,* and the ship had sustained some damage that needed immediate attention. Instead of trying to continue on their route, they'd sailed a short distance right here to await repairs in the village of Lillberg on the island of Skittmon, just off the coast of Sweden.

The ship had docked at a small pier, and the passengers and crew had been encouraged to go ashore and enjoy the charms of the island for as long as they were delayed here. London had just joined several people who came down the gangway onto the dock when an eerily familiar face had caught her eye. Her long-missing mom was right there among some villagers who had gathered to greet the ship.

And even though they had hugged after a fashion and talked a bit, London was still having trouble convincing herself that this was really happening. Worse, she couldn't collect her feelings enough to know how she really felt about this unplanned and unforeseen reunion.

What did I expect to feel? London wondered.

She'd surely anticipated feeling *something* if this ever happened. After all, she had only recently given up searching for Mom along every stop the *Nachtmusik* made on its tour of Europe. But right now, all she felt was jangled.

Did I expect to be overjoyed? she wondered.

Mom led London and Sir Reggie into a quaint little seaside café with cheerful, pastel wallpaper and pleasantly creaky wicker furniture. Fortunately, the waiter wasn't dismayed that a dog was with them. He cheerfully led them to a little table with three chairs where London, Mom, and Sir Reggie each sat down.

"Are you interested in some breakfast?" Mom asked.

"I've already eaten," London said.

"And Sir Reggie too?"

London nodded.

"No matter," Mom said. "It's always time for *fika* here in Sweden."

"Fika?" London asked.

"It's sort of like tea-time in England, except that it can happen multiple times a day, at pretty much any hour. The Swedes can be wonderfully laid-back that way. I recommend a nice cappuccino and a *mazarin.*"

With a nod toward Sir Reggie, Mom added, "Although I'm not so sure sweets are appropriate for our aristocratic friend."

No, probably not, London thought, remembering how sick Sir Reggie had gotten back in Copenhagen when he'd overindulged himself at a pastry festival.

"It's OK," London said. "I've got something for him."

She tossed him one of the specially made dog treats that she and other passengers carried around for him, and he caught it midair and munched it eagerly.

The waiter arrived, and Mom ordered for both of them in what sounded to London like flawless Swedish. London wished she had better mastery of Scandinavian languages.

As they waited for their order, Mom said to London, "So. Where do we begin catching up?"

London felt a bit lightheaded again and her mind boggled. She and Mom had only been reunited for a few minutes, but they'd already come to a hard part in their conversation.

Where do we begin indeed? she wondered.

CHAPTER TWO

London realized that she had no idea how to begin the conversation. What had she thought they might say, whenever she imagined this meeting?

No words came to her.

"Well?" Mom broke the silence, "What have you been up to all these years?"

London felt positively overwhelmed now.

"I guess I—I've been growing up," she replied.

Without a mother, she stopped herself from adding.

"Yes, you have grown up," Mom said with a nod of approval. "And a fine young lady you've turned out to be. And what a career you've had in the hospitality and travel industry! I've been following it all. You've worked at everything from bartending to bookkeeping until you started working as a tour hostess for Epoch World Cruise Lines. And now—you're the concierge aboard this unique ship!"

"Actually, I'm the social director," London said, correcting her.

"There's a difference?" Mom asked.

"Yeah, there kind of is," London told her. She felt tempted to add that she outranked the ship's actual concierge, but her mother just kept talking.

"Anyway, you haven't gotten married," Mom said, "Well, I can't say I blame you. Don't let anyone push you into anything you don't feel like doing. Parenthood is so awfully consuming."

London managed not to blurt out the obvious response.

How would you know?

She finally asked some questions that had been clamoring in her mind.

"Mom, where have you been all these years? Where did you go? Why did you leave us?"

Another silence fell as Mom drummed her fingers nervously on the tabletop.

"Yes … good questions," she muttered. "The truth is …"

Mom's expression clouded sadly. London sensed that she was trying to get up the courage to explain everything as honestly as she

5

could. But then Mom's eyes darted back and forth evasively.

"Well, I'm not quite sure of all that myself," she said.

"What do you mean?" London said with disbelief.

"My memories are … well, foggy," Mom said.

"Your memories of *what?*" London asked. "Your memories of leaving Dad and Tia and me?"

"Yes, I guess that is what I mean."

"Are you saying you've got amnesia or something?"

Mom tilted her head thoughtfully.

"I suppose that's one way of putting it," she said.

"Like you bumped your head and lost your memory?"

"Yes, it must have been something like that. Several years of it are … well, not all there."

London almost blurted, *I don't believe you.*

It seemed perfectly obvious that Mom didn't want to tell her the truth—whatever the truth might actually be. And try as she might to be patient and understanding, London was starting to get angry about it.

"Well, maybe I can refresh your memory," London said. "You had two small daughters and a husband, and we were all a very happy family. It was a crazy life, with both you and Dad working as flight attendants, but it was a good kind of crazy, and we had loads of fun and adventures. You took Tia and me traveling with you, and we grew up seeing the whole world and learning all kinds of wonderful things, including different languages."

Mom nodded and said, "And anyone can see you put those childhood experiences to excellent use. But you forgot to mention that your dad finally came out as gay."

"I was getting to that," London said. "The truth is, it was no big deal. You said yourself that you'd known Dad was gay long before even he did, and you were relieved that he was finally coming to terms with it, and you were happy for him. The two of you got a nice amicable divorce, and then nothing about our lives really changed."

"That's not exactly how I remember it," Mom said. Then she gave a deep sigh and added, "But you're right, he wasn't to blame. There were other reasons."

"What other reasons?" London asked.

Mom fell silent, and her expression turned more somber. Meanwhile, Sir Reggie looked worriedly back and forth between London and her mother, obviously sensing the tension in the air.

Just then the waiter came back with their cappuccinos and their pastries, which were shaped like miniature pies sprinkled with white powdered sugar and garnished with a raspberry and a blueberry. Mom smiled at the opportunity to change the subject.

"Try your *mazarin*, dear. I promise you'll love it."

Noticing an envious look from Sir Reggie, London took a bite of the *mazarin*, which was indeed very tasty, with a light, flaky crust and a moist almond-flavored filling. But then she put the pastry back on the plate. She wasn't exactly in the mood to really savor it.

"What now?" she asked Mom.

"What do you mean, what now?" Mom said.

"I mean, what happens now—between us? I'm not going to be in this little town for long, and I've got no idea what your plans are. Are we supposed to spend some time together somehow? Or are you going to just go running away again?"

Mom's eyebrows drew together into a hurt look.

"That's not a very nice way to put it," she said.

"I'm sorry, but I really need to know."

London and Mom locked eyes, as if they were challenging one another as to which of them would speak first. But before either one of them could say a word, London heard a light tapping sound nearby.

She turned and looked through the café's front window. Standing just outside was a dapper, white-haired man wearing a jaunty beret. He had gently clicked his knuckles on the window to get London's attention.

"Oh, my!" Mom said with a gasp. "Who is that charming gentleman at the window?"

"It's my boss," London said, waving to the man to come on inside.

"Really! Do you mean Jeremy Lapham himself, CEO of Epoch World Cruise Lines?"

She sure has been doing her homework, London thought.

"That's right," she said, stifling a sigh as Mr. Lapham came through the front door. It felt frustrating that she knew next to nothing about Mom—or at least nothing that would solve her own life's greatest mystery.

Walking toward their table, Mr. Lapham doffed his beret at the sight of London's mother and spoke to London.

"Well, well, well, London Rose," he said in excellent Swedish. "It seems that you've wasted no time getting to know the locals. Won't you introduce me to this charming Swedish lady?"

Mom giggled slightly, obviously delighted by Mr. Lapham's gallant

7

attention.

"Oh, I'm not actually a local," she said to him in English. "I'm an American like yourself. And I'm honored to make your acquaintance, Jeremy Lapham."

Mr. Lapham lifted Mom's hand to his lips and kissed it lightly.

"Ah, you have me at a disadvantage, madam," he said. "I do not yet know your name."

Stifling another sigh, London said, "Mr. Lapham, I'd like you to meet my mother, Barbara Rose."

Mr. Lapham's eyes widened with surprise.

"Your mother?" he said to London. "But how can this be? The two of you surely couldn't have arranged to meet here. Even I didn't expect to us to dock here a short while ago."

Mom's smile was positively glittering right now.

"It would seem that pure chance has brought us together, Mr. Lapham," she said.

Mom cringed a little at the way she said that word "us." It sounded almost as though it was meant to include Mom and Mr. Lapham but not London herself.

"Chance, dear lady?" Mr. Lapham said to London's mother. "Nay, I think destiny itself may have been involved. And not unexpectedly so—or at least not entirely."

Turning to London, he added, "Did we not receive a sort of augury that someone aboard the *Nachtmusik* was about to experience a 'transformative moment?'"

Yes, we did, London thought without saying so aloud.

Among Mr. Lapham's seemingly countless eccentricities, the millionaire CEO trusted many of his business decisions to the advice of an astrologer. London was still trying to get used to that.

Mom's face lit up with interest.

She said to Mr. Lapham, "A 'transformative moment,' you say? I am enthralled with curiosity. Please tell me more. And do sit down and join us. I cannot recommend this establishment's *mazarin* highly enough."

Mr. Lapham sighed sadly as he glanced at his watch.

"Alas, I do not have the leisure to do so," he said. "As it happens, I have just received a phone call about some urgent business to attend to back aboard the *Nachtmusik*. I spotted London sitting here in in this café and was hoping she could return with me, but now of course I wouldn't think of interrupting this remarkable reunion. But if Sir

Reggie happens to be available …"

At the sound of his name, Sir Reggie hopped down from his chair and eagerly put himself at Mr. Lapham's service.

Mom said to Mr. Lapham, "Oh, I wouldn't think of monopolizing London's time, not when she has professional duties to attend to."

"But madam, I'd hate to interfere—"

"Nonsense. You're not interfering with anything. London and I have all the time in the world to catch up."

All the time in the world? London wondered.

At the moment, that didn't seem especially likely.

"I must insist—" Mr. Lapham began.

"No, *I* must insist," Mom interrupted. "Business is business, and work comes before pleasure. London is all yours for as long as you need her."

"Very well, madam," Mr. Lapham said with a nod of his head.

London's head was reeling again.

Don't I get any say in the matter? she wondered.

But then, she figured maybe it was just as well that she didn't. She wasn't sure she'd be able to make up her mind. Things were just too bewildering right now.

She said to Mom, "But when are we … ?"

"Going to finish this interesting conversation?" Mom said. "Why, over dinner, of course."

Turning toward Mr. Lapham, Mom said, "Will she be available by 7:30?"

"I'll make sure of it," Mr. Lapham said.

I might as well not be here, London thought with frustration

"But where are we—?" London began.

Mom pointed and said, "You can see a restaurant just catty-corner across the street from here—the *Strömmingsvagnen,* it's called, and I hear it's very nice. They say it's animal-friendly, too, so by all means, bring Sir Reggie. Mr. Lapham, would you care to join us?"

London felt jolted by Mom's suggestion.

Doesn't she want us to spend some time alone together? she wondered.

Mr. Lapham seemed to sense London's discomfort.

"Thank you, but I wouldn't think of it," Mr. Lapham said. "The two of you have much to talk about, and I refuse to be a 'third wheel,' so to speak."

Kissing Mom's hand again, he added, "However, I do hope you and

I have time to get to know each other later on."

"I hope so too," Mom said with a flirtatious smile.

Feeling strangely unnerved, London rolled up what was left of her *mazarin* in a paper napkin.

She stammered to Mom, "I—I'll see you later."

"Yes, you will," Moms said with a smile.

Then London and Sir Reggie followed Mr. Lapham out of the restaurant.

"I do apologize, London," Mr. Lapham said as they headed back toward the dock. "If I'd had any idea, I'd have stayed away."

"It's all right, really," London said. "What's going on back at the ship?"

Mr. Lapham let a long, melancholy sigh.

"Well, as you surely remember, just yesterday I was planning to cancel our tour's final stop in Oslo on account of all the disagreeable murder and mayhem we've been coping with. But the passengers delivered to me a near-unanimous petition that we should finish our voyage, and of course I was pleased to comply."

With a shrug, Mr. Lapham continued, "But I'm afraid the sentiment is not quite so unanimous now that our ship was torpedoed by the dozing captain of a motorboat run amok. Three couples have asked to end their trip right here in this fishing town. Of course, they'll get their wish, but we have quite a few details to work out to make that happen. I do want them to end the tour happily."

London was saddened at the thought of anyone leaving the tour less than satisfied. She wondered which couples Mr. Lapham might be talking about.

"I'll be glad to help out," she said.

"Very good," Mr. Lapham replied.

Glancing back over his shoulder, he added, "Delightful lady, your mother. How long has it been since you last saw each other?"

"Twenty years," London said.

Mr. Lapham gasped.

"That long! Oh, this sounds like a 'transformative moment,' indeed."

London didn't say so, but the word "transformative" didn't seem quite right for her reunion with her mom.

"Scary" is more like it, she thought.

CHAPTER THREE

This is simply crazy, London thought as she waited in the lobby of Lillberg's hotel to finish up her afternoon tasks.

How could an unscheduled stop on the *Nachtmusik's* European tour have resulted in the seemingly impossible arrival of her mother?

Was it just a coincidence, or … ?

Worst of all, she had no idea what to expect to happen next.

Focus! she commanded herself.

Right now she had to finish dealing with the passengers who were departing right here in Lillberg. Although there was only one more stop scheduled on the tour, it unsettled London to say goodbye to them so soon. London had gotten close to these people during the voyage.

All afternoon, she had diligently gone about making hotel reservations and flight plans to get them back home to the United States—and most importantly, making refunds on their tickets and expenses, which Mr. Lapham insisted must be very generous.

Her final task was to check the passengers into this charming little hotel, where she stood waiting for them to arrive from the ship. They soon began to show up, followed by stewards helping with their luggage—and London struggled not to cry.

The first couple to arrive were a cantankerous pair who had recently struck up a surprising and sweet romance.

Cyrus Bannister said in his usual snide manner, "Ah, well—even the most catastrophic of tours must come to an end sooner or later."

"Oh, it hasn't *all* been terrible," Audrey Bolton reprimanded him. "It's been an adventure, anyway. Why, this was the first time that I've ever caught a killer! I'll be telling people that story for years."

London smiled, despite her sadness. It was certainly true that back in Bamberg, Germany, Audrey had popped up just at the right moment to shove a fleeing culprit into the river.

It's been an adventure, all right, London thought as they signed the hotel register.

The next to arrive were Rudy and Tina Fiore, a young honeymooning couple London had taken a liking to.

"Thanks for a wonderful trip," Tina said to London. "And thanks for somehow landing us in this adorable town. It's the perfect place for us to pause a bit before we go on our own way."

Rudy added, "We decided it would be a good time to see more of Sweden. Maybe we'll catch Norway on another trip."

After that couple went on, it came time to say goodbye to Walter and Agnes Shick, a kindly pair of pudgy elderly people. London had a special place in her heart for the Shicks, and she felt a wave of sadness as she saw tears in Agnes's eyes. Agnes reached out and gave London a hug.

"I'll miss you, London Rose," she said.

"I'll miss you too, Agnes," London said. "I'm just sorry things had to end this way."

"Me too," Agnes said, pulling out of the hug and wiping her eye.

Walter said to London, "I hope you understand. It all got to be too much for …"

He nodded toward Agnes.

"I understand," London said.

And she certainly did understand—or at least mostly.

London was the only person aboard the *Nachtmusik* who knew that Agnes and Walter had been in a witness protection program for 30 years. London didn't know what had happened all those years ago, but she did know that Agnes had been traumatized by it. She'd borne up as well as she could through five murders, but when the *Nachtmusik* had been rammed by a small boat, it had been too much for her.

Agnes stooped down and scratched Sir Reggie's head.

"And I'll miss you too, sweet fellow," she said.

When Sir Reggie let out a whine of agreement, Agnes was overwhelmed with emotion, and she and Walter hurried away.

"I'll miss them all," London said to Sir Reggie, who was standing at her feet.

Always sensitive to her moods, Sir Reggie nudged comfortingly up against her ankle. London scooped him up in her arms. It felt good to have a warm, sympathetic animal for company.

"Come on, Sir Reggie," London said, scratching his head. "Let's go meet Mom."

Carrying Sir Reggie in her arms as they went outside, London looked at the sky. It was just very nearly time for her rendezvous with Mom, although it was still surprisingly light outside. They were, after all, traveling farther north, where the summer nights were shorter than London was used to.

This was the first time London really had a chance to look around the little island fishing village of Lillberg. Its boat-filled docks and wooden houses looked like toys nestled among gigantic rocks where little vegetation grew.

London was struck by how different this town looked from the majestic cities the *Nachtmusik* had visited so far—Budapest, Gyor, Vienna, Regensburg, Bamberg, Amsterdam, and Copenhagen.

But Lillberg had a quaint charm of its own and, under normal circumstances, she thought it would make a lovely stop on their tour. Indeed, London saw a number of passengers taking advantage of the unexpected visit, walking along the cobblestone streets and looking into various shop windows as they enjoyed the smiles and greetings of the locals. She understood why the Fiores had decided to stay here awhile.

Finally, London and Sir Reggie arrived at the Strömmingsvagnen, the restaurant where London's mom had said they should meet. It was a picturesque, pleasantly weather-beaten clapboard building with smoke wafting out of a chimney.

London remembered Mom mentioning that the restaurant was "animal friendly." As London carried Sir Reggie into the front entrance, she was startled to see how true that was.

Several large cats were either prowling about searching for fallen table scraps or sleeping in empty chairs. They looked well-fed and groomed and clearly lived here. The customers, including several from the *Nachtmusik,* weren't the least bit disturbed by their presence.

For that matter, Sir Reggie wasn't disturbed either. London wasn't especially surprised, since her dog had become boon companions with Mr. Lapham's shipboard cat Siegfried during the last couple of days. Likewise, the cats here were unperturbed to see a dog come into their establishment.

"I guess they're used to dogs," London said to Sir Reggie, setting him down on the floor.

A waiter, clad in an old-fashioned sailor costume approached them, and in somewhat fractured Swedish, London asked him for a table for three and said they expected another guest. The waiter escorted London and Sir Reggie to a table for three, where they both sat down and made themselves comfortable.

Like so much else in Lillberg, London saw that the interior of the Strömmingsvagnen restaurant was cheerful and charming, with a low, wooden-beamed ceiling, a roaring fireplace, and anchor patterns on the wallpaper. It obviously wasn't a luxury restaurant but judging from the aromas that filled the smoky air, the food here was surely very good.

London glanced at her watch and saw that it was exactly the time she and Mom had agreed to meet. Then she gazed out the front window.

"No sign of Mom yet," London said to Sir Reggie. "Well, I guess I have no idea whether she's normally prompt or not. I've got a lot to learn about her."

She sat looking at the third chair at the table, the one that was still empty.

What are we going to say to each other over dinner? she wondered.

No matter how she tried to play out a conversation in her mind, it always seemed to end in an argument and even in tears. London couldn't shake off a sinking feeling that this reunion she'd craved for so many years was going to end very badly, for both herself and her mother.

If she ever does get here, she thought, looking worriedly at her watch.

CHAPTER FOUR

Be patient, London kept telling herself. *You've waited 20 years. Just a few more minutes isn't going to kill you.*

But the suspense was really getting to her.

Was waiting for Mom going to be even more frustrating than searching for Mom had been?

She tried to distract herself by looking over the menu, which featured a tantalizing range of seafood, including crab, oysters, shrimp, salmon, and cod.

The waiter must have noted her interest, because he soon came to the table.

"May I take your order?" he asked in English.

"No, I think we'll wait for our guest," London said.

"Perhaps an appetizer plate in the meantime?" the waiter suggested.

"Why, yes," London said, perusing the menu again. "Let's have a plate of your pickled herring bites. And a glass of white wine for me."

"Very good," the waiter said with a nod. Then he added in an equally formal tone, "And perhaps something for your small companion?"

Sir Reggie was sitting in his chair, looking at them expectantly and sniffing the air. London's dog was obviously hoping for something more than the treats she always had with her. But London hesitated, remembering how sick he had gotten the last time he'd overindulged.

"I don't know," she replied. "Seafood is probably too rich for him."

The waiter looked straight at Sir Reggie and asked, "What about something simpler? Perhaps a small serving of unseasoned chopped duck liver?"

Sir Reggie let out a yap of approval, as if he understood.

London and the waiter both laughed.

"He'll be happy with that," she told the waiter.

"Very good," the waiter said, then headed off to the kitchen.

As she and Sir Reggie waited, London kept looking out the window and drumming her fingers nervously on the table.

Mom was still nowhere in sight.

As London often did when she felt agitated, she began to think

15

aloud by talking to Sir Reggie. It always helped her make sense of things, and it usually calmed her down. Of course, she didn't believe that Sir Reggie really understood what she was saying …

Or maybe he does, she thought.

At times, the Yorkie seemed to grasp human language remarkably well.

"I still can't believe this is happening," she said to him. "You know, I spent the whole first part of the trip trying to track Mom down. I even picked up some clues along the way before I gave up hope. Remember that woman I met in Salzburg? Selma Hahn was her name, the director of the House for Mozart. But no, you wouldn't remember her, I don't think you were there when I talked to her …"

London's voice faded, as she felt again the shock of that moment.

Then she continued, "It was the very first hint I had that Mom was even still alive. Selma actually knew her. She had hired Mom as a language tutor for her daughter. They got to be good friends, but Selma could never get her to talk about her family."

London fell silent as she remembered Selma's exact words.

"Whenever she tried to talk about you, she'd look like she was about to cry."

And for a moment, London again felt as though she was about to cry herself.

She wondered—if Mom had felt so sad about her family, why had she stayed away from them all this time?

Just then the waiter returned with London's glass of wine, an appetizer plate, and a saucer with some chopped liver for Sir Reggie, which he set down on the chair where Sir Reggie was sitting.

While Sir Reggie savored his liver with gourmet-like appreciation, London debated whether to start in on the appetizers before Mom got here. She was feeling pretty hungry, so she picked up one of the eight morsels from the platter and looked it over. It was an attractive little item—a tidily-cut piece of fileted herring resting on a potato slice, all of it topped off with a dollop of sour cream and shredded red onion, sprinkled with what London guessed to be fresh dill and ground pepper.

Well, she wasn't in the mood to deny herself any longer, impolite or not.

She took a bite and was startled by a burst of flavor. She'd forgotten how pleasantly pungent pickled herring could taste, steeped as it was in a briny mixture of sugar and onion. A sip of her wine then went down nicely, a soothing contrast to the sharp flavor of the herring.

Sir Reggie looked up from his dish with interest as London took another taste of the herring bite.

"Sorry, Sir Reggie," London said. "This is definitely *not* for you."

Sir Reggie seemed happy enough to turn his attention back to his liver. London looked outside again. It was still very light outside, but London knew it was later than it looked. Mom was definitely not on time.

London sat staring at the remaining herring bites for a few moments.

Then she said quietly, "'Fern Weh.'"

Sir Reggie let out an inquisitive murmur, as if to ask her to explain what she meant.

London sighed and said, "According to Selma, Mom was traveling around Europe working as an itinerant language tutor. So when I saw that name on a message board back in Germany—an ad for a foreign language tutor—I thought maybe it was Mom living or working under an assumed name."

The dog looked so inquisitive, she felt the need to explain, "Because the German word *fernweh* means 'wanderlust.' That word seemed to fit Mom to a 't.'"

She thought for a moment, then added, "You know, Mom used to remind Tia and me that her name, Barbara, came from the Greek word *barbaros,* which means 'strange' or 'foreign.' 'That's what I am,' she used to tell us, 'just a wandering barbarian at heart.'"

London took a deep breath and went on, "So I called the number, but it wasn't in service, so I never found out whether Mom had left the ad or not. Maybe when she shows up I can ask her ..."

A little voice in her mind corrected her.

If she shows up.

London tasted another herring bite and took another sip of wine, but then she just sat staring in silence at the six remaining appetizers. The truth was, they weren't really whetting her appetite at all. She didn't feel like eating much of anything anymore.

Finally, she said to Sir Reggie, "She's not going to show up, is she?"

Sir Reggie replied with a skeptical but sympathetic whine.

London sighed again deeply as an unsettling feeling crept up inside her. It was a feeling she'd almost forgotten—that terrible mixture of anger, sadness, and fear she had felt as a teenager when Mom had first disappeared. She'd almost forgotten what an awful time that had been—not just for herself, but for Tia and Dad as well.

"I can't take this, Sir Reggie," she said. "If I stay here and keep waiting, I'll regress and wind up 13 years old again. But I can't just leave—can I?"

As if in reply to that question, London's cellphone buzzed. She saw that she had received an APB message sent to everyone who worked or traveled on the *Nachtmusik*.

Mr. Lapham asks that anyone who is ashore come back aboard immediately.

"What do you suppose this is all about?" she muttered. Then she called Amy Blassingame, the *Nachtmusik's* concierge. When Amy answered, London could hear a buzz of voices in the background.

"Amy what's going on?" London asked.

"London, you need to get back here right away," Amy said.

London felt a jolt of worry.

"Is something wrong?" she asked.

"I don't know," Amy said, sounding pretty anxious herself. "All I know is that Mr. Lapham says he's got some kind of an important announcement to make in just a few minutes, and he wants everyone on board ASAP."

London sat silently for a moment.

"Well?" Amy asked with a note of impatience. "Are you coming or not?"

"I—I guess," London said.

"Good," Amy said, and she ended the call.

London looked at Sir Reggie and said, "I guess we've got to go. And maybe it's just as well. I was about ready to lose my mind sitting here waiting like this."

London waved for the waiter and asked for the check for what little she and Sir Reggie had ordered. The waiter graciously said that Sir Reggie's duck liver was complimentary.

London handed a business card to the waiter when she paid him.

She told him, "If the guest I was expecting shows up, please tell her to give me a call."

As if that's likely to happen, she thought.

The waiter thanked London, and she and Sir Reggie headed outside and started walking back toward the *Nachtmusik*. She noticed several passengers hurrying in the same direction in response to the text message. Meanwhile, it was still very light outside, and London couldn't shake off the feeling that she really ought to wait a little longer for Mom.

Or maybe, after she'd dealt with whatever Mr. Lapham had to say, she could come back to town and search around and …

And what? she wondered.

She knew there was a regular ferry between the island and the mainland. Mom might well be off the island by now.

London reached down and picked up Sir Reggie.

"It's no use," she said to her dog. "If Mom really wanted to see me, at least she'd have told me her phone number. She just chickened out about the two of us getting back together again."

Either that, London thought, *or Mom's wanderlust has got the best of her all over again.*

Some things never change.

CHAPTER FIVE

As London headed toward the *Nachtmusik*, she realized that the other staffers and passengers who were on their way back to the ship were chattering with animation and concern. They had obviously also received the cryptic text message:

Mr. Lapham asks that anyone who is ashore come back aboard immediately.

"Let's just hope it's not another catastrophe," London said to Sir Reggie, who was trotting along beside. "I'm still trying to get over the last one—or maybe the last dozen or so."

The most recent catastrophe, of course, had been the *Nachtmusik* getting rammed by a wayward motorboat just this morning. But plenty of other recent crises were still fresh in London's memory, including a total of five murders that had happened during their visits to Gyor, Salzburg, Bamberg, Amsterdam, and Copenhagen.

London hoped with all her heart that Mr. Lapham wasn't about to announce that someone else had gotten killed.

At least whatever it is will get my mind off of Mom, she thought.

Maybe her mother had decided to disappear again, but London was determined not to let that interfere with her own life. Apparently she had work to do aboard the ship.

She picked up Sir Reggie again as they headed up the gangway. When she carried her dog into the bustling reception area, she saw that a lot of people were on their way to the nearby Amadeus Lounge.

Something seems to be going on in there, she realized. *Maybe it's the big announcement.*

As she followed them, she heard music from inside the lounge—a woman's voice accompanied by a piano.

London smiled at the familiar sound.

She said to Sir Reggie, "Well, whatever's going on, it hasn't stopped Letitia from singing."

On this voyage, passenger Letitia Hartzer had discovered a sort of calling as a popular singer right here in the Amadeus Lounge. She had also become one of London's best friends.

The big lounge was more crowded than usual, and when London entered, she couldn't immediately see Letitia or her accompanist. The performance had been set up on the far side of the room, next to the wide bar. London clung tightly to Sir Reggie and wended her way among the plush furniture and occasional potted plants and enthusiastic people in the audience.

Letitia was singing loud and clear in her heartiest mezzo-soprano:

"You like potato ..."

But then a higher soprano voice replied:

"... and I like potahto."

London felt a prickle of surprise as she heard the two voices continue swapping the lyrics of a familiar old tune, George and Ira Gershwin's "Let's Call the Whole Thing Off."

Who's singing with Letitia? she wondered. She was sure she hadn't heard that particular performer before.

When she managed to push her way closer to the little stage, her mouth dropped open with surprise.

As she'd expected, Letitia Hartzer was standing at a microphone, wearing the long sequined gown she always wore when she performed here at night. But London was unprepared for the singer she saw standing next to Letitia, sharing the same microphone.

Mom!

Mom was dressed in a less flashy but elegantly slinky black full-length gown. She and Letitia were singing in a lively bantering manner, exchanging humorous disagreements about pronunciations—*tomato* or *tomahto, pajamas* or *pajahmas, vanilla* or *vanella,* and the like.

They made a rather comical picture together—Letitia tall and stout, and Mom small and slight, almost like some kind of female Laurel and Hardy. They sang and swayed and even danced a little in perfect rhythm, as if they'd been rehearsing and performing this number for a long, long time.

But London was in for yet another surprise as she realized that the piano player was not Letitia's usual accompanist.

Instead, it was Mr. Lapham himself.

Merrily tickling the keys, he was dressed in his favorite casual attire—a velvet smoking jacket with a colorful silk scarf.

London was stunned.

"This has got to be a dream," she murmured to Sir Reggie.

But Sir Reggie didn't seem to think so, and he wagged his tail in time to the music.

For that matter, the audience certainly didn't think this was a dream. London looked out over the unusually large crowd and didn't see a single face that wasn't smiling with delight. Many listeners were tapping their feet and snapping their fingers, and a few were dancing.

Amy Blassingame, the ship's concierge, came up to London and Sir Reggie.

"Oh, London, you've been keeping secrets from me!" she said, tugging on London's sleeve. "You didn't tell me your mother was so wonderfully talented. For that matter, you never told me anything about your mother at all. Why didn't you tell me she'd be joining us today?"

London stammered, "Because I, uh, didn't know."

"Oh, London!" Amy chuckled incredulously. "I don't believe that!"

I hardly believe it either, London thought.

"You could have at least told me to have a room ready for her," Amy added.

A room! London thought.

It hadn't occurred to her until just this moment that Mom was joining them for the rest of the voyage. She was still reeling from confusion after having been stood up at the restaurant, only to find Mom here aboard the *Nachtmusik.*

How did this happen? she wondered.

And how did she feel about it?

She wanted to be happy to see Mom. But right now, she felt more dismayed.

Amy continued, "Fortunately, finding her a room wasn't too much trouble. Now that three couples have left us, three nice accommodations have opened up and I got them cleaned up quickly. I've already got your mother settled into the Schoenberg Suite. Of course, that's one of our very best, and I'm sure she'll be comfortable there."

The song ended to cheering and applause, and Mom and Letitia took gracious bows. Meanwhile, London saw Amy walk over to Mr. Lapham and share a few words with him.

London's eyes met Mom's, and Mom winked and waved and walked over to her.

"Oh, I'm so glad you could make it to our little cabaret, dear!" Mom said. "Isn't this fun? I haven't done anything like this for a long time."

London wasn't in the mood for chitchat. She crossed her arms and came right to the point.

"Where were you when we were supposed to have dinner together?"

"Oh, yes," Mom said with a tilt of her head. "We were planning to eat at that place called the *Strömmingsvagnen,* weren't we? Well, there was a change of plans. I ran into Jeremy this afternoon in the village while you were busy working, and he was really quite insistent that I come aboard the *Nachtmusik* for the rest of your cruise. He wanted to get me settled in as soon as possible, so I simply had to get my things together and come aboard right away."

With a chuckle she added, "Then Jeremy and I discovered each other's interest in music, and we got together with Letitia and started singing and playing together, and the next thing we all knew …"

Mom shrugged and said, "Well, I'm not telling you anything you don't already know. I called and left a message for you at the restaurant to let you know dinner was off and I'd see you in the lounge."

"I didn't get any message."

London's mother's brow knitted with concern.

"You didn't? That's odd. I'm sure I left a message on the restaurant's machine."

London didn't think Mom sounded so sure of that. In fact, she wondered whether Mom knew perfectly well she'd never left any such message. But she wasn't ready to accuse Mom of lying about it.

"Aren't you going to welcome me aboard?" Mom asked London.

London suddenly realized she hadn't so much as said anything nice to her mother since she'd come back to the ship.

"It's nice to have you here," London said, giving Mom a hug.

But once again the hug felt strange. She still couldn't get used to how much smaller Mom seemed now than she had all those years ago.

At that moment Mr. Lapham stepped onto the stage and walked over to the microphone. With his smoking jacket, silk scarf, comfortable pleated pants, and house slippers, London thought he looked like some kind of international playboy entertaining guests in his private penthouse.

"Ladies and gentlemen," he said, "Ms. Blassingame assures me that everybody is safely back aboard, and I can now share some good news with you. The damage to the *Nachtmusik* from today's collision was very slight and required only some very minor repairs—mostly just a bit of soldering for a few electronic circuits, and it's already finished. So we are about to set sail for Oslo at any moment now!"

Mr. Lapham's news was greeted by some happy applause, but also a few sighs of disappointment.

"Now, now, now," Mr. Lapham said, waving his finger at the complainers. "I know that our visit to the charming village of Lillberg has been an unexpected treat, and some of you would like to stay here awhile longer. But believe me, you will love Oslo even more, and we must squeeze the most enjoyment we can out of the last visit on our most eventful journey. You'll be glad of every minute we spend there, I promise."

With a cheerful wave to the crowd, Mr. Lapham went back to the piano.

Mom said to London, "Well, the show must go on, dear. We'll talk soon."

She rejoined Letitia on the stage, and Mr. Lapham played a piano intro that led into a Cole Porter number—"Begin the Beguine."

The two women sang this slower, sadder tune a bit tentatively at first, searching for their harmonies until they became more and more sure of themselves. By the time they got to the second verse, they sounded like they'd sung it a thousand times. And Mom's voice was every bit as fine as Letitia's.

The melancholy Cole Porter song startled her with a wave of emotion. When she tried to identify what that emotion was, a word came to mind.

Bittersweet.

But she still didn't know whether the feeling she had was more *bitter* or *sweet.*

Everything was too confusing.

Maybe I'll understand it better tomorrow, she thought.

Or maybe nothing will ever really make sense ever again.

Meanwhile, she felt the ship starting to move. They were setting out for Oslo.

London wasn't sure what to do next. Amy seemed to have everything running smoothly. And judging from the enthusiasm shared by the singers and the pianist and the crowd, the performance was likely to continue into the wee hours of the morning.

That conversation with Mom that she had expected to have at the restaurant wasn't going to happen here either. Not unless she barged up there and broke up the performance and spoiled everybody's evening.

But then London realized something with a shudder.

There's somebody I'd better tell about all this.

And it wasn't going to be easy.

"Come on, Sir Reggie," London said to her dog. "I've got a phone call to make."

Still apparently enjoying the music, Sir Reggie let out a mild whine of protest as they headed out of the lounge.

"Don't grumble," London said to Sir Reggie. "This phone call is going to be tough. And I'm liable to need a lot of emotional support from you by the time it's over."

CHAPTER SIX

Back in her stateroom, London sat down and just stared at her cellphone. When she heard a worried whimper, she realized that her little Yorkie was staring at her, obviously aware of her discomfort.

"Do I really want to do this, Sir Reggie?" she asked. "I just don't know what to say."

The dog let out a small whimper.

"You're right," London said with a sigh. "It's got nothing to do with what I *want* to do. It has to be done."

She looked at her watch and added, "It's late in the afternoon in Connecticut. I suppose this is as good a time as any."

She punched in a number and, in a few moments, she heard a little boy's voice answer the phone.

"Hello."

London gulped hard. Her seven-year-old nephew never turned the phone over to his mother before he'd made London feel thoroughly guilty about being so far away.

"Hi, Bret," she said. "This is Aunt London. How are you today?"

In the background, London could hear what sounded like a war going on, with explosions, gunfire, and zooming aircraft.

"I'm fine," Bret said. How are you?"

"Is school going OK?" London asked.

"I guess."

"That's good. How are your sisters?"

"They're trying to kill each other," Bret said.

London was startled, but only for a second. Of course, she realized that the sounds of battle were perfectly ordinary in that household. The older girls loved their violent computer games.

"Is your mom there?" London asked Bret.

Bret didn't reply, and London wondered if maybe he had set down the phone and gone to look for her sister, Tia. The sounds of digital battle seemed to grow more intense.

Finally, Bret asked, "Where are you, Aunt London?"

London stifled a groan of despair. Bret hadn't gone anywhere. He was still holding the phone.

26

He's not going to make this easy, she thought.

"Um, I'm aboard a ship. I work on a ship."

"I know that. Where is the ship? Where are you and the ship right now?"

"We're on our way to Norway, sweetie."

"Is that far away from where we live?"

"I'm afraid so," London said. "Remember when I called you last time, and I was in Europe?"

"Yeah."

"Well, Norway is across the ocean, like Europe, and it's way up north."

"Where the polar bears live?"

For a moment London wasn't sure how to answer his question correctly.

Then she remembered, "I think maybe there are some polar bears living in Norway."

"We never see any around here. If you see any polar bears, could you say hi to them for me?"

"I'll do that, sweetie. Could I talk to your mom please?"

Again there was a silence, but this time London was pretty sure that Bret still hadn't gone to look for Tia.

"We miss you, Aunt London," her nephew finally said.

"I know," London said, gulping hard again. "I miss you too. I'm sorry I'm so far away."

"When are you coming home?"

London slumped in her chair.

Home, she thought.

She realized she should have been braced for Bret to ask that question. He always did. And of course, she knew it made sense to the little boy to think that London's home was where he and his family lived. After all, whenever London wasn't voyaging around the world, she often stayed with them in their house.

"I don't know, sweetie," London said. "But I'll come and see you and your sisters and your mom and dad as soon as I can."

"OK."

"What's your mom doing right now?"

"She's fixing dinner."

"Could I talk to her, please?"

"I guess."

London heard some footsteps over the ongoing din of battle, then

27

some muffled words between Bret and his mother. Then Tia picked up the phone and spoke to her.

"Well, well, well. The prodigal sister calls."

"Hi, Tia," London said.

"Bret just said something about you and Norway and polar bears. I hope you aren't having some kind of a problem with a polar bear. Because I'm not sure there's much I can do if you're calling for my help."

"No, I'm fine, it's just …"

London fell silent for a moment, still searching for appropriate words.

Finally she said, "Tia, I've got some news, and I'm not sure how you're going to …"

London's voice faded again. Finally, she came out and said it.

"Tia, Mom's here."

London thought maybe she heard her sister gasp, but it was hard to tell over the background sounds of ongoing war. Then she heard some more footsteps, then the sound of a door shutting, and the war sounds became muffled.

"Couldn't you have given me some warning?" Tia said, her voice sounding shaky. "I had to come to another room. I don't want the kids to hear us talk about … this … about her."

Before London could muster an apology, Tia rushed on, "What do you mean anyhow? What do you mean by 'here?'"

"Aboard the *Nachtmusik.*"

"Is she there right now? I mean, in the same room with you?"

"No," London replied. "Mom is …"

She quickly decided against mentioning that, at that very moment, Mom was performing in a cabaret act in the ship's lounge.

"I think she's relaxing," London finished.

"What's she doing there?" Tia asked. "How did she get there?"

"That's kind of hard to explain," London said.

Tia let out a loud groan of dismay.

"Oh, London. Don't tell me you went *looking* for her. We talked about that the last time we talked. You promised you wouldn't do that."

I don't remember promising that, London thought.

Anyway, London actually had stopped looking for Mom back in Amsterdam, after following a completely erroneous clue that led her to a brothel in Amsterdam's red-light district. She'd given up the search right then and there—for good, she'd thought.

28

"I wasn't looking for her," London told Tia, at least somewhat truthfully. "She just, well, showed up."

"I don't believe it," Tia said.

I don't blame you, London thought. *I hardly believe it myself.*

London continued, "Look, the ship had a small accident, and we had to dock in a little Swedish fishing village, and …"

London's voice faded.

She knew what she was about to say was going to sound ridiculous.

"She just happened to be there," London said.

"Where?"

"On the dock. When we landed. As soon as I stepped off the boat, there she was."

"And how did she *happen* to be there?" Tia asked.

That's a good question, London thought.

All Mom had told her at the time was that she somehow knew London had been on her way to Oslo.

"You'd be surprised at the things I know," she'd said.

"She hasn't told me yet," London said.

There was a tense silence on the other end of the line, and then Tia asked, "London, are you sure it's her?"

"Absolutely," London said with a nervous laugh.

"Are you still in that little fishing village?"

"No, we're sailing again. To Oslo. We'll get there tomorrow."

"And you're letting her come with you?"

London was jolted by the question. It hadn't occurred to her that she might have had any choice in the matter. And of course, she actually hadn't had choice. Mr. Lapham had pretty much taken the decision upon himself to bring her aboard without consulting London about it. Mom had been there, performing in the lounge, when London had returned to the ship.

London sighed and said, "Look, Tia, she's here now, and that's just the way it is. What am I supposed to do, tell her to jump into the sea?"

"It's a thought."

London heaved a long, heavy sigh.

"Tia, I know this is hard to deal with. I'm having trouble dealing with it too. I just thought you should know."

"Know what? You haven't told me much of anything. Has she told *you* anything we might want to know—like where she's been for 20 years, and why she took off in the first place, leaving you and me and Dad all scared and hurt like that?"

29

"She hasn't told me anything like that, no," London said.

"Well, why hasn't she?"

London stammered, "Tia, there—there hasn't been a whole lot of time to talk. All this just happened today."

"Are you sure she's not just avoiding talking to you?"

At that, London fell silent. Of course, Tia was right.

Mom is avoiding talking to me.

That was the reason for the casual conversations, for Mom turning her charm on Mr. Lapham and everybody else who was around, for Mom going into performance mode … even for the missed dinner.

She told Tia, "I'll get her to explain all that tomorrow."

"Well, that'll be great, London. Just great. And when you know the truth, do me a really big favor, OK?"

"What is it?"

"Don't call me and tell me about it. I can't believe you're calling me about it right now. And most of all, I don't want to talk to Mom. Didn't it occur to you I wouldn't want to hear about this stuff?"

"I thought—"

"Well, I *don't,* London. I stopped thinking about Mom years ago, completely gave up on any notion that she might be part of our lives again. And things were good that way. For me, anyway. "

London was speechless for a moment.

Finally, she said, "Tia, I don't know what to do."

"I think you should jump in a lifeboat and get away from Mom as soon as you can," Tia said.

Another silence fell.

"I don't really mean that," Tia said. "If you're happy to see Mom again, then I'm happy for you. It's just that … well, this whole thing just makes me feel really confused. And I'm worried about you, London. I'm worried that you're going to get hurt."

"I'll be OK."

"I hope so."

"There's one more thing, though. I haven't decided whether to call Dad and tell him …"

"Don't."

"But maybe he'd want to know—"

"Don't, I said. At least not until you can tell him more than you've told me. It would really upset him, London. There's no need for that."

"OK," London murmured.

London could hear a loud crash in another room of Tia's house.

30

"I'd better go," Tia said. "I think the girls are destroying something. Take care. Love you."

"Love you too," London said.

They ended the call, and London sat staring dumbly at the phone. Apparently sensing London's need for sympathy, Sir Reggie jumped up into her lap and snuggled against her.

London petted her dog and said, "Tia thinks I should jump in a lifeboat and get away from Mom. What do you think?"

Sir Reggie let out a worried whine.

"Oh, don't worry," London said. "If I do, I'll be sure to take you with me."

Sir Reggie sighed, sounding rather reassured.

"I guess it's time for bed," London said to her dog. "I hope we can get some sleep."

Lord only knows what tomorrow will bring, she thought.

CHAPTER SEVEN

London felt an eerie chill.

She knew that she was standing in the passageway just outside her stateroom, but she didn't know where she'd been just a moment before, or where she'd planned to go, or what she expected to do now.

She didn't see anybody else in the passageway. Although she felt the Nachtmusik *heaving up and down as it sailed on open waters, she didn't hear the slightest sound—not even the ship's engine.*

"Why is everything so quiet, Sir Reggie?" she asked.

But when she looked down, she saw that even her dog wasn't there.

Am I all alone on the ship? *she wondered.*

As if in reply, she heard a distant piano and someone singing. Although the music was very faint, London recognized the melody.

"Begin the Beguine."

London smiled. That must be Mom doing her cabaret act up in the lounge with Letitia and Mr. Lapham.

She walked down the passageway to the elevator and pushed the button. But when the doors opened, she found herself facing an empty elevator shaft. Looking down the long shaft, she could see water splashing at the distant bottom. Looking upward, she saw a starlit night sky. There was no sign of an elevator car in either direction.

Somebody ought to get that fixed, *London thought as she backed away and allowed the doors to close. She made her way to the nearby spiral stairway and climbed up two decks to the reception area.*

Now she could hear the music much more clearly than before.

When she walked inside the Amadeus Lounge, she was surprised to see that only one person was in the huge room—Mr. Lapham, who was playing the piano on the little stage.

"I thought I heard Mom singing," London told him.

"No, it's just me playing all alone," Mr. Lapham said.

"Where's Mom?" London asked him.

"She jumped into the sea," Mr. Lapham said with a smile.

London felt as though an arrow had been shot through her heart.

"Didn't she tell you?" Mr. Lapham said. "Oh, that's right, she asked me to tell you. She didn't want to cause you any more hurt, she

said. She also said not to worry about her, she's just fine, she jumps into the sea like that all the time."

London felt tears burning in her eyes.

Mom will do anything—*anything*—just to avoid me, *she thought.*

Even jump into the sea.

And now I'll probably never see her again.

She looked around and asked, "Where is everybody else?"

But when she looked back to the stage, she saw that Mr. Lapham too was gone. And now there was truly nothing to be heard—not even the sound of a piano. There was only the slow, silent heaving of the boat.

She walked out of the lounge and up the stairs to the open-air Rondo *deck. Again, she saw nobody anywhere—not in any of the deck chairs, or in the swimming pool, or playing shuffleboard, or looking out over the rails.*

She quickly realized where everybody must have gone.

They jumped into the sea—like Mom.

Then she looked up and saw that even the bridge was vacant.

Who's steering the ship? *she wondered.*

But it seemed like a silly question. There was no engine running, and yet the Nachtmusik *kept moving forward through the surging waters.*

The boat was obviously on its way to its own chosen destination.

A profound loneliness came over London, and she knew she had a terrible decision to make.

Was she going to stay here and let the Nachtmusik *take her to its final destination?*

Or was she going to jump into the sea like everybody else?

"What am I going to do?" *she cried aloud.*

London awoke to the touch of Sir Reggie's cold nose against her cheek and his worried whimper.

I must have yelled in my sleep, she realized.

"It's OK, Sir Reggie," she said. "It was only a dream."

London got up and gave Sir Reggie his breakfast and got dressed and ready for her day. All the while, she kept trying to put the dream out of her mind. But it still nagged at her. The *Nachtmusik* was now out on the open, choppy waters of the Skagerrak strait on its way to Oslo, and the ship was heaving up and down, just like it had been in her dream.

As she brushed her short auburn hair and looked into her blue eyes in the bathroom mirror, London kept seeing another face superimposed there. Mom had those same sharp blue eyes, and her hair had once been an even brighter shade of red.

London felt as though she could see her mother looking back at her from behind the glass.

Maybe I'm still dreaming, she thought.

Maybe all of yesterday was just a dream.

Maybe it had only been a dream that Mom had come aboard the *Nachtmusik* yesterday. And maybe London's conversation with Tia had been part of that same dream.

Was she still asleep and dreaming even now?

Her scalp twinged sharply as she tugged at a snag in her hair, proving that she was awake.

"No, I'm quite awake," she realized

And Tia had been right about one thing—Mom owed them an explanation for the last 20 years. London felt a nagging worry that learning the truth today wasn't going to be easy.

London finished arranging her hair, then stepped out of the bathroom, where she found Sir Reggie finishing his breakfast.

Then she heard a knock at the door, and her spirits suddenly lifted at the sound.

"There's *my* breakfast," she said to Sir Reggie as she walked to the door. "And right on time, too."

During the course of the voyage, London had struck up a tentative romance with the ship's handsome Australian chef, Bryce Yeaton. Since Mom's arrival, she'd barely had time to give Bryce any thought, but now she was grateful that he was apparently still being attentive. Every morning at exactly this time, Bryce sent a steward to deliver a delicious breakfast to London's stateroom.

But when she opened the door, she was let down by what she saw. The steward hadn't arrived with his usual cart laden with delicious food.

Instead, he simply smiled and said with a tip of his cap, "Mr. Yeaton told me to drop by and tell you he's looking forward to seeing you in the Habsburg Restaurant."

Then he walked away without saying another word.

Huh? London wondered as she shut the door.

She couldn't remember any changes to the usual plans.

She shrugged and said to Sir Reggie, "Well, I guess we're expected.

Let's get going. Maybe Mom is up there already."

But as London and Sir Reggie stepped out into the passageway and headed for the central elevator and stairs, the door to the neighboring stateroom opened behind them.

"Oh!" a familiar voice said. "London!"

She whirled around to see her mother standing there.

Mom said with a smile. "Good morning, dear! I was just on my way to fetch you!"

"Uh, good morning, Mom," London said.

"You look surprised to see me," Mom said.

"Well, yes, I guess I kind of am," London said. "The last I'd heard, you were going to be staying up in the Schoenberg Grand Suite."

"Oh, I decided I didn't like being two whole decks above you," Mom said. "I asked that nice concierge of yours—Amy is her name, isn't it?—if you and I could be closer together. I don't need a grand suite all to myself. This little stateroom is more to my liking. And now we're neighbors! Isn't that lovely?"

London stammered, "Yes, it—it's lovely. But what happened to the two guys who were sharing this room before?"

"Oh, that's a long story," Mom said with a laugh. "Come on, we've got a reservation for breakfast."

A long story? London wondered as Mom led the way toward the elevator. *A reservation for breakfast?*

Her mind boggled at all the "long stories" that still needed to be told. How had Mom talked Bob Turner and Stanley Tedrow into vacating their room for her?

As they reached the elevator, the doors opened, and two passengers got off. They gave both London and her mom a cheerful greeting and went on their way, chatting excitedly about the next stop in Norway.

Then an enormous, incredibly fluffy black and white cat strode majestically out of the elevator car. Mom let out a squeal of delight and stooped down and petted the animal.

"Oh, hello there, Siegfried!" she said. "How nice to see you this morning! Have you got any interesting plans for today?"

London was startled anew to realize Mom had already befriended Mr. Lapham's cat.

What else has she been doing since she came aboard?

Siegfried and Sir Reggie greeted each other cordially, then wandered off along the passageway together.

Mom laughed and said, "Well, I guess the two of them are off on a day of exciting adventures. Jeremy tells me they've gotten to be great friends. Imagine, a dog and a cat, getting along like that! What was it Jeremy called them? Oh, yes—'harbingers of world peace.' Well, why not? We can hope, can't we?"

London shook her head with wonder at how quickly Mom was making herself at home aboard the *Nachtmusik.*

Of course that's a good thing, she told herself.

Before she stepped into the elevator, she found herself hesitating and glancing downward to make sure this was no empty shaft reaching deep into the water.

"Come on dear," Mom laughed, stepping inside the car. "People are awaiting us."

London felt oddly, unexplainably uncomfortable as she joined her mother and listened to her chatter during their ride up to the *Menuetto* deck.

When they walked into the Habsburg Restaurant, Bryce himself was waiting for them, handsomely dressed in his white chef's tunic and floppy white hat. He looked as handsome as always, with his gray eyes, dimpled chin, and carefully groomed stubble of beard, although London thought he did look rather tired.

"Ah, two of my favorite ladies!" Bryce said, giving London a kiss on the cheek—a bit less wholeheartedly, London thought, than he might have kissed her without Mom around.

"Is our table waiting, Bryce?" Mom asked him.

"Of course! Come in, come in!"

London's jaw almost dropped as Bryce showed them to a table.

She's even made friends with Bryce!

CHAPTER EIGHT

London felt her mind reeling with perplexity as she watched Bryce gallantly helping her mother into a chair.

Is there anybody *on the ship Mom hasn't gotten to know?* London wondered.

It was hard to believe Mom had just arrived here late yesterday.

London stepped forward a bit shakily and sat down across the table from her mother.

Bryce asked, "What will you be having for breakfast this fine morning, Barbara?"

"Just the same as my daughter," Mom replied. "Eggs Benedict."

London struggled to remember if she had even tried that dish by the time she'd last seen Mom. She didn't believe so, and she certainly hadn't mentioned Eggs Benedict in any of their recent conversations—if you could even call them conversations.

So how did she know?

"I thought that would appeal to you," Bryce said to Mom with a laugh. "Coming right up for both of you."

Before Bryce could leave the table, London caught his sleeve and said quietly, "Bryce, we've got to talk."

Of course, that was a true understatement. Now that the voyage was coming to an end, they both had major decisions to make—including about whether to continue their relationship.

"I agree," Bryce replied. "Let's do that soon."

Then Bryce headed back to the kitchen.

Mom winked at London and said, "Oh, what a handsome boyfriend you've got!"

London sputtered, "How—how did you know ...?"

"How did I know what, dear?"

"That—that Bryce is ... anything to me?"

"Well, he did give you a little kiss just now," Mom said. "Not much of a kiss, though. I do hope you're past the peck-on-the-cheek phase."

"Mom, just tell me," London said, rolling her eyes.

"OK, I make friends fast," Mom said with a shrug. "I'm sure you do too. After all, it's just something we learn in the hospitality business, isn't it? Anyway, Bryce came to hear Letitia and Jeremy and me perform last night. When we finished, he and I sat up talking for a while."

So that's why Bryce looked tired, London realized.

When she'd left the Amadeus Lounge last night, she'd been sure that the performance was going to last a good while longer. Mom and Bryce must have stayed up talking very late.

"So," Mom asked, "what kind of plans are you and this handsome Aussie making for the future? Where are you going to live? How big a house are you going to buy? How many children do you plan to have?"

The questions took London by surprise all over again.

"Mom, Bryce and I, we ..."

"Well?"

"Well, we've only known each other since the beginning of the voyage."

Mom let out a grunt of disapproval.

She said, "And the voyage is going to be over in—what?—another day or two. If you want to have a future with this young man, you'd better start cracking."

At long last, London couldn't keep her jaw from dropping. She really had no idea how to reply to this sudden blitz of maternal advice. But in a way, Mom was right. She and Bryce had a lot of deciding to do.

She was relieved when breakfast was served so quickly and she realized that Bryce must have started getting it ready ahead of time. But of course, he and Mom must have discussed Eggs Benedict last night, and he'd known in advance what she was going to order.

What else did they talk about? London wondered.

"Oh, my, this is delicious!" Mom said as she took her first taste of the dish, with its incredibly rich and buttery Hollandaise.

London remembered something her sister had said on the phone last night.

"Are you sure she's not just avoiding talking to you?"

London didn't doubt that Mom was doing just that.

And it's got to stop right now, she thought.

"Mom, you have a lot of explaining to do," London said firmly as she started eating.

"Where would you like me to begin?" Mom asked with an imperturbable smile.

"Well, let's start with yesterday," London said. "Maybe you can tell me how you happened to be there when the *Nachtmusik* docked in Lillberg."

Mom laughed and said, "Well, that was rather a coincidence, but only partly. You see, for years I've always tried to keep track of your travels and activities. I like to think of it as 'vicarious mothering.' I found out you'd be working aboard the *Nachtmusik* as concierge ..."

"Social director," London said, correcting her.

"Oh, yes—Amy is the concierge, isn't she? Well, I've been using the internet to keep tabs on your trip every single day. Even though I knew where you were, I couldn't make up my mind to just barge back into your life. In fact, I had decided not to do that."

"And yet ...," London ventured.

Her mother just kept talking, "So of course I knew your last stop was going to be in Oslo, which is not on my current travel schedule. But as it happened, I'd been working on the mainland right there in Sweden, just a short ferry ride from that island village ..."

Mom paused and squinted.

"I work as an itinerant language teacher; did you know that?" she said.

"Yes, I did," London muttered.

It was, in fact, one of the few things she really knew about Mom.

Mom continued, "Well, early that morning I heard on the radio that the *Nachtmusik* had run into a bit of trouble and was stopping for repairs in Lillberg. It was as though you had suddenly taken a detour to come to see me. So naturally, I jumped on the first ferry over to the island, and I got there just in time to meet you at the pier."

Mom laughed and added, "So you see, it was partly a coincidence, and partly—well, something else. Surely Jeremy was right when he spoke of auguries and transformative moments and destiny and all that. It really is rather uncanny, don't you agree?"

Yes, I guess I do, London thought without saying so aloud.

And she had a feeling Mom was telling the truth about how they'd reunited at long last, at least as much as she was willing to say.

But so far, they hadn't ventured very deeply into the mysteries surrounding her mother.

She remembered her sister's questions.

"Has she told you anything we might want to know—like where she's been for 20 years, and why she took off in the first place, leaving you and me and Dad all scared and hurt like that?"

How do I even ask? London wondered.

Could she just blurt out Tia's questions right here at this table set with sparkling linen, silver utensils, and the remains of a delicious breakfast?

Before she could formulate a single query, the flash of light on mirrored sunglasses caught her eye. She was actually relieved to see the two men who were approaching.

Bob Turner, the ship's rather bumbling "security expert," was wearing his mirrored glasses as always. With him was Stanley Tedrow, a short, stooped, elderly aspiring mystery novelist with squinty eyes. They'd been roommates in the stateroom next door to London's—at least until last night.

Both of them seemed delighted to see Mom.

"Hey, if it isn't our lovely chanteuse!" Stanley said.

"Yeah, and you're a pretty good singer, too!" Bob added.

"Why, thank you," Mom replied, with a wink and a smile to London at Bob's ignorance of what "chanteuse" meant.

"What a great little ensemble you and the boss and Letitia make," Stanley added.

"I'm glad you enjoyed it," Mom said.

"Oh, and thank you for the great favor you did for us yesterday," Bob said.

"Oh, it was really you gentlemen who did *me* a favor," Mom said with a modest shrug. Then turning to London, she explained, "You remember how I was supposed to get the Schoenberg Grand Suite, but I wanted to be closer to you? Well, Stanley and Bob were willing to switch rooms with me."

"And did we ever get a bargain out of the deal!" Bob said. "I'd forgotten how big those grand suites are."

With a salute, Bob wandered off toward an empty table.

Stanley whispered to London and Mom, "And we got out of that dinky room just in the nick of time. Bob was really driving me crazy. I was afraid we were going to kill each other. It helps a lot to have more space to spread out."

Stanley followed Bob over to a table for two.

"Aren't they just the most amusing fellows?" Mom said to London. "Did you know Bob is helping Stanley with his writing? He started out by sharing his crime expertise with him, but now he's also working as Stanley's editor and agent."

"Yes, I knew," London said, finishing the last bite of her breakfast.

Feeling determined not to drop the questions that needed to be answered, she added, "But Mom, you've still got a lot of explaining to do."

"Yes, I know—about the last 20 years," Mom said with a sigh. "Well, it's like I said yesterday, a lot of it is rather foggy."

London stifled a groan of annoyance.

The whole amnesia thing again, she thought.

London still wasn't ready to believe that wasn't just another evasion. But before she could challenge Mom about it, Amy Blassingame came hurrying over to the table.

"Barbara Rose!" the concierge said. "Just the person I want to see! Didn't you tell me yesterday that you were a pretty good bridge player?"

"I believe I may have mentioned that, yes," Mom said.

"Well, we've got a bridge club that meets every morning at this hour in the lounge. But one of our players came down with a pretty serious case of seasickness and can't make it. Could you fill in?"

"I'd be glad to," Mom said.

"Wonderful!" Amy said. "Please come and join us as soon as you can."

Amy hurried away just as Mom was finishing the last bite of her breakfast.

"Well, that was positively delicious, dear," Mom said to London, putting her napkin on the table. "You'd better hang onto that dashing Australian. Husbands who can cook are few and far between."

Mom hurried away.

Escaped again, London thought, sitting at the table alone. So far, Mom was successfully singing and talking and charming her way out of any serious explanations.

London was teetering between exasperation and confusion when her cellphone rang.

The call was from Mr. Lapham.

"Good morning, London," the CEO said. "I wonder if you could stop by my suite for a chat. I've got a rather urgent matter I'd like to discuss with you."

"Of course," London said.

She finished the last bites of breakfast and left the dining hall. As she took the staircase up to the *Menuetto* deck, her was still mind abuzz.

This is really not a dream, she reminded herself. *I am wide awake, and my mother is here on the ship, playing bridge with some of our passengers.*

But then another possibility occurred to her.

Maybe I've gone completely insane.

CHAPTER NINE

A new worry crowded its way into London's already overloaded brain. As if there weren't already enough issues to deal with, she had to wonder just what Mr. Lapham wanted to talk about. Her boss seldom asked to speak with her unless there was some urgent matter at hand—although what he considered urgent had sometimes been mystifying to her.

As she headed up the stairs to the *Menuetto* deck, she thought about some recent events. The CEO resided in the ship's large and elegant Beethoven Grand Suite. When the tour first started, that space had been occupied by Lillis Klimowski, Sir Reggie's wealthy former owner and also the first of five people London had found dead during the *Nachtmusik's* uncannily murder-prone European tour.

After Mrs. Klimowski's untimely demise, Sir Reggie had happily moved in with London, and the ship's would-be security man Bob Turner had taken over the suite. During his short stay there, Bob had revealed himself to be a thorough slob, and the accommodations had looked anything but "grand."

When she arrived and knocked on the door, London heard Mr. Lapham call for her to come in. Once inside, she saw that the CEO had restored the Beethoven Suite to its former glory. The seating area and the bedroom were again recognizably separate spaces, and framed pages from 18th- and 19th-century music scores had been returned to their original places on the walls.

The CEO was sitting in an armchair surrounded by pages of well-read newspapers in a number of different languages. Aside from the loose newspaper pages, everything was immaculately neat. London thought that even the stern portrait of Beethoven that presided over it all looked a tiny bit more cheerful.

"I'm glad you could stop by, London," Mr. Lapham said with a pleasant smile. "Do sit down and make yourself comfortable."

As London took a seat in a smaller armchair, the CEO tapped out a musical beat on the arm of his chair as he sang a couple of lines of the Gershwin brothers' "Let's Call the Whole Thing Off." London was struck by what a fine tenor voice he had. She hadn't known until last night that he was an excellent pianist.

What other talents does he have that I don't know about? London wondered.

"Ah, what a delightful tune!" Mr. Lapham said. "I'm glad you could catch a bit of our cabaret last night. It was a pleasure to accompany your mother—and Letitia as well, of course. They have an excellent chemistry together. Your mother is especially talented ..."

Mr. Lapham's voice faded, and his eyes twinkled at the memory.

"Yes, very talented, indeed," he added quietly. "And very remarkable."

London suddenly knew something she had half-consciously suspected.

He's smitten with Mom.

London pushed down the confused feelings which that thought stirred up. She wasn't ready to consider how she felt about the possibility of a romance between her mother and her boss. She had no idea whether his feelings for Mom were requited—and she wasn't sure she wanted to know.

Mr. Lapham finally leaned toward her and said, "Let me get right to the point, London. You have been a *rock* during this tumultuous voyage."

Then he added with a chuckle, "I mean that metaphorically, of course. Rocks—large ones, at least, and especially boulders—are not normally to be desired aboard a ship. But you have been a rock of stability and professionalism—a sort of rock that never sinks, as it were. I am very grateful for all that you have done to maintain some semblance of sanity aboard the *Nachtmusik.*"

London felt a surge of gratitude.

"That's very kind of you to say, sir," she said.

Mr. Lapham nodded and continued, "Now as you well know, Oslo will be the last port in our rather fraught journey. I expect to sell the ship during the next few days, and that will be the last I expect to see of this fine but star-crossed ship."

Of course she was struck by the words "star-crossed." She knew that Mr. Lapham attributed the *Nachtmusik's* many troubles to a number of supernatural factors, including the astrological influence of the newly discovered dwarf planet Eris and its moon Dysnomia. London did her best to keep an open mind about what struck her as some pretty unconventional notions for a millionaire businessman.

Mr. Lapham cradled his fingers together with a thoughtful

expression.

"Meanwhile," he said, "I want to make sure that everyone on our excellent staff and crew is treated as they all deserve—especially you, if I may say so."

"I appreciate that, sir," London said.

Mr. Lapham said, "Despite the catastrophes that have befallen us, I have confidence in our company's future in international river tours—and so do my spiritual consultants, including my astrologer, Alex."

London felt a twinge of uneasiness as she began to realize what might be coming.

Scratching his chin, he added, "To that end, I have purchased a new boat named the *Galene*. I intend to launch her on a two-week tour of the Seine next month. Our passengers will be treated to all sorts of delights—Claude Monet's house in Giverny, the magnificent cathedral in Rouen, the ruins of Richard the Lionheart's Château Gaillard, Napoleon's Château de Malmaison, the beaches of Normandy, and of course Paris itself. If the first tour is a success—and I am sure it will be—I will keep it going indefinitely."

Leaning toward London, he added, "I would be very pleased if you accepted your current position aboard the *Galene*—with a considerable raise in salary, I should add, and a promise of a secure future."

There it was—a new job offer. But she didn't know what to say.

"I'm honored, Mr. Lapham," she replied.

The CEO smiled knowingly.

"But you aren't ready to leap at the opportunity," he said, not unsympathetically.

London shook her head silently.

"Let me guess," Mr. Lapham said. "Your reticence has something to do with your budding romance with our ship's medic and head chef, Bryce Yeaton."

London felt herself blush deeply.

Mr. Lapham laughed warmly and said, "Oh, no need for embarrassment, my dear. I for one am greatly in favor of workplace romances among my employees. It adds a bit of spice to things."

London felt a flash of hope.

She stammered awkwardly, "Do you—I mean, is Bryce going to be—?"

"Working aboard the *Galene?*" Mr. Lapham said. "Alas, I don't think so. In fact, I am in negotiations with a new chef whose credentials are very good. My understanding is that Mr. Yeaton has an excellent

45

offer from Aeolus Adventures to serve as head chef aboard their cruise ship the *Danae."*

London's eyes widened with surprise. She and Bryce had talked about this offer and what effect it had on the possibility of a future together. She had no idea that Mr. Lapham even knew about it.

"Did he tell you that?" she asked.

"Oh, no, of course not," Mr. Lapham said with a chuckle. "Since when do employees keep their bosses in the loop about their job prospects? But I do make it my business to … well, to keep tab on my employees' business. And the cruise industry is a tight community rife with gossip. It would have been difficult *not* to find out about such a grand offer."

Drumming his fingers on the arm of his chair, Mr. Lapham added, "However, I have not heard … if you don't mind my asking—have *you* been offered a job aboard the *Danae?"*

"No," London said, wincing slightly.

In fact, she found it a sensitive subject.

"I think we need to make this decision together," Bryce had said.

But they'd scarcely had any time together to discuss much of anything—least of all where they would soon wind up and how their relationship was going to continue.

Mr. Lapham shrugged and said, "I must say, the *Danae* position is much better than anything I could possibly offer Bryce. He'd be a fool to turn it down—strictly from a business angle, I mean."

He paused for a moment, then added in a kindly voice, "But then, there are angles other than business to consider, aren't there?"

London felt a lump of emotion in her throat.

"Yes, sir, there are," she said.

Mr. Lapham leaned back in his chair and said, "I hope you understand, I need an answer to my offer very soon—by the end of today, in fact. As it is, I'd already find myself tight on time if I have to find someone else for the job."

London managed to keep her mouth from dropping open.

I have to decide by tonight? she thought.

But she reminded herself that he did have a business to run.

Then Mr. Lapham laughed and said, "And frankly, if you don't mind my saying so, you two 'crazy kids' need to make up your minds just what you're going to do with the rest of your lives. I feel like knocking your two heads together!"

London laughed a little too.

He certainly is being very nice about all this, she thought.

But then, she already knew that her eccentric boss didn't have a mean bone in his body.

"I'll make a decision by tonight, I promise," she said.

"Good," Mr. Lapham said. "Oh, by the way—your mother is a delightful woman. Of course, after not seeing each other for 20 years, the two of you must find this unexpected reunion to be ..."

He paused as if looking for the right words.

"Well, I'm sure it's stirring up some complicated emotions," he said.

"It is, sir," London said.

"I think I can assure you that your mother wants to put things right between the two of you."

London felt a bit lightheaded with surprise.

What makes him think that? she wondered.

She wanted to ask but had no idea how to go about it. Was it possible that Mr. Lapham now knew more about Mom than London herself did?

"I guess I'd better get back to work," she said, getting up from her chair. "Thanks so much for the job offer. It's very kind and generous of you, and it's always an honor to work for you. I'll make a decision soon."

"Please do that," Mr. Lapham said.

London swayed a bit dizzily as she left the suite and closed the door behind her. She stood in the passageway trying to regain her bearings despite the continual heaving of the ship.

How much more unreal can things get? she wondered.

For one thing, just how much talking had Mom and Mr. Lapham done last night?

Just how much had Mom told him about herself?

It was starting to seem as though everybody aboard the *Nachtmusik* had befriended Mom—and also that everybody was more comfortable with her presence here than London herself was.

Still bemused by this odd new situation, London made her way back to the ship's reception area, with its elevator and stairs. Before she could decide what part of her job she should get back to first, her thoughts were interrupted by a familiar German-accented voice.

"Hallo, London—just the person I wanted to see."

She turned and saw the ship's historian, Emil Waldmüller, walking toward her. The rather haughty but not unhandsome dark-haired scholar with black-rimmed glasses was smiling that dry, ironic smile of his.

He glanced at his watch and said, "The two of us have some work to do before we reach Oslofjord, eh? Plans, reservations, tour ideas, the usual sorts of things. Let us go to the library and get to it."

He's absolutely right, London thought.

Of course, she'd rather take this time to talk with Bryce. But she knew he was frantically busy in the kitchen, so now was not the time. Besides, she was glad to have something professional to deal with in the midst of all the personal chaos of her life right now.

She and Emil started toward the lounge and adjoining library but stopped in their tracks when they heard a woman singing just behind them. It wasn't a very good voice, so it definitely wasn't Letitia—or Mom.

When they both whirled around, London was surprised to see a short woman with a smooth helmet of dark hair singing lyrics from some old standard tune and swaying to the music. The ship's concierge, Amy Blassingame, chirped, "Oh, what a marvelous singer your mother is, London!"

Then Amy smiled impishly up at Emil, and asked, "Don't you agree that 'Stardust'—by *Hoagy Carmichael*—is one of the loveliest songs ever?"

Emil let out a grunt of anger, then turned and stalked off, leaving London and Amy behind.

CHAPTER TEN

As London watched Emil stride away, she heard a gloating chuckle from Amy.

Then Amy said, "That man has no sense of humor."

London's first impulse was to make some excuse and get away from this latest drama between the ship's historian and the concierge. She already had enough questions on her mind, and this pair's on and off feuds were nothing new. They'd even had a brief, unlikely romance, but had quickly broken it off.

But she was intrigued by the odd emphasis Amy had put on the name of the composer, Hoagy Carmichael—especially right after complimenting Mom's singing. She had to wonder which comment had made Emil so angry.

"What was that all about?" London asked.

Amy sounded surprised, "Weren't you there when it happened? No, that's right, you'd already left. During the cabaret, Mr. Lapham and Letitia and your mother started taking requests from the audience. In his best know-it-all manner, Emil stood up and asked them to perform 'Stardust'—by Harold Arlen."

"Oh dear," London said, starting to get the picture.

"Oh dear indeed," Amy said. "Your mom very sweetly explained to the whole audience that 'Stardust' was actually written by Hoagy Carmichael, not Harold Arlen. Then Letitia graciously stepped out of the way, and your mom sang 'Stardust' as a gorgeous solo with Mr. Lapham playing the piano. She sang it quiet and intimate-like right in Emil's face, exactly as if she were performing for him and no one else. It was like putting a spotlight on his humiliation. He stormed out as soon as she'd finished the song."

Now London understood the cause of Emil's fury. The historian was not only haughty and elitist—he was also thin-skinned, with an enormous but very fragile ego. That ego had taken a few blows during the last few days, especially after Mr. Lapham's arrival. Mr. Lapham was every bit as knowledgeable as Emil about all sorts of things, and he didn't mind showing off his knowledge.

Last night he got the same treatment from Mom, London thought.

49

And Emil doesn't deal well with embarrassment.

"I shouldn't get such a kick out of it," Amy said with a guilty giggle. "But I guess I can't help twisting the knife a little—especially since it was a woman who got the best of him last night. I can't help thinking it kind of serves him right. What are you up to?"

"I have to do some work with Emil about the upcoming tours," London said.

"Oh, I'm sorry for disrupting things," Amy said with a giggle that contradicted her apology. "I'll get out of your way. I'm sure he'll be fine in a few minutes, at least if you throw him a few compliments."

Amy scurried off, and London made her way to the library, which was just off the big lounge.

Poor Emil, she thought.

As London had expected, the library door was closed. Even though the book and video collection were open to the passengers on the *Nachtmusik,* the historian sometimes shut himself up in there to listen to music and ruminate on his thoughts.

She knocked cautiously on the door and asked, "Emil, may I come in?"

"Of course you may come in," Emil's voice snapped from inside the room. "Why shouldn't you come in? The library is open to all."

London stepped into the cluttered room. Emil was sitting at the large table where passengers sometimes gathered for his lectures or workshops. His arms were crossed, and his brow furrowed in a haughty frown.

London said, "Uh, Emil—do you want to talk about it?"

"Talk about what?" Emil replied through clenched teeth.

"Well—whatever happened at the cabaret last night," London said.

"I don't know what you mean. Sit down and let's get to work."

There's no point in arguing about it, London thought with a shrug

Relieved at the prospect of doing something productive, she sat down at the table with Emil and started to work. There was plenty do in preparation for their arrival in Oslo, including sorting through logistics of the island-hopping some of the passengers were planning to do in Oslofjord.

Emil's mood improved as he and London went about their tasks together. When the time came around for Emil to give a little introductory lecture to passengers on the open-air *Rondo* deck as the *Nachtmusik* neared its destination, she thought the historian was pretty much his old self again.

London walked up the stairs with him and out into the bright sunlight. It was a lovely day, and quite a few passengers were gathered near the ship's prow to hear what Emil had to say. Amy was among them—and so were Mr. Lapham and Mom, who were standing together.

This should put Emil back into a good frame of mind, London thought. *It's where he shines best.*

Emil stepped up to the bow, where two landmasses were just then coming into view.

"Ladies and gentlemen," he said, "we are about to enter the fjord leading to Oslo. The area around Oslofjord has been inhabited at least since the Stone Age or the Bronze Age, included by the Vikings."

Pointing ahead, he continued, "Up ahead on an island to port you can see the Svenner lighthouse, and to starboard on another island you can see the Torbjørnskjaer lighthouse. These two lighthouses mark the entrance to Oslofjord, and—"

London felt a warning chill when she heard Mom's voice call out to him.

"Excuse me, Herr Waldmüller …"

Oh, no, London thought.

Emil turned and glared at her and growled, "What is it, Ms. Rose?"

Smiling sweetly, Mom said, "Well, I think you are mistaken about the lighthouse to port. That's actually the Færder lighthouse."

Emil's face turned an alarming shade of red.

Still standing next to Mom, Mr. Lapham spoke up.

"I believe the lady may be correct, Emil."

Mom added, "Yes, I'm quite sure of it. The Svenner lighthouse is on an island farther west, and we can't actually see it from where we are."

Emil's face twitched and his fists clenched, but he managed to keep himself under control.

In a raspy voice he said to Mom, "Madam, I have a pretty good command of the geography of these parts. And I have very little doubt that the lighthouse to port is really the Svenner lighthouse, and that the Færder lighthouse is the one farther away. But we can check the facts of the matter after my lecture. If I am wrong, I will gladly concede my error. Meanwhile, allow me to proceed."

Looking rattled and agitated now, he pointed and said, "Also over to port, you'll soon see a charming little village come into view— Åsgårdstrand, it is called. It famous for being the home of that great modernist painter …"

Emil paused, and all the blood suddenly drained from his face.

Oh, no, London thought.

The familiar name was surely on the tip of Emil's tongue, but London realized that he was so flustered that he just couldn't bring it to mind. That kind of thing never happened, not with this historian. How was he going to pull this lecture off?

And again, Mom spoke up.

"I believe you're thinking of Edvard Munch, who is especially famous for painting *The Scream.*"

Emil's eyes bulged, and for a moment he seemed to be having trouble catching his breath.

Finally, he managed to gasp out the words, "This … is … intolerable!"

As she watched Emil stagger off toward the elevator, London realized something surprising.

At least one person aboard the Nachtmusik *doesn't seem enamored of Mom.*

But the *Nachtmusik* still had an important stopover in Norway, and the whole crew needed to be at their best. She had hoped that Oslo would offer a warm and wonderful finale to their sometimes-disconcerting European Tour.

This is bad, London thought with dread. *This is really bad.*

CHAPTER ELEVEN

As Emil went stalking away, Mom trotted over to London and asked in an innocent voice, "Was it something I said?"

London was about to reply, *Yes, Mom, it was definitely something you said.*

Then she realized that the passengers clustered right there on the open deck were looking rather confused. They were still waiting for the promised lecture on the Oslofjord, which the *Nachtmusik* was now passing through.

This was not the time to get into a public tiff with her mother.

Fortunately, Mr. Lapham took charge of the situation. As Emil stalked off, the CEO stepped toward London and said, "Let's go talk to him. Surely we can fix this."

Then he turned toward Mom and added, "Uh, Barbara, could you fill in lecturing for a few moments? I'm sure our guests would appreciate it."

Mom's face lit up with enthusiasm.

"Of course!" she cried happily, turning to the audience.

London was a bit surprised at Mr. Lapham's request. He seemed to have considerable confidence in Mom's knowledge of Oslofjord. She wondered if the CEO had thought of the possible effect on Emil of having Mom taking over his duties, even temporarily. But this was also not the time to get into a discussion with her boss.

Anyhow, she saw that the passengers looked perfectly happy with the substitute. It occurred to London that Mom was already a celebrity for those who had enjoyed her performance in the lounge last night.

As London hurried after Mr. Lapham, who was following after Emil, she could hear Mom explaining more about Munch's familiar painting *The Scream*.

"Munch actually painted *The Scream* while looking out over this fjord as the sun set and the clouds turned red. He wrote in his diary, 'I sensed a scream passing through nature; it seemed to me that I heard the scream.'"

She certainly seems to know what she's talking about, London realized.

53

She and Mr. Lapham caught up with Emil just as he stepped into the elevator. They stepped right into the car with him, and then the door began to close.

"Wait for me!" someone cried out behind them.

Mr. Lapham stopped the door from closing, and Amy dashed into the elevator car with them. The concierge appeared to share their concern over Emil.

The elevator door finally closed, and the four people all turned and looked at each other.

"Emil, where are you going?" Mr. Lapham asked as the car began to make its descent.

"To my stateroom, of course," Emil said, crossing his arms. "I plan to stay there until this voyage is quite over. And then—well, who can say? The whole world awaits, I suppose. Who knows what my future may bring?"

"But you still have work to do here," Mr. Lapham said. "We depend upon your considerable expertise."

"Oh, I hardly think so," Emil said with a smirk. "You yourself began encroaching on my duties back in Copenhagen. And now that—that *woman* up there has completely usurped my position. She has brought any need for my services to an end."

Amy reached up and touched him on the shoulder. "Don't you think you're overreacting, dear?" she said, with a distinct note of sympathy in her voice.

I guess she still cares about him, at least a little, London thought.

But Emil brushed the hand aside.

"Overreacting? Not a bit. Mr. Lapham, I will write my resignation letter and give it to you as soon as possible. Meanwhile, you might as well turn all my duties over to the interloper. I am quite through with them."

London herself had no idea what to say during the elevator ride. It especially troubled her that her own mother's behavior had caused this outburst.

The elevator doors opened on the *Allegro* level, and Emil got out and strode down the passageway toward his stateroom.

Amy followed after him saying, "Now, Emil, calm down, OK? … Just listen to me … There's no reason to be like this …"

Emil opened the door to his stateroom and stormed inside and closed the door before Amy could follow him.

Amy knocked on the door, calling out his name.

She might wind up knocking for a long time, London thought. She knew that their prestigious historian was nothing if not stubborn.

Meanwhile, Mr. Lapham was looking thoughtful. He asked London, "Do you think he'll come to his senses?"

London considered the question. She'd seen Emil in all sorts of moods, including some pretty foul ones. But she'd never seen him act anything like this before. He was usually more careful to maintain his dignity.

"I'm not sure," she said to Mr. Lapham. "This seems to have gotten to him more than most problems do."

"He's not handling this one very well," Mr. Lapham said with a sigh. Then he added, "Perhaps we didn't either."

Amy was still standing outside of Emil's door. The small concierge looked determined, as though she intended to stay at her post until the historian either came out or let her in.

Mr. Lapham said to London, "There's nothing more to be done here for now. We'd better head back topside and see how things are going there."

London and the CEO got back into the elevator and returned to the open-air *Rondo* deck. When they stepped outside, London quickly saw that Mom had Emil's erstwhile lecture audience wrapped around her little finger. Everyone was smiling and listening raptly as she kept right on talking.

"… and if I'm not mistaken, we are right this minute sailing over the Oslofjord Tunnel, which opened in the year 2000 and runs all the way across the fjord, reaching a depth of about 440 feet below sea level."

Then with a chuckle, she added, "I should mention that we're using the word 'fjord' a bit loosely. Geologically speaking, Oslofjord isn't a fjord at all. True fjords are flanked by mountains that were cut apart by giant glaciers back during the Ice Age. If you've never seen a real fjord, I hope you do sometime. The cliffs and mountainsides are really quite breathtaking."

She pointed out over the water, which was now scattered with boats of all kinds and sizes, and also to the shore, which was dotted with houses and villages.

"Anyway, the Oslofjord is actually a bay," she said. "Or rather a pair of connecting bays, the *indre,* or 'inner,' and *ytre,* or outer. The city of Oslo awaits us at the far end of the *indre* …"

Mr. Lapham nudged London as Mom continued her impromptu

spiel.

"We're lucky to have your mother aboard, eh?" he said.

Maybe, London thought.

But then again, Mom's expertise wouldn't be needed if she hadn't succeeded in driving the normally stoic Emil Waldmüller to the brink of insanity. Still, London couldn't deny that Mom was giving an amazing performance.

"I'd like to know how she knows all this stuff," she said to Mr. Lapham.

"Didn't you know?" Mr. Lapham said. "She lived in Norway for a couple of years. She even conducted tours in Oslo. She knows even more about Oslo than I do—and I know quite a lot. She's just what we need right now."

Well, there's one more thing I didn't know about her, London thought, stifling a sigh.

She wondered wryly whether she could learn everything about her own mother just by going around the *Nachtmusik* asking people questions.

Why does everybody else seem to know more about her than I do?

And is she ever going to tell me anything about her life, and why she left us?

CHAPTER TWELVE

London felt increasingly exasperated as she and Mr. Lapham stood listening to Mom's lecture.

Why do Mom and I keep missing any chance to really talk? she wondered.

It was starting to seem ridiculous. Of course. both she and Mom had been at a loss for words when they'd first seen each other back in Lillberg. That was understandable. But surely, they should have been able to do at least a little catching up by now.

So why hadn't it happened?

For her part, Mom always seemed to have an excuse not to talk, and some of those excuses had struck London as pretty lame. She doubted that Mom had really left that message on the restaurant's machine telling her about a change of plans.

And then London had gotten back to the ship to find Mom in the middle of a wildly popular cabaret performance.

Just another way to avoid talking? London wondered.

Then there had been their breakfast this morning, and they'd actually talked a little then, but even so Mom had somehow managed to avoid telling London anything she really wanted to know.

That amnesia thing, London thought, remembering how Mom had again insisted that her memories were "foggy."

London glanced over at Mr. Lapham, who was laughing at something funny Mom had just said.

Mr. Lapham seemed to have gotten to know Mom surprisingly well.

Mom had also taken up singing with Letitia.

She'd even hit it off with Bob and Stanley and switched staterooms with them.

Weirdest of all, she'd spent time talking to Bryce.

Even I haven't had time to talk to Bryce! London thought.

And she and Bryce had an awful lot they needed to talk about.

But then an unsettling possibility began to dawn on London.

Is it really me?

Am I really the one doing the avoiding?

Do I even really want to know why she disappeared twenty years ago?

Mom wound up her lecture, and her listeners applauded and then started asking questions. London drew a deep sigh. Her mother was busy with admirers, and London herself had things to do. She turned and walked away toward the elevator.

*

London was rushing about making sure everybody was ready for their arrival when she felt the *Nachtmusik* slowly coming to a halt. The engines soon stopped, and London heard the sounds of men mooring the ship to the pier.

We're here, she realized. *We're in Oslo.*

As she hurried down the passageway toward the reception area, Sir Reggie himself came trotting toward her from the opposite direction. He was carrying his leash in his mouth.

"Oh, you want to go ashore too, do you?" she said.

Sir Reggie sat and let out an anxious whine.

"Well, I don't know ..."

Sir Reggie's whine grew higher and louder.

London said to him, "You know, our normal rule is that you can't go ashore in any city until I find out how dog-friendly it is."

Sir Reggie tossed his head back and forth to make the leash wave and rattle.

"Well, maybe just this last time," London said. "Our first destination is the Akershus Fortress, and I hear that people walk dogs there all the time. It should be OK."

She fastened the leash onto Sir Reggie's collar, and the two of them walked through the reception area to the top of the gangway.

"Oh, my goodness!" she murmured aloud when she saw the view outside.

Only a short distance away from the pier, stone walls rose in a steep cliff. Atop that foundation towered a massive stone castle with its turrets and fortifications.

"There it is, Sir Reggie," London said. "Akershus Fortress."

She and her dog continued down to the bottom of the gangway, where passengers were gathering. Amy was checking off passengers' names and making sure she knew what they planned to do and where they expected to go during their stay in Oslo.

Many were heading out to explore on their own, including the Royal Palace, the Munch Museum, and the Oslo Opera House. About 25 passengers had chosen to start sightseeing right here with a tour of Akershus Fortress.

When Amy got a break, London approached her and asked, "Were you able to talk to Emil?"

Amy shook her head.

"I knocked on his door until my knuckles got sore. There's no getting through to him when he gets like this. I think he really means it. He's finished working aboard the *Nachtmusik* for good."

"Oh, dear," London said.

"That means more work for you, doesn't it?" Amy said, smirking a little. "I hope you feel ready to fill his shoes today."

As Amy turned back to her task, London realized she didn't feel ready at all. As always, she'd done a good bit of homework about their destination, but she'd expected to also rely on Emil's much more encyclopedic knowledge.

Then she noticed Mr. Lapham and Mom standing together talking intently.

As she picked up Sir Reggie and went to join them, London remembered Mr. Lapham's comment.

"We're lucky to have your mother aboard, eh?"

She thought maybe her mother was going to take over some of the tour guide responsibilities. But when she approached, she recognized anxiety in their voices and faces.

"Are you sure you're up to this?" Mr. Lapham said, holding Mom's hands reassuringly.

"I—I think so," Mom said.

"Because I can take over tour guide duty while we're at the fortress. I know a good bit about it myself."

"No, don't be silly," Mom said, forcing a smile. "I've got to face my demons straight on."

Mr. Lapham chuckled and said, "Well, they're not necessarily *your* demons."

"Even so. I can't let them get the best of me."

"Very well, then," Mr. Lapham said. "But just remember, you can change your mind at any moment. I'm always here to pitch in."

"Thanks, I'll keep that in mind," Mom said.

What's this all about? London wondered.

After Mom's cabaret act last night and her lecture about Oslofjord,

59

London found it hard to believe she'd suddenly come down with a case of stage fright.

Just then, Mom stepped away from Mr. Lapham and clapped her hands and called out for everybody to hear her.

"Everybody who's scheduled to tour Akershus Fortress, follow me and let's get started!"

Still holding Sir Reggie in her arms, London trotted alongside Mom as she led the group up a steep cobblestone path toward an arched opening in the massive stone walls.

"Is everything OK, Mom?" London asked.

Mom laughed a bit awkwardly.

"Of course, everything is fine, dear. Why wouldn't everything be fine?"

London shrugged and said, "Well, I happened to overhear ... you said something about demons ..."

"Oh, that," Mom said, patting her on the cheek. "It's nothing for you to worry about, dear. We've all got our demons, don't we? I know how to keep my own demons in line."

Wagging her finger at London, she added, "I hope you do too. Demon-taming is an important life skill. Too many people don't know how to properly go about it. They let their demons run the whole show."

Mom brought the group to a halt just outside the arched stone gate.

Seeming her usual confident self now, Mom clapped and called out again, "Ladies and gentlemen, we are about to enter Akershus Fortress, which was built around 1300 by King Haakon V. As you can well imagine, these mighty fortifications have successfully resisted many sieges over the centuries. Let's explore, shall we?"

London set Sir Reggie down to walk beside her as the group followed Mom through the tunnel and up a steep slope of cobblestones onto the vast castle grounds with their formidable stone towers and buildings.

"First of all," Mom said, "let's go have a look at the city that Akershus Fortress is here to protect. After all, it's *still* a military facility, even though it's open to the public. Who knows—maybe this fortification might get put to use again, someday. I hope you're ready for a bit of a climb!"

The group good-naturedly grumbled as they climbed up more paths and stone steps. Even Sir Reggie was soon panting from the effort. Finally, they reached the top of the massive, grass-covered ramparts lined with antique cannons.

Like everyone else, London let out a gasp of amazement.

From this high place, they could see the whole city of Oslo, and also the entire *indre*—inner—fjord, including the strait where the *Nachtmusik* had sailed from the broader *ytre*—outer—fjord earlier this morning.

Boats of all shapes and types sailed over the fjord, and countless docks far below were crowded with boats and ships ranging from three-masted schooners to modern vessels like the *Nachtmusik.*

Like most of the others in the tour, London felt out of breath from the climb. Nevertheless, Mom pointed out over the water and started talking to the group.

"Let's just take a moment and imagine what this fjord might have looked like during the Viking Age, from 793 to 1066 A.D. Picture those majestic Viking ships with their rows of oars, their square sails, and their curved prows, all of them coming and going among the settlements along the shore. In fact, the whole region around the Oslofjord was called *Viken* back in those days ..."

Mom finally seemed to run out of breath.

She shook her head with a laugh and said to Mr. Lapham, "Jeremy, I seem to be a bit winded. Would you care to share a bit of your expertise while I collect myself?"

"I'll be glad to," Mr. Lapham said.

London couldn't help but notice that Mom was asking Mr. Lapham to fill in instead of her. But she figured it was just as well. Her knowledge of this particular tourist site was a bit shaky.

For his part, the CEO seemed eager to pitch in and unfazed by the climb.

Of course, he likes to drop out of helicopters, London thought, remembering his daredevil airborne arrival on the *Nachtmusik.*

Mr. Lapham stepped in front of the group and spoke.

"Oslo was founded by King Harald Hardraade in 1040, around the end of the Viking Age." Pointing far beyond the fortifications, Mr. Lapham said, "Harald originally founded what he called the city of Ánslo to the west of the Akerselva, that charming little river you can see cutting through today's city right over there."

Mr. Lapham thought for a moment, then added, "When Haakon V built this fortress here some 250 years later, it seemed ideally situated to protect the city, as you can well imagine—although it wasn't of much help against the Black Death. That plague killed about three-quarters of the populace in 1350. Cannons and walls aren't exactly rat-proof—and that's how the plague was spread, by rats."

With a sigh, Mr. Lapham said, "Also, the city of Ánslo in its original location had an unfortunate tendency to—how shall I put it?—burn to the ground over and over again. Every 20 years seemed to bring a catastrophic conflagration."

Mr. Lapham added wryly, "Of course, that was long before the invention of smoke alarms and sprinkler systems and fancy fireproof construction materials, and the building codes of the time were probably rather lacking in the necessary rigor. All told, the original site did seem to be a bit unlucky."

Mr. Lapham shrugged and said, "Finally, after a three-day fire in 1624, King Christian IV decided he'd had enough of such disasters. He decided to pack up the whole city and move it to the other side of this fortress."

Pointing across a busy inlet toward a bustling modern urban area, Mr. Lapham continued, "The king commanded everybody to rebuild it from scratch over to the east of Akershus Fortress. He renamed it Christiania, and so it was called until 1925, when it became Oslo again."

Then he pointed out over the water.

"As you can see, the *indre* fjord is dotted with charming little islands, some 40 of them within Oslo's city limits. When we finish touring the castle, we'll do a little island hopping. I promise it will be great fun. Now let's retrace our steps and have a look around the fortress."

Sighing with relief that their climbing had come to an end, the group followed Mom and Mr. Lapham back down the way they'd come.

They soon arrived at a tunnel with steps that led down into some kind of a gloomy-looking cellar.

When Mom shuddered sharply at the entryway with its open barred gate, Mr. Lapham put his hand on her shoulder.

"You needn't do this, my dear," he said. "You could stay right here while I show them around down there."

Mom took a deep breath and drew herself up and laughed nervously.

"Don't be silly, Jeremy," she said. "It's time."

Time for what? London wondered as she picked up Sir Reggie and held him tightly. As she and the group began to follow Mom and Mr.

Lapham, single file down the narrow stairway, London remembered what Mom had said a short while ago.

"I've got to face my demons straight on."

London felt a cold shiver as she wondered what kind of "demons" might lie ahead.

CHAPTER THIRTEEN

The spooky mood of the stone walled stairway seemed to be contagious. The passengers spoke to each other in nervous whispers as they continued on their way down. Even Sir Reggie shivered in London's arms and let out an apprehensive whimper.

It's the kind of place that might harbor actual demons, she thought. *If any such thing really existed.*

Finally, they all reached the bottom of the stairs and found themselves in the midst of stone passageways with iron gates and barred cells.

Mom's voice echoed eerily as she spoke softly.

"Akershus Fortress was used for many years as a prison, and we are now in its infamous medieval dungeon. Prisoners suffered misery, starvation, and torture down here."

Leading the group deep into the passageway, Mom continued, "All kinds of celebrated outlaws have been locked up in these cells, including Ole Høiland, the so-called 'Norwegian Robin Hood.' Ole was caught and imprisoned several times and kept managing to escape. He even escaped from this place once, but the last time he was locked up here was too much even for him. He committed suicide in his cell in 1848."

Mom shivered a little, then added with a forced chuckle, "Judging from how nervous I must seem, you're probably wondering whether I was once a prisoner here myself. No, I'm glad to say I wasn't. But I *was* a tour guide here at the fortress for a few months, until I had an experience that sent me looking for another job ..."

Mom's voice faded, then she held her fingers to her lips.

"Listen very closely. Does anybody hear anything?"

The group fell silent and listened for a moment—London as intently as all the rest. Even Sir Reggie perked up his ears and seemed to listen. Then the visitors shook their heads and murmured no.

Mom smiled and said, "That's just as well. People here sometimes claim to hear pretty frightening sounds. Some people say that Akershus Fortress is the most haunted place in Norway."

A few members of the group chuckled skeptically.

Mom laughed a little as well.

"I don't blame you if you don't believe in such things," she said. "And with some luck, we'll leave here today without anything happening to change your minds. But over the centuries, visitors have reported hearing screams and rattling chains, and even seeing a lot of weird things."

"Such as?" asked one of the passengers, sounding a bit nervous now.

London's own curiosity was definitely piqued.

Mom said, "Well, for one thing, tiny burning women called 'nightpyres,' who fly through the air and cackle and have horrible grins. They're not supposed to be bad spirits, really. In fact, they warn of dangerous fires breaking out in the castle."

Nightpyres, London thought with fascination. *Sort of like medieval fire alarms!*

Mr. Lapham added, "Visitors also say they feel and hear mysterious breathing out of nowhere, and sometimes they get pushed or shoved when nobody is near them. I've heard *lots* of stories about this place."

Mom took a long deep breath, then said, "When I worked here as a tour guide, I didn't see or hear any of *those* things. But one day I came down here early in the morning before anyone else did, and before I could turn the lights on, I saw ..."

Saw what? London wondered as Mom's voice faded for a moment.

Mom inhaled sharply and pointed, "Well, it was quite dark, but I *thought* I saw a shadowy cloaked woman wandering right over there. I was about to ask her who she was when she turned toward me."

Mom hesitated and then said, "But she didn't have a face."

A silence fell on the group.

London herself asked her, "What did you do?"

Mom shuddered and replied, "I suddenly turned on the lights, and she vanished."

London felt Sir Reggie tense up in her arms. Even her little dog was spooked by the story.

"Are you sure you didn't just imagine it?" one of the passengers asked Mom.

London was wondering the same thing. She still didn't know how prone Mom might be to flights of fantasy.

"Oh, it's very possible," Mom said nervously. "This place *does* have quite an effect on the imagination."

Several others muttered in agreement. London certainly felt under

65

the thrall of the place's atmosphere.

"Maybe it was even some kind of a prank," somebody else said.

"Maybe," Mom said. "But when I mentioned the woman to the other tour guides, they said other people have seen her wandering around the castle. She even has a name—Mantelgeisten, she's called."

Mom shook off her unease and added, "Well, I never saw her again. So let's get on with our tour."

Mr. Lapham smiled approvingly at Mom, then he nodded and walked with the others as they continued on through the dungeon.

"Oh, by the way," Mom said to the group, "I hope nobody saw a weird snarling dog or a black galloping horse back the way we came in."

A dog? London wondered. *A horse?*

The tourists murmured no.

"That's good," Mom said, wiping her brow with relief. "Otherwise, somebody would be in real trouble."

Apparently, everybody was too spooked to dare to ask her what she meant.

As they continued on their way toward the end of the dungeon, Mr. Lapham touched Mom on the shoulder and said in an admiring tone, "You're a brave woman, Barbara Rose."

"Why thank you, Jeremy," Mom replied.

As Mr. Lapham continued on ahead, Mom gave London a nudge.

"How did you like *that* little number?" she said to London with a wink, then hurried on ahead.

Little number? London wondered.

What did Mom mean by that?

Had she just made up that story about seeing Mantelgeisten?

If so, she fooled everybody, London thought. *Including Mr. Lapham.*

And if so, London didn't think that was a nice thing to do. She figured she'd better talk to Mom about it whenever she got a chance.

Along with everything else we've got to talk about, she thought with a sigh.

Mom finally led the group out of the dungeon and passed on into a marble room with walls and a ceiling that together formed a continuous arch. It contained two enormous coffin-like cases.

"This is the Royal Mausoleum," Mom explained, pointing to the cases. "The two sarcophagi contain the remains of Norwegian monarchs who reigned and died during the 20th century. Inside the white sarcophagus are King Haakon VII and Queen Maud. Inside the dark green sarcophagus to the left are Haakon and Maud's son, King Olav V, and his wife, the Crown Princess Märtha."

Mr. Lapham put in, "King Haakon VII and his son Olav V were both very fine fellows. During World War II they stood side by side resisting the Nazi occupation for as long as they could. Haakon's son Olav became known as *Folkekongen*—'The People's King'—on account of his easygoing, egalitarian manner."

With a laugh, Mr. Lapham added, "King Olav liked to go out driving in public lanes, and he even traveled by the public railway whenever he went skiing. When someone asked him why he dared go out without bodyguards …"

Laughing as well, Mom finished Mr. Lapham's thought, "Olav replied, 'I have four million bodyguards.'"

Mr. Lapham nodded and said, "And indeed he did. The whole population of Norway adored him."

Nodding toward a large space on the floor to the left of the sarcophagi, Mom said, "You can see that a space is reserved for a sarcophagus for Olav's son, the currently reigning King Harald V, and his wife, the Queen Consort Sonja."

Mom pointed around the room and said, "Sealed up in these walls are the remains of earlier Norwegian monarchs, including those of King Haakon V, the founder of Oslo and the builder of this fortress."

Sir Reggie leaned against London's shoulder and napped as Mom led the group on through a series of magnificent halls and chambers. Finally the group emerged outside again, where they stood facing the stone wall of a seemingly nondescript building with gables and a red-tiled roof.

Mr. Lapham walked over near the wall, then turned toward Mom and asked, "Is this the place where it happened?"

"That's the exact spot," Mom said.

The spot where what *happened?* London wondered.

She could tell by a general murmur that others were curious as well.

Mr. Lapham turned toward the group and said, "Tell me—what does the word 'quisling' mean to you?"

A mutter of disgust went through the group. Even Sir Reggie let out a low growl, but London thought that might be because he was dreaming.

A woman said, "It means a traitor to one's country."

"It does, indeed," Mr. Lapham said. "And you may feel blessed that your own very names don't become literal synonyms for humanity's worst characteristics. Allow me to explain."

Pacing in front of the wall, Mr. Lapham continued, "Akershus Fortress has successfully protected Oslo and all of Norway from all enemy sieges since it was first built back around 1300. Alas, it was surrendered without a fight to the German army in 1940 when the Norwegian government went into exile."

Mom added, "The Nazis turned this into a place of shame, where many members of the Norwegian resistance were executed. Of course, there were a few Norwegians who collaborated with the Nazis. The most notorious of those collaborators was Vidkun Quisling."

Mr. Lapham went on, "Quisling was a Norwegian army officer who urged the German invasion of Norway, and who declared himself head of the government when the Nazis took control of the country in 1940. He did everything he could to promote Nazism during the occupation and sent 1000 Norwegian Jews to their deaths. Of course, the people of Norway came to hate him."

Mom walked over to the wall and said, "When the war ended, Quisling was tried and found guilty of treason."

She patted the stones and added, "And he was shot to death by a firing squad right here."

The group fell silent as they absorbed this historical fact.

Then Mom smiled and said, "Well, on that note, I guess our tour of Akershus Fortress has come to an end. Let's head back the way we came and get ready for our next adventure."

She led the group back through the fortress grounds, and they soon arrived at the dock where the *Nachtmusik* was docked. Now four inboard motorboats were also docked nearby.

London set Sir Reggie down and clapped her hands and called out to the tourists, "OK, folks, now we're going to begin the fun part of today's activities. We're going to split into four groups and go fishing and island-hopping on these three boats, and then ..."

She was interrupted by an unexpected—and unwelcome—arrival.

CHAPTER FOURTEEN

"Is it OK if I join you?" the tall, imposing man called out from the *Nachtmusik* gangway. As he approached, London stifled a sigh. Scott Raife wasn't her favorite passenger, and judging from a collective murmur of dismay, others in her tour group felt the same way.

She even heard a soft grumble from Sir Reggie.

It wasn't that she'd had any specific issue with Scott. In spite of his pushy, macho attitude, she hadn't even heard of any actual conflicts between him and other passengers or crew. But his overly hearty manner and loud, blustery voice could be grating, and London had so far managed to keep her distance from him.

Now he strode up to her with a wide grin on his stubble-bearded face. Up close like this, she could see that his muscular frame was starting to bulge around the middle with age.

"I heard we're going fishing," he said. "I'm ready for that."

"I didn't realize you signed up for the boat trip," London said. She certainly hadn't planned on bringing him island-hopping. But she did a little mental math and figured there would be room on one of the waiting boats. She couldn't actually turn him away.

"Well, here I am," he replied. "Your very own maestro with a rod and reel."

"You brought your own rod and reel?" London asked.

Scott gestured to the long, cylindrical case slung over his shoulder. "What do you think this is? It's a Penn International fishing rig—a rod and reel that I paid a thousand bucks for, especially for this trip. I figured I'd get a chance to use it sooner or later."

London squinted uncertainly.

"Um, Scott, I'm not sure you'll be needing that," she told him.

"I only use the very best," Scott said. "So I brought it with me."

"Well, yes, but …"

"But what?"

Nodding toward the four boats, London said, "The pilots we signed up with said we wouldn't be needing any equipment of our own."

Scott scoffed loudly and said to the group, "Well, maybe none of the rest of you will need any equipment. But I'm planning to do some serious game fishing. Maybe I can even teach the locals a few things."

London shrugged. She doubted that the man's self-confidence was backed up by actual skill, but she thought that there would probably be no harm in letting him bring along his expensive new plaything.

She turned to Mr. Lapham, and the two of them set right to work dividing the tour group up for the four boats. Since she didn't want to let Mom get out of her sight, London made sure she was included in her own group.

Maybe I'm afraid she'll run off again, she thought.

She also included Scott in her group, because she figured he might be a problem for anyone else. And after all, this sort of thing was London's job.

The other two passengers in her boat would be Gus and Honey Jarrett, a middle-aged couple London had gotten to know and like. She was glad to see that, for once, Honey wasn't wearing high heels and had limited her usual frills to a ruffle on the bottom of her blouse. Gus was sporting a fisherman's cap, and Honey had a sailor hat perched on her dyed red hair.

Seeing that London's quota was filled, Mr. Lapham assigned himself to another boat. He herded all three of the other groups to their respective fishing boats and boarded one himself.

As London turned back to her charges, a large, powerful man wearing a nautical cap and a life vest climbed off of the nearest boat and greeted them with a robust grin. He had a barrel chest, a broad cheerful face, and rough skin and a swaggering walk that London guessed came from spending much of his life on a boat.

"Welcome, folks," he said in Norwegian-accented English. "I am Iver Nilsen, and I am the captain of the *Kråkebolle.*"

London introduced herself and her four passengers, then suddenly realized that the dog at her feet might be a problem.

"Oh, dear," she said to Sir Reggie as she picked him up in her arms again. "I should have thought about you earlier."

Turning to Captain Nilsen, she asked, "Could you wait here for just a few minutes while I take Sir Reggie back to our ship?"

The captain walked toward Sir Reggie and peered at him closely.

"It depends," he said. "Does this 'Sir Reggie' of yours really want to be left behind? Should he not really be given a choice in the matter?"

Scratching the dog's head, the captain added, "What do you say, my friend? Would not you rather join us out on the wild fjord than spend your day aboard some boring tour ship?"

To the amusement of the others, Sir Reggie let out a yap that clearly said "yes."

"Are you sure it will be all right?" she asked the captain.

The captain shrugged his enormous shoulders.

"As long as Sir Reggie is not afraid of the water," he said. "My guess is that this beast is not afraid of anything. He strikes me as very, eh … *intrepid* I think is the English word."

Sir Reggie let out a yap of enthusiastic agreement.

"Let us consider it settled, then," the captain said.

But then Captain Nilsen crossed his arms and frowned at another passenger.

"What is that you have brought with you, Mr. Raife?" he asked, indicating the case over Scott's shoulder.

"Fishing gear," Scott said.

"Well, you will not be needing it," Scott said. "Best you take it back to your ship or stow it under the *Kråkebolle's* bow."

"Aren't we going to be fishing?" Scott asked.

"Yes, but for mackerel," Captain Nilsen said. "We have got everything you need right here."

London sensed that Scott was daunted by the captain, who was a bit shorter than he was but undoubtedly a great deal stronger. Nevertheless, Scott was not about to let his intimidation show to the others.

"The rest of you can fish for mackerel," he said. "I've got my eye on bigger game."

"Is that so?" Captain Nilsen asked with a wry squint. "What kind of game do you have in mind?"

"Why, sea trout, of course," Scott said.

The captain let out a skeptical laugh. London was surprised to hear her mother chuckle as well.

The captain shook his head and said, "I am afraid you are not likely to have much luck catching sea trout on this trip. And besides …"

Captain Nilsen broke out laughing again, apparently quite amused by Scott's expectations.

"Well, have it your way," he said to Scott. "I do not suppose you will do any harm."

Then with a wave to the group, he said, "Come aboard, all of you, and let us get started."

Captain Nilsen helped Honey Jarrett into the boat—a delicate task, since the woman was, as usual, wearing a tight short skirt. Her loudmouthed but always affectionate husband Gus also gave her hand.

Still staring at the captain from the dock, Scott grumbled, "I wonder why he doesn't think I'm going to catch any sea trout. I bought the right gear for it—the right lures too. And the Oslofjord is a good place for sea trout."

To London's alarm, Mom decided to offer her own opinion.

"Maybe it's because it's easier to catch that kind of fish here in the fjord when the weather is cooler. Also, it's best to do it from dry land— a rocky place is good. I don't know much about mackerel fishing, but I do know the captain will keep the boat moving. It will be really hard to catch sea trout from a moving boat."

Scott's face reddened with anger.

"Let me be the judge of my prospects, ma'am," he growled at Mom. "I've got a pretty good idea what I'm talking about. I'll have you know I'm no mean excuse for a sportsman. I've gone rock climbing in the Rockies. And sky diving. And I ran with the bulls in Pamplona."

Mom snickered a little.

"Catch a lot of sea trout doing that stuff?" she asked.

Scott's eyes bulged and he growled aloud. But before he could think of a sharp comeback, the captain called out to him.

"It is your turn to come aboard, Mr. Raife."

Scott sputtered wordlessly and waved his finger at Mom, then followed the captain into the boat.

In her horror, London flashed back to how Mom had managed to humiliate Emil yesterday with her know-it-all attitude.

Is she always going to do this? she wondered.

"Mom, when are you going to learn to keep your mouth shut?" London said.

Mom stared at her with an innocent expression.

"What?" she said. "Was it something I said?"

"Just watch what you say, OK?"

"Don't I always?" Mom asked.

At that moment, Captain Nilsen reached out to give Mom a hand into the boat. She managed to board gracefully, while a scowling Scott Raife stood glaring at her.

London sighed and whispered to Sir Reggie, "This could turn out to be a pretty rocky ride."

CHAPTER FIFTEEN

Was it a mistake to put Mom in my group? London wondered as her mother climbed aboard the boat. She saw that Scott Raife was taking his fishing pole out of its case, conspicuously ignoring Mom.

At least a fight hasn't broken out yet, London thought. *If only Mom doesn't say anything else to make trouble.*

London handed Sir Reggie over to Captain Nilsen, who put him into the boat. Then London was the last to come aboard.

The *Kråkebolle* was long and low with just a small roof over the pilot's controls. A rolled-up canvas attached to that roof looked as though it could be extended over the whole cockpit, but London was glad that they would be enjoying the sunshine and open air today.

The passengers rode on padded seats that lined both sides of the cockpit. Mom had plopped down on the port side next to the Jarretts and was already exchanging playful comments with Honey. London sat down on the starboard side, and Sir Reggie hopped into her lap.

London thought that if Scott would sit down next to her, maybe she could keep him distracted from any possible barbs that Mom might deliver. He wasn't the company she preferred, but she'd do anything to keep peace aboard the boat.

As a slim, rather frail-looking young man unmoored the boat from the dock. Captain Nilsen introduced him in a playfully facetious tone.

"This hulking beast of a sailor is my son, Sander. He will be serving as my first mate—or trying his best at it, anyway. My regular man has gone off to seek bluer waters, you might say."

Sander waved to the group good-naturedly, apparently not bothered by his father's description.

"All had better get into life vests," Sander said in English, although he was clearly not quite as fluent as his father. "Under the seats," he added.

London, Mom, and the Jarretts rummaged around under the seats and found the orange life vests. As they put them on, the already buxom Honey giggled as she fastened the straps.

"It looks good on you," Gus told her.

"We can just consider it a Mae West moment," Honey replied.

Both Mom and Captain Nilsen laughed heartily along with Gus at the reference to the old-time movie star with the generous bust. During World War II, the British Royal Air Force tagged inflatable life jackets with her name.

Sander looked confused and Scott Raife looked positively grumpy. Still standing and examining his brand-new fishing gear, he grumbled, "I won't be needing a vest."

"You don't think so, do you?" Captain Nilsen inquired.

"Not a chance," Scott said. "I was a champion diver in high school. I put myself through law school, working summers as a lifeguard. I'm an excellent swimmer. Life vests cramp my style."

Captain Nilsen laughed ominously and held out a life vest for Scott.

"It is a rule on my boat that everybody wears a life vest," he said. "If you do not follow my rules, you will get a chance to show what an excellent swimmer you are sooner than you may expect."

Trying vainly not to look intimidated, Scott put on the life vest.

"What about poor Sir Reggie?" Honey asked with a snap of her chewing gum. "Doesn't he get a life vest too?"

"He's too little," Gus said.

The captain let out a hearty laugh as he reached under a seat.

"Not at all!" he said. "I have got just the thing right here."

He pulled out a tiny little life vest that looked like a toy and handed it to London. London's eyes widened with surprise.

"You mean you carry a special life vest for really small dogs?" she asked.

"Not exactly," Captain Nilsen said, laughing some more. "My cat Baldr sometimes likes to come fishing with me. Nothing excites him more than a really big catch! I had this specially made for him. It happens to be just the right size for Sir Reggie. I hope he does not mind sharing a life vest with a cat."

Gus chuckled and said, "I'm sure he won't. One of his best friends is a cat."

Of course London knew that Gus was referring to Sir Reggie's well-known friendship with Mr. Lapham's cat Siegfried. Indeed, Sir Reggie sniffed the vest with mild curiosity and allowed London to put it on him. When she was finished, she thought he looked markedly more comfortable in his life vest than Scott Raife did in his. The little dog scrambled into the seat next to London, and the ill-humored man finally sat down on the other side of her.

Captain Nilsen then attached the Norwegian flag, with its red background and its blue cross edged in white, to the stern of the boat. Finally, at the captain's order, Sander climbed into the boat, sat down at the controls, and fired up the engine. The *Kråkebolle* pulled smoothly away from the dock. In a few moments they were on their way across the enormous fjord, away from the city and toward the numerous local islands.

As they moved through the water, Sir Reggie put his front paws up against the seatback and stared raptly over the railing at the water, his tongue hanging out as he enjoyed the wind in his face. Seagulls darted near him and cawed as if to say hello, and he yapped out greetings in return, obviously having a wonderful time.

"I know just how you feel," London said, sitting next to the dog and scratching his head.

She found the salt air to be nothing less than intoxicating. Although the *Nachtmusik* had been sailing on open seas since it left Amsterdam a few days ago, standing high up on the *Rondo* deck, the *Nachtmusik* simply couldn't compare to riding so close to the surf and feeling the spray of water on one's cheeks.

The refreshing feeling almost made her forget about the huge, life-changing decision she would have to make in just a few hours, or about the confusion she felt about having Mom back in her life.

London could see that Honey and Gus were also enjoying the ride as they held hands and pointed out interesting sights to each other. Mom seemed positively hypnotized by the view. The captain, sitting among the passengers, was watching them and basking in their delight. Scott Raife, by contrast, sat there with his brand-new fishing pole across his lap, appearing rather unsure of himself.

He doesn't look like someone who's run with the bulls in Pamplona, London thought.

She wondered if maybe he'd been making all that stuff up about skydiving and cliff climbing. For all she knew, he couldn't even really swim. She felt that it was definitely a good thing that the captain had forced him to wear that life vest.

Honey held out her arms in the breeze and said, "It's such a nice sunny day, just so perfect—not too hot, and not too cold."

London smiled in unspoken agreement. She was glad she had issued instructions to the passengers suggesting they not dress too warmly.

"Who'd believe we're so far north?" Gus added.

London could see that the captain was about to explain the pleasant temperature, but Mom beat him to it.

"Oslofjord is protected from cold sea winds by the land surrounding it," she said. "It also gets warmed by the Norwegian Current, which brings tropical waters up from the Gulf Current to the south. I'll bet you find the islands especially pleasant. They're among the warmest islands in Norway, and they're just full of lush plant life."

The captain smiled as he listened to Mom, apparently not offended that she'd spoken up before he did. From a curl at the edge of his smile and a twinkle in his eye, London could see that he found Mom quite fascinating. She wondered if maybe he was developing a crush on her, like Mr. Lapham.

Maybe so, she thought.

London was bemused by the sheer range of reactions Mom seemed to stir up in people. Fortunately, most people took an immediate and strong liking to her—but not everybody.

Not Emil, London reminded herself.

And apparently not Scott Raife, either. As he sat by himself holding his fishing rod, he kept glancing at Mom with a sour expression.

A few people seemed to take a strong dislike to Barbara Rose. But Mom didn't appear to have any interest in winning them over. In fact, she often made things worse with comments that only aggravated the situation.

I have no way at all to predict what Mom might do next, London realized.

That thought made her shiver in the warm misty breeze.

CHAPTER SIXTEEN

London struggled to put her concerns about Mom aside. After all, even Sir Reggie seemed to be having a good time.

I should have a good time too, she thought, scratching the dog's head again.

As the boat coasted over the water, Captain Nilsen paid increasingly close attention to his surroundings.

Finally, he called out to his son in Norwegian and ordered him to slow the boat down. Sander did as he was told, and the noise from the engine diminished considerably as the *Kråkebolle* reduced its speed.

Nilsen got up from his seat and removed the flag that was flying from the stern of the boat. He rolled it up and stowed it away under the seats,

"We are now ready to fish for mackerel," he said, holding up two rectangular wooden frames.

"We will use these," he said. "We find that our traditional fishing tackle makes fewer problems for our guests who are not accustomed to deep sea fishing with large rods and reels. These lines pull out smoothly, and when we set the lures for the right depth, everything goes well."

With a brief glance at Scott Raife, the captain handed one of the frames to Gus and Honey and the other to London and Mom.

"Just hold them by the sidebars," he told them, picking up another frame to show them what he meant.

London saw that fishing line was spooled around rods that connected the sidebars, and they could unwind it without ever touching the line or the weights and hooks that were attached. Following Nilson's instructions, the teams of two began to unspool the lines, which pulled out smoothly.

Sir Reggie stood watching attentively as they lowered the lines into the water so that they trailed behind the moving boat.

"Be careful now," the captain said. "The hooks are very sharp."

Indeed, the novice mackerel anglers had to pay close attention as they unspooled a series of five slender shiny lures, each accompanied by a sharp hook.

The lures were spaced a yard or so apart along the line. Shortly beyond the last of the lures was tied a stone that was larger and heavier than the two weights at the far end of the line.

The captain explained, "The stone will pull the lures down to a depth where we should be able to catch some mackerel. The last time I was here, I came by a pretty good catch about five or six meters down."

"That's somewhere between 16 and 20 feet," Mom explained to Gus and Honey, whom she thought maybe weren't familiar with the metric system.

"That's right," Captain Nilsen said. "And our speed is about two knots. So if we release about 20 meters of line—that's about 66 feet—the lures will trail at about the right level."

The two teams lowered the lines as they were told.

Captain Nilsen then crossed his arms and said with a smile, "Now we wait and give the mackerel a chance to get interested."

London noticed that Scott Raife had been watching all this happen with interest. But now that the lines were lowered, he feigned scorn with a snort of laughter.

"That doesn't look like real fishing at all," he said.

Captain Nilsen chuckled and said, "Well, we'll soon see if the mackerel agree with you."

Scott then stood up between the two fishing teams and lifted his own expensive a rod and reel. He made a clumsy attempt at casting, but the lure wound up dangling a few feet off the end of his rod. London felt positively embarrassed for him.

London's mom nudged her and said, "Judging from his technique, I guess he's maybe practiced casting in his backyard, but that's about all."

London felt pretty sure that Mom was right, but she hoped that Scott hadn't overheard the snide comment.

Scott made another attempt, and at least the lure landed in the water, but instead of letting out more line so his lure could trail behind the boat, he reeled it back in again.

Mom said to him, "Would you like some help with that?"

When London gave her a sharp poke in the ribs, Mom looked at her and said, "Well, I'm just asking."

Scott glared at Mom angrily, then tried again. This time his cast was more or less successful, and he let the line troll in the water behind the boat.

Gus asked the captain, "Isn't he going to get his line tangled up in ours?"

The captain chuckled, obviously amused by Scott's clumsiness.

"Oh, I do not think there's much chance of that," he said. "Our lines run a lot deeper. I do not believe his will even go deep enough for mackerel."

"What do we do now?" Honey asked the captain.

"Wait a bit," the captain said. "Just be patient. Ninety percent of fishing is waiting."

As the four novice anglers sat near the stern waiting for mackerel to bite, London found herself watching Mom, who seemed to be lost in thought.

Or maybe in memories? London wondered.

Everyone else was staring out over the water, and London thought maybe she wouldn't be heard over the rumble of the engine.

"What are you thinking about?" London asked her mother.

Mom snapped out of her reverie.

"Why nothing, dear," she said. "Why do you ask?"

That startled expression made it clear to London that Mom had been thinking about a great deal. She felt a swell of frustration at the silence—and even evasiveness—that always stood between them.

She took a deep breath and said, "We're going to have to really talk, you know."

Mom squinted with feigned incomprehension.

"Why, we've been talking nonstop since yesterday, haven't we?" she said.

London sighed and said, "No, Mom. We've barely talked at all. And not about anything that really matters."

Mom shook her head. "You're expecting too much from us both, dear. We've got 20 years to catch up on. You can't just do that in a few minutes."

"Maybe we should get started," London blurted, a bit more loudly than she'd meant to.

Out of the corner of her eye, she saw Honey glance over at her and Mom. Gus was staring rather stiffly out over the water, as though he wouldn't let himself look their way. Even if they couldn't hear what London and Mom were saying, they must have picked up on the palpable tension building up between them.

"This is not the time or place," Mom said.

"I guess not," London admitted. "But when? Will there ever be a right time and place?"

Mom thought for a moment, then said, "We're going to be making a stop on Trollskog Island, aren't we?"

"That's right," London said.

Mom squeezed her hand and said, "Well, I hear it's a lovely place, covered by woods and wildflowers. Let's take a walk while we're there."

London smiled and said, "That sounds like a great idea."

At that moment, the captain stood up and said, "Now let us check our lines and see if we have anything."

Mom and London began to pull in their line, and Honey and Gus began to pull in theirs. When they got to the part of the line with the lures, London could feel right away that nothing had changed. She and Mom hadn't caught anything.

But Honey let out a squeal of excitement.

"Oh! I think we've got something!" she said.

Sure enough, as Honey and Gus pulled in their line, a couple of fish came into view just beneath the water's surface. Captain Nilsen helped the couple lift their fish out of the water.

He held up the line with two sparkling blue-green fish with dark-striped backs and silver-white bellies. They were each about a foot long.

"They're not very big," Honey said, sounding disappointed.

"Oh, they are just the right size," the captain assured her as he unhooked the two fish and dropped them into a bucket that was hanging off the back of the boat.

"But now that we've caught them, what are we going to do with them?" Gus asked.

Captain Nilsen let out a hearty laugh.

"Why, eat them, of course!" he said. "We are just getting started, I assure you. With any luck at all, we will wind up with a fine catch to have an island picnic."

London and Mom had already let their line out again, and now Honey and Gus did the same. Meanwhile, Scott Raife did his best to ignore the activity as he pulled in his fish-free line and cast again.

Scarcely five minutes had gone by when London noticed that the line she shared with Mom tightened a little.

She looked up at the captain and asked, "Do you think …?"

Captain Nilsen laughed again.

"I most certainly *do* think!" he said. "But give the fish just a little longer. The four of you have a total of ten lures, after all. See how many you can catch at one time."

Honey and Gus's line was twitching a little by now. Sir Reggie stood gazing back and forth from the fish in the bucket to the lines in the water, wagging his tail and whining eagerly.

"Be patient, pal," London said to the dog.

After a few minutes, Captain Nilsen signaled both groups to bring in their lines. Sure enough, Gus and Honey had caught four mackerel, and Mom and London had caught three.

Fifteen minutes later, the two teams brought in full loads of five mackerel each. Although he kept right on trolling his line, Scott now looked rather uncomfortable.

But just when the two teams had finished bringing in their third haul of ten fish, Scott let out a whoop of excitement.

"I've got something!" he yelled.

Everybody turned and looked. Sure enough, Scott's reel whirled and buzzed as something in the water ran away with the line.

Captain Nilsen's brow knotted up anxiously.

"Oh, no," he said.

He doesn't sound like he thinks this is a good thing, London realized.

CHAPTER SEVENTEEN

As the fishing line zipped out, Scott tried to grab the whirling handle of his reel. London watched as he yelped with pain as the handle battered his fingers, and he drew his hand back sharply.

The line was still flying out, pulled by whatever he had hooked.

"Give me the pole," Captain Nilsen said, stepping toward him.

"Not a chance," Scott snapped defiantly," This is my catch."

He made another grab at the reel handle, and this time he caught it. His hands were strong enough to halt the whirling handle, and the line ceased racing out into the water. But the pole almost leaped out of his hand and into the water. It doubled over as he tried to pull it back.

Mom called out to him, "You've got the drag set too tight."

"The drag?" Scott yelled back at her.

Mom rolled her eyes at London and said to her, "He doesn't even know what I'm talking about."

I guess not, London realized.

London hadn't done much fishing in her life, but even she knew what Mom meant. The drag was the friction that the fish had to overcome in order to pull the line out of the reel as it swam away. Before beginning to fish, an experienced angler would set the tightness of the drag to suit the game he was trying to catch. And it would be better set too loose rather than too tight.

Still, London wished her mother would keep her criticisms to herself.

Captain Nilsen said to Scott, "The lady is right. If you do not loosen the drag, the line is going to break—or else you are liable to lose the pole *and* the fish. And then the fish will be encumbered with your gear. Here, let me take care of it."

"No," Scott growled.

"Do you want to start swimming?" the captain asked.

Scott reluctantly handed the pole to the captain, who immediately displayed superior grace and strength. As he held the pole with one hand, Nilsen used the other to twist a knob on the front of the reel. Then he grabbed the pole with both hands as the reel let out the fierce, snarling sound of the reset drag, and the line rushed faster out into the water.

"We're going to lose him," Scott protested.

"Not at all," the captain said, handing the reel back to him. "Just follow my instructions."

Visibly struggling to fight down panic, Scott did exactly as he was told. He stopped the reel from spinning and pulled it back until the drag started to growl again. Then he let the fish run with the line before he pulled back the pole and reeled while the drag snarled loudly. He repeated this process again and again.

Honey and Gus had paused from their mackerel fishing to watch what was going on. Sir Reggie also sat staring with fascination.

Scott gasped to Captain Nilsen, "I hadn't expected a sea trout to be this big."

"This is not a sea trout," Nilsen replied. "Which means we have a problem."

Still following the captain's moment-by-moment orders, Scott alternately reeled the fish in and let the line run out, letting the fish tire itself. Finally, everybody on the boat could glimpse the catch just below the surface. London could see that it had a white stripe along its mottled greenish brown back.

"You're right," Mom said to the captain. "That's no sea trout. That's a cod."

And a big one, too, London realized.

Scott's rod bent sharply as he drew the fish close enough to the boat for the captain to catch it in a net. Everybody aboard the boat gasped with amazement as the captain lifted the cod out of the water.

It was about a yard long, and London guessed that it weighed some 60 or 70 pounds. She was amazed that Scott had managed to bring it in, even with the captain's diligent help and advice.

"Wahoo! Just look at my fish!" Scott yelled Whooping with triumph, he waved his hat in the air. "Doesn't that beat a whole mess of mackerel? Why, all of us are going to have a regular feast—including the dog!"

Indeed, Sir Reggie's eyes grew big at the sight of the impressive catch.

Captain Nilsen lifted the fish within arm's reach. Then without a word, he unhooked the lure from the fish's mouth, lowered the net back into the water, and allowed the big creature to swim away.

Scott let out a shout of protest.

"Why did you do that?"

"Because I had to," the captain said, wiping his hands with a rag. "It is illegal to catch cod in this part of Oslofjord."

"What?" Scott demanded. "But why?"

"Fish stock has dropped drastically in the fjord," the captain explained. "It is on account of overfishing and climate change. Oh, there are still plenty of mackerel. But fishing for cod is not allowed until the stock builds up again—if that ever happens."

London detected a note of sadness in his voice. The captain had surely borne witness to the fjord's decline and was bitter about it.

"But you let me catch one," Scott objected angrily.

The captain stared at him and snorted with contempt.

"Well, you said you wanted to catch sea trout. But actually, you are such a terrible fisherman, I was convinced you would not catch anything at all. Cod are especially rare in this part of the fjord, and you were going about everything all wrong anyway. I never thought for a moment you would actually catch one of them."

With a shrug the captain added, "Accidents will happen, I suppose."

"Accidents?" Scott growled. "You call my bringing in the biggest catch of the day an accident?"

"Never mind," Captain Nilsen said, trying to turn his attention back to the mackerel fishers.

Scott grabbed the captain by the shoulder.

"You didn't have to let it go," he snarled. "I mean, it's just a fish, right? Just *one* fish. What would be the harm? Nobody even had to know, except the seven of us people and the dog. I'm sure all of us know how to keep our mouths shut."

The captain's scowl darkened.

"I would advise you to remove your hand from my shoulder," he said.

But Scott didn't budge his hand.

He continued, "And anyway, we're on our way to some nice island to cook up our catch and eat it, right? Well, we could have done that with the cod. Once we finished eating it and getting rid of the bones, how could anybody prove I'd even caught it in the first place?"

In a single deft move, Captain Nilsen grabbed Scott's hand, forced it behind his back, and pushed him against the railing.

"Because that is not how we do things on my boat," the captain said sternly. "Do you understand?"

"I—I understand," Scott gasped, suddenly terrified.

"Are you sure of that?" Captain Nilsen said, tightening his grip on

Scott's hand. "Perhaps you would prefer to swim after all."

"No, no, I understand," Scott said.

But Captain Nilsen still wouldn't let go of him.

London cautiously stepped toward the two men and put her hand on Nilsen's shoulder.

"I—I think he's learned his lesson," she told the captain.

"I'm glad to hear it," Captain Nilsen said, releasing Scott's hand and helping him into a seat.

Meanwhile, the other passengers had been watching the scene with stunned expressions.

Now that it was over, Mom said, "Really, Captain Nilsen—was a show of violence really necessary?"

The captain tipped his cap at her and smiled.

"My apologies, madam. I did not mean to cause you any concern. I am passionate about such matters, and I sometimes let my commitment get the best of me."

Mom said, "I don't believe I'm the one you ought to apologize to."

London gave Mom a swift nudge in the ribs to remind her to mind her own business.

But it didn't seem to be necessary. Captain Nilsen simply ignored her remark without saying a word.

At that moment, Sander called out from the controls.

"We are nearing the island. Come and look."

London picked up Sir Reggie, and she and the passengers moved forward in the boat until they could see through the front windshield. There were plenty of islands all around the boat, but the one they were approaching seemed especially charming. Facing them on its nearest shore was a white building that looked like a church with an unusually tall steeple. Beyond the building, the entire island seemed to be covered with woods.

"There it is," Captain Nilsen said with a note of fondness in his voice. "Trollskog Island. That is our destination. The building you see is an abandoned lighthouse. It hasn't been used for years. The island is a public nature preserve, so we must behave like respectful visitors. No hunting, no fishing, no picking flowers—and of course, no littering."

Then the captain added a bit more sternly, "Oh, one other thing. Nobody climbs up into the lighthouse tower. And I do mean nobody."

Sander glanced back at the others with a wink.

"Nobody except Father himself, is his meaning," Sander said. "With Father—how do you say it in English?—rules are made to be twisted."

The captain didn't look pleased by his son's remark. But before he could make any protest, Sander pointed and exclaimed in Norwegian.

"Father, look. I think there is trouble."

Captain Nilsen let out what sounded like a curse in Norwegian.

Sure enough, London saw that a plume of smoke was rising up on the island from somewhere back among the trees.

CHAPTER EIGHTEEN

As London stared at the plume of smoke, Honey let out a gasp of alarm.

"Is the island on fire?" she cried.

Judging from the amount of smoke, London didn't think it could be a really big fire. But Captain Nilsen definitely looked upset about it.

The captain didn't reply to Honey's question. Instead, he ordered Sander out of the way, then sat down and took over the boat's controls. With a grim expression, Nilsen piloted the *Kråkebolle* toward their destination.

The lighthouse they were headed for was situated at the end of a wide stone pier that protruded into the water. Instead of the tall, rounded lighthouse towers that London was used to seeing elsewhere, this one was a quaint old white clapboard building. The open tower that jutted from the roof resembled an oversized church steeple. It all looked dilapidated and abandoned.

The captain deftly pulled the boat to a flight of stone steps that led up to the pier. On the shore, trees grew close to the rocky waterfront, which had just a narrow beach.

The captain stopped the engine, and Sander set to work mooring their vessel. Leaving Sander with that job, Captain Nilsen got out of the boat and hurried up the stairs.

London, Sir Reggie, Mom, Gus, and Honey all scrambled up after him. Without a glance back, the captain strode off toward the plume of smoke that still wafted from somewhere beyond the trees.

The captain's fists were clenched at his sides, and London could tell that he was very angry. She hesitated for a moment, wondering if she and the passengers should wait here until the captain returned. But Mom was already following the captain, and Gus and Honey tagged along after her.

Sir Reggie was staring impatiently at London, as if he wanted to go with them. London shrugged, and she and her dog both hurried after the others.

Just a short distance through the open woods, they came out onto a broad stretch of sand along a wider beach. A youngish couple clad in expensive-looking outdoor gear was seated there on two logs, roasting marshmallows over an open fire.

London heard several members of the group let out sighs of relief that no dangerous brushfire had broken out on the island.

Honey commented, "How cute," and the couple looked up with smiles on their faces.

But the captain's grim attitude didn't change. He strode over to the fire and glared down at the pair and their marshmallow feast.

With crossed arms, he told them sharply, "No open fires are allowed on the island."

"Really?" the young man asked, not looking particularly alarmed.

"We didn't know," the young woman added nonchalantly.

Growling with anger, the captain began to kick sand onto the fire to smother it.

The young couple scrambled to their feet, looking worried now.

"Are we in some kind of trouble?" the man asked. "Who are you, anyhow?"

Instead of answering their questions, the captain kept kicking sand on the flames.

Just then Sander caught up with the group, and with a cry of disapproval he joined his father, scooping up handfuls of sand and throwing them onto the fire.

When the fire was out once and for all, Captain Nilsen growled at the couple, "Who are the two of you? Judging from your accents, I take you to be American."

The young man had recovered his composure. "Why yes," he replied calmly. "My name is Carter Wuttke, and this is my wife, Mardi."

Honey asked half-jokingly, "Are you from the chocolate Wuttke family?"

"As a matter of fact, I am," Carter said. "Ludwig Wuttke was my great-great-great grandfather."

Gus's eyes widened as he said, "Wow, that must make you the heir to the Wuttke candy fortune."

Giving her husband a disapproving shove, Honey said, "Show a little couth, sweetie. He probably doesn't want anybody to make a big deal out of it."

But judging from the couple's expressions, London didn't think they were bothered by being recognized for the millionaires they surely were. Like just about everybody else in the world, London was familiar with Wuttke candies. She knew that the candies were manufactured in a town in upstate New York that was named "Wuttke" after the company's founder. Rumor had it that the Wuttkes owned the entire town.

Carter extended his hand to Captain Nilsen.

"We apologize," he said. "I'm sure we should have checked out the regulations."

Captain Nilsen frowned for another moment, then shook Carter's offered hand.

He said, "My name is Iver Nilsen. I own the boat that just arrived over at the lighthouse."

Honey added, "Captain Nilsen is kind of a stickler for rules."

"He sure is," Gus added.

Sander put in, "Father has reason to be."

Captain Nilsen explained, "This island is a nature preserve. That's why no open fires are allowed."

"We're terribly sorry," Carter said quite sincerely. "We really had no idea."

Mardi added, "We came to Oslo on vacation. I guess we don't know all the rules yet."

Captain Nilsen still didn't look very happy.

"How did you get to this island?" he asked the couple.

"We rented a boat," Carter said. "After we'd done a little island hopping, we decided to check out this one. It seems to be completely uninhabited." He pointed farther along the beach and said, "We found a wooden dock over on that end of the island. That's where we docked."

Mardi giggled and added, "I guess we just wanted to act like kids again and have a marshmallow roast. It was silly, I know. If we'd had any idea that it was against the rules, we'd never have done it."

Captain Nilsen shuffled his feet a bit, looking more or less satisfied with what he'd heard.

Sander seemed eager to lighten the general mood.

"I have kind of a, uh, idea," he said to the Wuttkes in his clumsy English. "If you two are hungry still, you should join us maybe at the lighthouse. We have a biggest catch of fresh mackerel, plenty for us and you also, if it sounds good."

Carter looked at Mardi and smiled.

"Sound good to you, dear?" he said.

"Oh, yes," Mardi said. "I've never tried mackerel. I'll bet it's delicious."

"Come with us, then," Sander said with a wave.

Sander's father didn't look exactly thrilled at this idea, but he didn't raise any objections. As the group started back toward the lighthouse, London noticed for the first time that Scott Raife wasn't with them. He hadn't followed them to the campfire.

I guess he stayed back at the boat, she thought. *Probably sulking.*

Meanwhile, London listened to a conversation taking place between Captain Nilsen and the Wuttkes as she and Mom walked behind them.

Carter said to the captain, "You know, the reason Mardi and I were island-hopping was because we were thinking about buying one."

"You mean buying an island?" the captain grunted disapprovingly.

"Well, yeah," Carter said. "We've heard that folks are buying Norwegian islands these days."

The captain shook his head vigorously.

"You won't have any luck buying this one. It is not available. It belongs to the municipal government. That is how it got turned into a nature preserve."

"I see," Carter said, sounding more pensive than disappointed.

The captain let out a sarcastic laugh.

"What do the two of you want with a whole island, anyway?" he asked. "Build a hotel on it, maybe?

"Oh, that's the last thing we've got in mind," Carter said.

"And we wouldn't be buying it for ourselves," Mardi added.

"Who would you be buying it for, then?" the captain said.

Carter let out a self-effacing laugh.

"Well, as you may have guessed," he said, "Mardi and I have more money than we could possibly need. Fortunately, there's a long tradition of philanthropy in the Wuttke family. We do our best to help good causes. We've heard that the Oslofjord is suffering from environmental issues. So we thought maybe we'd buy an island and donate it to the IGEF."

The captain's eyes widened with surprise.

"You mean the International Gaia Engagement Fund?" he said.

"That's right," Carter said. "I take it you've heard of it."

"Indeed, I have," Captain Nilsen said.

Carter said, "We hear that the whole ecosystem around here is in trouble."

"Birds are even starving to death!" Mardi said.

"That is right," the captain said. "Mussels and fish are disappearing, and birds cannot find enough to eat. There is also pollution, garbage, and plastic in the fjord. We are all doing our best to make things better, but ..."

The captain fell silent, shaking his head.

Carter said, "An organization like the IGEF can help a lot. If it owned this island, you could be sure it would stay pristine and beautiful for many generations. But I guess that's not an issue, since it's not privately owned."

"That's true, but ..."

Captain Nilsen's voice faded for a moment as they kept walking along.

Finally he said to the couple, "I have got some connections. I might be able to help you make some kind of deal. In fact, ... you might be surprised what kind of a deal you might get. Surprised and very pleased. Let's talk it over after we eat."

"We'd like that," Carter said.

London noticed a skeptical look on Sander's face as his father talked to the couple.

"Father, remember—this island is public, eh, property land," he said in his awkward English.

"I know that," Captain Nilsen

"It is belonging to the city of Oslo," Sander added.

"I said I know that," the captain snapped at his son a bit impatiently.

In Norwegian, Sander said, "It is not your decision to make."

"Do not argue, Sander," Captain Nilsen said in Norwegian.

Then, turning to the couple again, he said, "Yes, let's do talk after we eat."

"That would be great," Carter said.

Mom turned to London and said, "Isn't that lovely? Something really good is liable to come from our little outing."

London silently agreed. She, too, had heard of the International Gaia Engagement Fund, and knew of its excellent reputation. It really did feel good to think this excursion might make things at least a little better for the fjord's ecosystem.

But as the group approached the stone pier with the lighthouse on the far end, London didn't see Scott Raife anywhere. The last time she had seen him, he'd still been there on the boat, smoldering with anger over his humiliation.

Where is our grumpy macho man? London wondered uneasily.

CHAPTER NINETEEN

"Stop worrying!" Mom said, giving London a playful jab in the ribs.

London squinted at her with surprise and asked, "How did you know I was worried?"

Mom shrugged and said, "I'm your Mom. Mothers pick up on these kinds of things. It's natural. It's intuitive. It's normal."

The irony felt so sharp that London almost gasped.

Normal? she wondered. *What could Mom possibly know about being a normal mother?*

But London didn't say anything about it. The last thing she wanted right now was for the two of them to get into a fight. Besides, Mom was probably right this time. She shouldn't be worrying about Scott Raife. He was a grown man and perfectly capable of strolling around an island on his own if that was what he wanted to do. In fact, wandering about alone might be the best way for him to stay out of trouble.

As they walked along the pier, Captain Nilsen said something to his son in Norwegian. London could understand their Norwegian well enough to know Captain Nilsen was ordering Sander to bring in the bucket of mackerel they had caught. With a nod, Sander climbed down the stone steps into the boat. The captain stood there for a moment, giving him additional directions.

The rest of the group continued along the pier toward the lighthouse. Gus and Honey were leading the way, followed by London, Mom, and Sir Reggie. The newcomers, Carter and Mardi Wuttke, trailed along behind, looking at everything with interest and commenting quietly to each other.

Suddenly Gus came to a halt and called back to the captain, "Do you normally leave this place unlocked?"

The door to the clapboard building was standing wide open.

The captain caught up with them and squinted at the open door uneasily. "Unlocked, yes. Believe me, there's nothing in there anyone would want to steal. But it looks like somebody's been in there."

Turning to Carter and Mardi, he asked, "Did you come in here earlier?"

The Wuttkes shook their heads no.

The captain grumbled, "I do not much like people coming and going here as they please."

The group followed the captain into a rundown room with creaky wooden floors and heavy ceiling beams. Inside there was only a large wooden table, a few bits of other furniture, and a big old stove connected to a propane tank. London also noticed that part of one wall was covered by a large pegboard laden with hand tools.

The captain strode across the barren room and through another door.

London heard him shout, "What are you doing here?"

She and the rest of the group hurried after him.

They stepped into a large square room where a rickety-looking ladder ran up the wall into the lighthouse tower. Sunlight filtered down from the open area high overhead where the light used to be.

Scott Raife was standing right beneath the tower and staring up into it with apparent fascination.

"What are you doing here?" the captain demanded again.

"I'm just having a look around," Scott replied with a shrug. "I was curious. I've never been in a real lighthouse before. I found the door to the building unlocked and came right on inside for a look around. Was there anything wrong with that?"

The captain pointed to a rickety-looking ladder than ran up the wall toward the top of the tower.

"Did you climb up into the tower?" he demanded.

Scott looked a little unsettled by the sharpness of the question.

"No," he said.

The captain said, "Because I told everybody earlier, nobody is allowed to climb this tower."

Scott smirked and said, "Except you, right? That's what your son said."

"That is none of your business," the captain said.

"Well, I didn't climb up there," Scott said defensively, crossing his arms. "And I don't plan to, either. But you sure do make a lot of rules. And I for one am getting tired of them."

The captain turned to the rest of the group and said, "I am only concerned about your safety. The ladder is in very poor repair."

London heard Gus Jarrett mutter to Honey, "Kind of a shame. I'll bet it's a spectacular view of the whole fjord."

Honey scoffed and muttered, "From the looks of that ladder, it sounds like a pretty good rule to me."

London looked upward and silently agreed with Honey. The platform where the lamp had once shown out over the fjord was some 30 feet off the floor, and the rungs of the ladder didn't look like they were in good shape. If the captain himself did climb up there, it would be because he knew every rung well enough to stay safe.

"Right," she said to Honey. "Broken bones would be no fun."

"Broken bones or worse," Carter Wuttke agreed.

"Yes," Captain Nilsen added, "Someone could get killed if they fell from up there."

The captain led the group back into the larger room, where Sander was laying out their enormous catch of mackerel on the large wooden table. It was obvious there would be more than enough fish for everybody, including Carter and Mardi.

"Would anybody like to help with the cooking?" the captain asked the group.

Mom hopped up and down and said, "Oh, absolutely! Come on London, let's do this."

London smiled. She thought that helping to prepare a feast would probably be fun. It did cross her mind that it would be nice if the ship's chef could be here too—and not just for his cooking skills.

At the same time, she felt a nagging anxiety at how uncertain things were between her and Bryce. She still hadn't made up her mind about whether to take the job aboard the *Galene,* and she had no idea whether Bryce had decided to take the job aboard the *Danae.*

So much is up in the air, she thought.

Meanwhile, she was glad when Captain Nilsen and Sander took on the disagreeable task of cleaning the fish. The captain slit their bellies and emptied their entrails into a bucket, then cut off their heads and tails.

During that process, most of the group decided they would rather enjoy the fine weather outside. Honey wanted to stay and help cook, but Gus pulled her out through the door "to do a bit of exploring."

Sander washed the fish in fresh water from a hand pump in the kitchen.

Meanwhile, London and Mom took stock of the ingredients and supplies. A pair of potted herb plants, one oregano and the other thyme, were growing in the window.

"Everything is freshly grown," the captain boasted, watching Mom and London as he continued cleaning the fish. "Even the lemons! I have a small lemon tree at home on Lindøya island."

"Is there enough sunlight this far north to grow lemons?" London asked with surprise.

Mom chuckled and said to London, "You forget, dear, that days are long here this time of year, even in southern Norway. The sun rises earlier and sets later than what you're used to."

"That is right," the captain said. "Of course, there is much less of the sun during winter months, and I have to bring the tree indoors and put it under artificial grow lights. By the way, Lindøya is a nice little island."

"Yes, I've been there," Mom said.

"Perhaps we can stop there for a visit later today," the captain said.

"That would be lovely," Mom said.

Following Mom's instructions, London set to work on the fish. First, they covered multiple baking sheets with cooking parchment, then sprinkled the parchment with olive oil.

They placed several fish on each sheet, scoring them with a knife on each side, then adding freshly milled salt and pepper. They inserted half-moon slices of lemon into the incisions and also inside the fish, along with the fresh oregano and thyme. After another sprinkling of olive oil, the fish went into the oven.

London found herself smiling and even laughing as she and Mom worked together.

She certainly knows how to cook, London thought.

For the first time since Mom had turned up, London was actually having a good time with her.

Memories of her whole family came flooding back—Dad, Mom, Tia, and herself dashing around a kitchen to prepare some really special meal. Mom and Dad were both expert cooks, and oftentimes the whole operation would break down into a lighthearted spat over the recipe, followed by a round of uncontrollable laughter and eventually by a delicious meal.

It was good to feel a little of that joy again.

I wish Tia were here, she thought.

Dad too.

Soon the aroma became irresistible, and Scott, the Jarretts, and the Wuttkes reappeared for the meal. As each batch finished roasting, Captain Nilsen put the mackerel on earthenware plates with steel forks and knives while Sander poured white wine into earthenware cups. The diners carried their meals outside and found places to sit on the pier and the rocky shore.

On her way out of the building, London's eyes were again caught by that large pegboard with all the hand tools on it. She was impressed by how neatly the tools were arranged, and how carefully everything seemed to be fitted into its place.

I guess the people who visit here take good care of things, she thought.

Outside, she found Sir Reggie, who had been waiting patiently during the preparation of the food. But now he sat up and begged. When that had no effect, he did several rollovers and bows. The people cheered and applauded, and London had to stop them from letting the little dog gorge on mackerel.

"It's too rich for him to eat much," London told them, giving him a treat instead. "He'll just get sick again."

Mom and London sat down on the edge of the pier with their legs hanging over the water.

"Have you ever tried freshly-caught mackerel, dear?" Mom asked. "I mean, straight-off-the-fishing-line fresh, not out of a can?"

"I don't think so," London said.

"Well, it's so good, I positively *envy* you the experience. Go ahead, have a taste."

London poked her fork into one of the sliced openings and tugged under the shiny skin to pull loose a bit of incredibly tender meat. When she put it in her mouth, she realized Mom wasn't exaggerating.

The fish had a bold, oil-rich flavor that reminded London of salmon with a hint of tuna, but it was sweeter than most sea fish she was used to, so she wasn't bothered by an overly "fishy" taste. And of course, the simple recipe of thyme, oregano, and lemon added exactly the right touch of flavoring. The white wine was obviously inexpensive, but it went very nicely with the fish.

Sir Reggie was still staring at them, his mouth watering at the smell of the roasted mackerel.

"Sorry, Sir Reggie," London said, giving the disappointed dog a treat. "I told you before, this is definitely too rich for you."

With a grumble, he finally gave up begging and settled down between them.

London and Mom looked around at the others as they ate. Gus and Honey appeared to have struck up a sparkling conversation with Carter and Mardi Wuttke, and Sander kept circulating among the travelers to make sure everybody was happy.

"Everybody seems to be having a great time," London said.

"All except him," Mom said, pointing a short distance along the pier where Scott Raife was sitting by himself, scowling at his plate of fish while he poked it with a fork and the blade of a Swiss Army knife, which he seemed to showing off.

Mom patted the rocks next to herself and London and called out to Scott in a friendly voice.

"Would you care to join us?"

Scott barely looked up from his fish and said nothing.

"That's a nice knife you've got," Mom called out, trying to get some conversation going with him.

"Thanks," Scott grumbled. "I ought to be using it right now on some cod."

Standing nearby, Captain Nilsen let out a growling chuckle.

He said, "That little thing wouldn't do you much good for any real fishing."

He pulled out the big knife he'd used to gut the mackerel and fingered its blade and said, "Now *this* is the kind of knife you can really get some use out of."

Scott's face reddened at this new slight, but he didn't say anything.

Mom muttered to London, "I think it's time the captain stopped finding ways to embarrass that rather silly man. I've got half a mind to talk to him about it."

Although London felt much the same way, she sensed it would be best not to aggravate the captain further.

"I'd rather you didn't," London said to Mom.

"Why not?"

Because you'll only make things worse, London thought without saying so aloud.

Besides, London sensed that Mom was, as usual, already looking for some excuse to avoid the conversation they needed to have.

And it's definitely time we did that, she thought.

CHAPTER TWENTY

How on earth am I going to get this conversation started? London wondered.

She decided to dive right in.

"Let's talk, Mom," she said.

"Now?" Mom said almost inaudibly as she picked at her fish.

"Yeah, now."

An awkward silence fell. Sir Reggie looked back and forth between Mom and London apprehensively.

Come on, get going, London told herself.

But the questions she needed to ask seemed so enormous.

Like, where were you for 20 years?

She decided that it might be better to start with something less overwhelming. The question that popped into her mind was something that had been bothering her ever since their visit to Akershus Fortress.

"Mom, why did you lie about seeing that ghost?" London asked.

Mom looked up in surprise. This was obviously not what she had expected.

"What ghost?"

"The ghost in the dungeon. The shadowy cloaked faceless woman you said you saw down there."

"What makes you think I was lying?"

London rolled her eyes as she remembered Mom's nudge and wink as they'd left the dungeon.

"How did you like that *little number?"* Mom had asked with a voice filled with mischief.

London said, "Come on, Mom. You practically told me it was a lie."

"Well, it wasn't *completely* a lie," Mom said. "Lots of people say they've seen that woman. I've talked to a few of them. OK, so I never saw her myself. What's the big deal? It's called *showmanship,* dear. Don't tell me you haven't spiced up a story to make it more entertaining when you were conducting a tour."

Not like that, I haven't, London thought.

Besides, that wasn't exactly what was bothering London about

98

Mom's story.

"You even made Mr. Lapham believe it," she said. "He was all worried about you before the tour. He offered to conduct the tour himself so you wouldn't have to relive the whole thing. But you insisted. 'I've got to face my demons,' you told him. Why did you trick him like that?"

"Oh, that," Mom said. "Well, I guess you could call that a bit of old-fashioned flirting."

"Flirting?" London said with surprise.

"Sure. Don't tell me you've never pretended to be scared of something in order to get a guy's attention. Or acted helpless or clumsy or incompetent or anything sympathy-inspiring to feed a male ego."

"No, I don't think I ever did," London replied. "I thought that kind of 'feminine wiles' thing went out in the 1800s, along with fainting spells."

Mom shrugged and said, "OK, so I guess it is kind of a generational thing. But Jeremy and I are both of an age, and you have to admit, my little ruse had its desired effect on him. He's a very attractive man. I felt that when I first laid eyes on him. And anyone can see he feels the same way about me."

"Oh, Mom—"

"He's being coy, though. Maybe even playing a bit hard-to-get. It's up to me to reel him in."

Reel him in? London thought.

She wasn't prepared for fishing metaphors.

London said, "I really think it was wrong to mislead him like that."

"Well, what do you expect me to do about it now?"

"I think you should tell him the truth. And apologize."

"Oh, London—"

A short silence fell between them.

"Maybe you're right," Mom said.

"Yeah, I'm pretty sure I am."

"OK, I'll take care of it," Mom said.

A longer silence fell. London realized that she herself was doing some avoiding now. She and Mom had both finished their fish and their wine. It was time to get right to the point.

"Mom, why did you leave us?" she said. "And don't tell me you don't remember. I just won't buy the whole amnesia thing."

Mom heaved a long, sad sigh.

"Well, I don't know how well you remember how things were

before I left, after your dad and I got divorced …" she began.

Pretty well, London thought.

Mom continued, "It was all perfectly amicable, of course. But it wasn't exactly fair. I retired and became a stay-at-home wife and mother in a nice house in a nice suburban neighborhood, while your father kept gallivanting around the world as a flight attendant, and …"

She paused for a moment, then said, "London, I don't want you to think I didn't love taking care of you and your sister. But it was just such a different kind of life than I was used to. I never really adjusted. Do you understand?"

London was looking into her mother's eyes now. She could see a world of sadness there. Her throat caught as Mom's phrase echoed through her mind.

"… such a different kind of life …"

Maybe she couldn't understand what her mom had done—at least not yet. But at least she could feel a tingle of sympathy for how unsuited she'd felt for the life she'd tried to live back then.

Before either London or Mom could say anything more, London's phone rang. She saw that the call was from Bryce.

London wavered about taking the call. She certainly didn't want to delay the long-overdue conversation with Mom. On the other hand, her situation with Bryce seemed equally urgent.

"I'd better take this," London said to Mom.

"That's OK," Mom said. "I'll just take our plates back to the kitchen."

As Mom headed away, London stayed sitting there on the pier and took Bryce's call. Sir Reggie hopped up into her lap.

"Hi, London," Bryce said. "I just thought I'd check in. How are you doing?"

"OK, I guess," London said, happy to hear the sound of his voice. "How are you?"

"Well, I'm not sure. Things felt a little weird this morning when I met you and your mom for breakfast. I could tell it was kind of awkward for you. I didn't mean for it to be."

London stifled a groan.

"I guess it was kind of weird," she said, petting Sir Reggie.

"Look, your mom and I sat up talking late last night, and the one thing she really hadn't told me was that things still aren't quite right between the two of you. I should have figured that. I didn't mean to put you in an awkward situation. I also feel kind of bad that I spent so much time talking to her when you and I are so long overdue for a talk of our own."

London smiled a little. Bryce was nothing if not empathetic. She liked that about him. At the same time, she hesitated before asking him the question that was uppermost in her mind. Finally, she just came out and asked it.

"Have you made a decision about that head chef offer from Aeolus Adventures?"

Bryce was quiet for a moment, heightening London's anxiety.

"No, I haven't," Bryce finally said. "I just don't think I can make a decision like that by myself. We've got to sort it out together, London."

"I know," London thought out loud.

Then she remembered her conversation with Mr. Lapham this morning and his offer of job aboard the *Galene*.

"I need an answer to my offer very soon," Mr. Lapham had said. *"Today, in fact."*

That was another decision that she and Bryce really needed to consider together.

"Bryce, I've got some news, too. We really do have a lot to talk about. But not right now, not over the phone. Can we get together when I get back to the ship?"

"That would be great."

She and Bryce ended the call. London sat staring at the phone for a moment, full of questions about what the future had—or didn't have—to offer. Then she got to her feet and looked around. She saw that the Wuttkes and Jarretts, accompanied by Sander Nilsen, were heading together along the pier toward the island.

But Mom wasn't with them, and London didn't see Mom anywhere along the pier.

"Do you know where Mom went?" she asked Sir Reggie.

The dog nodded toward the lighthouse. London remembered how Mom had volunteered to take their dishes back. She and Sir Reggie went to the lighthouse and peeked inside. Captain Nilsen was washing dishes in water he'd heated up on the stove.

Nobody else was there with him.

London asked the captain, "Was Mom here a few minutes ago?"

"Yes, she brought some dishes," Captain Nilsen said.

"Did she say where she was going then?" London asked.

"Sorry, but no," Captain Nilsen said. "Everybody just headed back outside."

London's pulse quickened and she felt a chill of alarm.

"Where did she go this time?" she asked Sir Reggie.

Sir Reggie replied with an indecisive growl.

London took a deep breath to calm herself.

"Well, surely there's nothing to worry about," she said to Sir Reggie. "Mom probably just panicked about the things we need to talk about and tried to get away. That doesn't really matter. After all, Trollskog is a tiny island. She couldn't have gotten far."

London and Sir Reggie trotted after Sander, the Wuttkes, and the Jarretts, and called out to them, "Hey, has anybody seen my mother? I mean just now."

The five people looked back at her.

Mardi said, "I thought I saw her heading this way just a couple of minutes ago."

Honey added, "I think our would-be fisherman was with her."

She went away with Scott Raife? London thought with disbelief.

It seemed like only a short while ago that Scott couldn't stand the sight of Mom. Things always seemed to be changing with her, sometimes so fast that London couldn't keep up with them.

"Did you notice which way they went?" London asked the couples.

Carter Wuttke said, "I think the two of them headed along that way."

He was pointing toward a path that led into the woods. London thanked them, and she and Sir Reggie dashed ahead of them down the path. The air was clear, flowers were in bloom, and sea birds fluttered in the air. Under different circumstances, London knew that this would be a lovely place to explore.

"Maybe later we can enjoy a little walk," she said to Sir Reggie.

But she soon came to a place where the path forked in not two but *three* separate directions.

"Which path did they take, Sir Reggie?" she asked her dog.

Sir Reggie let out a whine of uncertainty.

"You're not much of a bloodhound, are you?" London said with a sigh.

She couldn't make out any footprints on the stony ground. But she did notice that the middle path led uphill, apparently toward the highest place on the island.

"Maybe we can see them from up there," London said to Sir Reggie.

It was a short but strenuous climb to the top of the hill. London was gasping for breath by the time she stood on its rocky height.

She turned all around and took in the stunning view. At one end of the island stood the lighthouse on the stone pier, while at the other end was the wooden dock where the Wuttkes had moored their rented inboard motorboat. As London looked all around, it seemed as though she could see every nook and cranny of the little island. She could certainly see the all the well-kept paths, the rocky shores, and a few stretches of sand.

The hilltop also offered a wonderful view of Oslofjord and its many islands. The fjord was scattered with literally hundreds of sailing vessels, ranging from ocean-going ships to small rowboats and sailboats of all shapes and sizes. London was briefly startled by the sight of a wooden vessel with identical curves at both the prow and stern. At first it seemed to be remarkably large.

A Viking ship? London wondered.

But she quickly realized the apparent size of the vessel was really an optical illusion. It was really just a small rowboat shaped in the fashion of a Viking ship.

As London gazed at it and other boats, she wondered whether Mom and Scott had left the island aboard one of them.

If so, why? London wondered.

She really had no idea. The only people she could see on the island were the Wuttkes, the Jarretts, and Sander, who were now walking together along a beach.

London sighed and said to Sir Reggie, "Have you got any idea what happened to Mom and Scott?"

The dog made no reply.

"Maybe they doubled back to the lighthouse," London said. "Maybe they're inside the building again. It's the only place I can think of. Let's go check it out."

She and Sir Reggie retraced their steps back down the hill all the way to the shore, then went straight to the lighthouse. The door was standing wide open, and they walked on inside. Nobody was in the kitchen area, not even the captain.

Suddenly Sir Reggie growled. He seemed anxious and agitated.

"What's wrong, pal?" she asked.

Sniffing uneasily, Sir Reggie walked toward the door that led into the tower. London followed him and opened the door.

She let out a horrified cry at what she saw.

103

CHAPTER TWENTY ONE

A man's body lay in a twisted heap at the base of the ladder. His eyes were wide open and frozen with shock and terror, and his back was twisted so badly that it must have been broken.

It was Captain Nilsen.

Even though the result seemed obvious, London stooped down to feel for his pulse.

She wasn't surprised that there was no pulse.

"He's dead, Sir Reggie," she said in a hushed voice.

Sir Reggie stepped around the body and peered at it as if he didn't quite believe what London had just said.

London fought down a dizzying wave of horror. She'd learned from experience—too much experience—that she needed to have her wits about her at a time like now. Even though the man was dead, she still had no time to lose. She needed to call the proper authorities.

Before coming to Oslo, she'd made sure the city's emergency number was on automatic dial on her cellphone. Now she pulled out her phone and hit the number.

A woman's voice answered, *"Hva er did nødssituasjon?"*

Even with her limited command of Norwegian, London knew what the woman had said:

"What is your emergency?"

The problem was, London wasn't nearly up to the task of explaining the situation in Norwegian.

"Snakker du engelsk?" she asked—*"Do you speak English?"*

"Yes," the operator replied in English.

London felt a weird calm settling over her. She felt eerily detached from the situation, as if the whole thing were happening to somebody else. She even felt as though she might be listening to someone else speak her own words.

Symptoms of shock, of course, she knew.

"I need to report a death," she said.

"Where are you right now?" the operator said.

"I'm on Trollskog Island, inside the lighthouse there."

London could hear the operator's fingers rattling on the keyboard.

"I am sending someone there right now," the operator said. "Meanwhile, I need to ask you a couple more questions. Are you able to identify the deceased?"

"Yes, his name is Iver Nilsen."

"And can you determine the cause of death?"

London glanced up the ladder and saw that one of its upper rungs was broken through.

"I believe he fell from high up in a lighthouse tower," she said.

"You have been very helpful," the operator said. "Do you need someone to stay with you on the line until help arrives?"

Of course, London knew the woman was concerned about her mental state.

"No, I'll be all right."

"Please do nothing to disturb the scene. Do not touch anything at all unless you have to. And do not leave the immediate area."

"I won't."

"And stay close to the scene."

"I will."

The operator thanked her and ended the call, leaving London and Sir Reggie alone in the lighthouse tower, looking at the dead body.

London said to the dog, "She didn't ask me whether I thought it was foul play. I sure hope not. It's bad enough that the poor man died in such an awful way."

London shivered under the dead man's gaze. It felt almost as though he was trying to tell her something with his eyes alone. If so, London had no idea what it might be. And standing here staring wasn't going to help the situation.

"Come on, Sir Reggie," she said.

Together they walked out of the tower into the large room that had served as a kitchen a little while ago. London remembered the kindly captain and his son bustling around getting the mackerel ready to cook, then later how the captain had washed the dishes in here.

How suddenly things can change! she thought.

As she stepped out of the building onto the stone pier, the crisp breeze reminded her that she wasn't the only person left on the island. And one of the others was the dead man's son.

London suddenly felt a spasm of dread.

I've got to tell them, she realized.

She remembered the last time she'd seen Sander, the Wuttkes, and the Jarretts from the hilltop. They'd been walking together along the

105

island's beaches. She also remembered the operator telling her not to leave the immediate area.

London looked down at Sir Reggie and said, "Sir Reggie, I need your help."

The dog looked up at her and tilted his head expectantly.

She said, "Could you go look for the others? I'm talking about Mom and Scott Raife too."

The little dog looked a bit confused, so London pointed and said, "Find somebody."

Sir Reggie perked up his ears at the word *find*.

"Find Mom," London said, then added, "Find anybody. I need them to come back here right away.

Sir Reggie let out a yap of assurance and hurried off. As London watched the dog dash across the pier and head out along the shore, she marveled at how well the little creature seemed to understand.

Smarter than a lot of people, she thought gratefully.

While she waited, she stood on the edge of the pier staring forlornly out over Oslofjord, trying to understand what had just happened.

Captain Nilsen had warned all the passengers that the ladder was unsafe for climbing—although according to Sander, the captain was prone to disobey his own order. London had no reason to think his death was anything but an accident. But she knew she needed to leave that conclusion to the authorities.

Meanwhile, some odd words drifted through her mind.

"The problem is truly in the stars."

That was how Mr. Lapham had explained why the *Nachtmusik* kept running into such serious troubles.

London still couldn't bring herself to believe in the CEO's rather arcane theories. She didn't think that astrology or numerology or any of his miscellaneous other-than-normal influences could be blamed for all their tribulations.

After five different murders, she'd learned to rely on more earthbound clues. She'd had to turn detective and pretty nearly singlehandedly find the culprits. The auguries and omens of Alex, Mr. Lapham's trusted astrologer, had been no help to her at all. She didn't want to go through all that again.

London's thoughts were interrupted by the sound of Sir Reggie yapping urgently. She turned and saw her little dog trotting back to the pier, followed by the people he'd been sent to find—except, unfortunately, for Mom and Scott.

Honey called out to her as they approached, "London, what's the matter?"

Gus added, "Sir Reggie's acting weird."

London swallowed hard at the sight of Sander trailing behind the others. She would have to tell him that his father was dead.

This is going to be really hard, she thought.

She stepped toward the slim, pale, rather fragile-looking young man. Remembering that his English wasn't nearly as good as his father's, London decided to try her best to talk to him in her limited Norwegian.

"Sander, something has happened to your father," she managed to say.

Sander's eyes widened with alarm.

"What is it?" he replied, also in Norwegian.

"There has been an ... an ..."

London's voice faded as she struggled to remember the Norwegian word for "accident."

Fortunately, she sensed that Sander was starting to understand what she was having so much trouble trying to say.

Sander said in a hoarse voice, "Is he ... alive?"

London silently shook his head.

"Then where ... ?" Sander began. Then he seemed to be seized by a moment of realization.

"The tower?" he asked.

London nodded.

With a horrified cry, Sander turned and ran toward the lighthouse.

"Sander, wait!" London called after him in the best Norwegian she could muster. "You must not touch anything!"

She wasn't sure he'd even heard her as he dashed into the front door. She started after him, then realized that the Wuttkes and the Jarretts were right at her heels.

She whirled and said to them, "Stay behind me. And give us some room."

The four people nodded with stunned expressions.

London took off again toward the lighthouse with Sir Reggie at her heels. She reached it just in time to see Sander disappear through the open door into the tower.

Then she heard Sander let out a wail of grief and horror. She entered the tower in time to see the young man fall on his knees in front of his father's body. He was on the verge of gathering the corpse into his arms.

"No!" London cried, pushing him back as gently as she could.

She struggled to explain in Norwegian, "You must not touch him. Police are coming. They want everything to stay just like this."

Sander obediently drew back from the corpse.

He sobbed as he spoke in Norwegian to the dead man, and London was only able to pick out bits and pieces of what he was saying.

"Father, why? ... You said yourself, the ladder was dangerous ... You wouldn't let anyone else climb it ... Why couldn't you follow your own orders? ... I warned you over and over ... Why were you always so stubborn? ..."

London turned and saw the Wuttkes and the Jarretts standing nearby. Poor Mardi Wuttke had turned pale. She seemed about to faint, but Carter managed to steady her just in time.

"Come on, let's get you out of here," Carter said, gently leading his wife out of the tower.

By contrast, Gus and Honey looked stunned but not overwhelmed. London quickly recalled this wasn't the first corpse they'd known about during this voyage. Back in Bamberg, they had actually seen a man who drowned in a vat of beer.

"Poor Captain Nilsen!" Honey said as London led them into the other room, leaving Sander alone with the body. The five people found places to sit, and Sir Reggie hopped up into London's lap.

"Do you think it was ... ?" Gus said to London.

Although Gus's voice faded, London knew that he was wondering the same thing as she was—whether the man had been murdered.

"I don't know, Gus," London said.

"It had to have been an accident," Honey said, pointing up at the broken ladder rung. "Look, you can see exactly where it happened—and how."

I hope you're right, London thought.

"Besides," Gus added, "Who else could have even been here?"

The truth was, as London mulled over what had happened, it really did seem most likely to be an accident. Captain Nilsen had stepped on a weak rung that had broken under his weight, and he had fallen to his death.

At least she hoped it was that simple.

Things were bad enough without foul play being involved.

Honey said, "Nobody would have hurt Captain Nilsen. He was as sweet as a lamb."

Gus scoffed and said, "Don't forget, he did keep threatening to throw Scott Raife overboard."

"Yeah, well, Scott would have had it coming," Honey said with a shrug, "What an obnoxious guy."

Gus looked around and added, "Where is Scott, anyway?"

And where is Mom? London wondered.

This was surely the worst of all times to have two people disappear.

At that moment, she heard the noise of an approaching engine. The police boat had surely arrived.

Things are about to get really tough, London realized.

CHAPTER TWENTY TWO

When London hurried outside, she saw a boat the size of a small yacht with a large, glass-enclosed cabin like a ship's bridge. Large letters on its side formed the word *POLITI*.

"That thing's not going to be able to moor here," a voice grumbled from behind her.

London turned and saw that the Jarretts had followed her out, along with Sir Reggie. They were all staring at the daunting vessel pulled up across the pier from Captain Nilsen's much smaller *Kråkebolle*.

"It's way too big," Gus added to his comment.

"He looks like he knows what he's doing," Honey said. "I bet he makes it."

As they watched, the pilot skillfully brought the boat up against the pier, where crew members began to moor it in place.

"He's very good, just like I said," Honey declared.

A tall and imposing woman with a strong jaw and intense gray eyes climbed out of the boat. She was wearing a black baseball cap and a black jacket with black-and-white checkered rectangles. Her shoulder insignias each had two stripes and a single gold star. She was followed by several police officers and a pair of medical examiners who hauled a gurney up onto the pier.

The tall woman's eyes immediately fell on London, as if she knew this was the person to talk to.

She tipped her cap to London and said in Norwegian, "I am *Politiførstebetjent* Monica Kolberg. I understand there has been a death here. Could you please tell me where to find the body?"

London understood the word *Politiførstebetjent* to mean "Police First Constable."

She pointed and struggled to say in Norwegian, "The body is … over in the tower there."

The constable nodded toward the medical team, who carted the gurney on into the lighthouse.

"Are you the one who called the emergency number?" the constable asked.

"I did," London said.

110

"So you were the one who discovered the body?"

"That's right."

"And what is your name?"

"London Rose."

The constable squinted as if the name struck her as vaguely familiar. London could guess why it might be, and it worried her. She knew that rumors about her reluctant sleuthing activities had been circulating all over Europe, especially in law enforcement circles. Not all of those rumors were true—and some were not very flattering.

"So I take it you are American," Kolberg said.

"That is right," London said, realizing that the constable was referring to her accent. "So are the other people here, except for the dead man's son. And I am a bit embarrassed to say ..."

Kolberg smiled before London could confess that she spoke little Norwegian.

"Do not worry," she said. "Go ahead and speak to me in English. I know it quite well. Come and show me what happened."

Followed by the Jarretts and Sir Reggie and the pair of policemen, London led the *Politiførstebetjent* into the building. The Wuttkes were still sitting in the larger room, looking as shocked and bewildered as before. Honey Jarrett picked up Sir Reggie and said, "You stay out here with us, young man."

Sir Reggie made no objection, so he and the Jarretts stayed with the Wuttkes while London led the constable and policemen on into the tower.

The body of Iver Nilsen still lay twisted on the floor. Poor Sander hovered over him, with tears running down his cheeks.

London murmured to the constable, "The dead man is Iver Nilsen, the owner of the boat you saw on the pier. This young man is his son, Sander."

Kolberg nodded with a concerned expression, clearly unfazed by the sight of the corpse but nevertheless worried about Sander's emotional state.

"It appears that Herr Nilsen fell from the ladder," the constable said quietly, glancing upward.

"I think so," London replied, "He actually warned the rest of us that it wasn't safe."

"But he did not heed his own advice," the constable said with a shake of her head. "A pity. I suppose that may be all there is to it."

I hope so, London thought.

The constable stooped down and took a careful look at the body. Then she signaled the medical team. Sander stood by weeping and babbling incoherently while the team put the corpse onto the gurney.

London felt a stab of sympathy for the son's stunned bereavement. She felt as though she couldn't begin to understand how horrifying this was to him.

As they carted the body out of the tower, he began to follow them.

Kolberg stopped Sander with a gentle touch on the shoulder.

"I will need to talk with you," she said to him in Norwegian.

"I understand," Sander said, trying to pull himself together.

Kolberg quietly ordered the two policemen to gather evidence inside the tower. Then she, London, and Sander left the tower and joined the Jarretts and the Wuttkes and Sir Reggie in the larger room. Honey put Sir Reggie down, and he trotted over to take his place beside London.

Everybody sat down except *Politiførstebetjent* Kolberg, who paced thoughtfully and then took out a pencil and notebook.

"I need everybody's names," she said

The Jarretts identified themselves. When Carter and Mardi said their names, the constable tilted her head and asked, "Are you of the candy Wuttkes?"

"That's right," Carter said.

"Your candy is very popular here in Norway," Kolberg said.

"I—I'm glad to hear it," Carter stammered, still shaken by what had just happened.

Kolberg frowned slightly and said, "No one has introduced me to the dog."

"His name is Sir Reggie," London told her.

Kolberg nodded with approval and said, "A Yorkshire Terrier, I believe. An excellent breed."

Then she said to the whole group, "I take it you are all Americans—except for young Nilsen."

Everybody nodded and said yes.

"And what are the circumstances that brought you Americans here today?" she asked.

London said, "We arrived in Oslo this morning on the *Nachtmusik,* a cruise ship owned by Epoch World Cruise Lines."

Kolberg's eyes widened at the name of the ship.

Then she said to London, "Oh. I *thought* I had heard your name before. You are the American crime solver."

London stifled a groan of despair.

As if things weren't bad enough already, she thought.

"Actually," she said, "I am the *Nachtmusik's* social director."

"Yes, yes, that too, I have heard," the constable said, peering attentively at London. "I had pictured you as taller. And older. With one of those checkered hats with a button on top and a bill both on the front and back. And a large pipe."

"Like Sherlock Holmes?" Gus asked.

"Right, like Sherlock Holmes," the constable agreed.

London tried not to show her dismay. Since she'd become an accidental detective, she'd found herself compared to Nancy Drew, Miss Marple, and Hercule Poirot. This was the first time she'd been likened to Sherlock Holmes. She didn't think any of those comparisons were meant to be complimentary.

During her previous encounters with local European law enforcement, the police she'd dealt with hadn't always been pleased to meet her. By contrast, Kolberg seemed to be rather impressed.

"Tell me, Frøken Rose," she said. "Do you think this was an accident?"

London felt truly taken aback. High-ranking law enforcement officers seldom if ever asked for her opinion.

"I—I don't know," she said. "I only hope it's not …"

"Foul play?" the constable said, finishing London's thought. "Yes, I hope not too."

Then she said to the group, "Now tell me how you all happen to be on this island."

Carter said, "Mardi and I rented a boat to do some island-hopping. We stopped on this island because we liked how it looked."

London said, "I chartered Herr Nilsen's boat for some of my passengers. He brought us here."

"Where were all of you when the … fatal incident occurred?" Kolberg asked.

"We were all out for a walk along the beach," Gus said.

"All of you?"

Carter shrugged and nodded toward London, "All of us except her."

London's stomach sank at the prospect of explaining her own alibi.

"And where were you at the time?" Kolberg asked London.

London gulped hard and said, "I was outside looking for a couple of missing passengers. One of them is a man named Scott Raife. The other is …"

113

London hesitated, then said, "My mother, Barbara Rose."

The constable squinted again.

"Missing, you say?" she said. "Do you mean from the island?"

"I'm not sure," London said. "I think possibly so."

"Do you have any idea how they might have left? Or why?"

"I'm afraid not," London said.

Before Kolberg could ask any further questions, one of the police officers she'd left in the tower came out and asked to speak to her. The two of them stepped aside, and the officer spoke quietly while showing Kolberg what London assumed to be some images on his cellphone.

When the policeman went back into the tower, Kolberg looked at the group with a markedly more suspicious expression than before.

"I am afraid the investigation has taken an unfortunate turn," she said.

London's heart sank.

It's as bad as I feared, she thought.

CHAPTER TWENTY THREE

London's companions gasped and looked back and forth at each other with alarm.

Sander started crying again.

"I cannot believe this," he sobbed in Norwegian. "I cannot believe this."

Honey asked the constable, "Do you mean that poor man really was murdered?"

Politiførstebetjent Kolberg said sternly, "I will ask the questions, if everybody does not mind."

Honey closed her mouth firmly.

The constable paced the floor for a moment, then asked the group, "Did any of you have any sort of altercation with the deceased? Or do you know of anybody who did?"

Before anyone could answer that question, the outside door swung open. Mom was standing there in the doorway.

"What's going on?" Mom asked anxiously. "What are the police doing here?"

Before anybody else could say anything, Gus Jarrett stood up and spoke sharply to Kolberg.

"I'll tell you somebody who had an 'altercation' with him. Scott Raife, the guy this woman ran off with a while ago."

Honey rolled her eyes and reprimanded her husband, "Come on, Gus. Don't go jumping to conclusions already."

"Well, it's true, isn't it?" Gus said. Then he asked Mom, "Where is he, anyhow? Where did he go?"

London stopped herself from asking, *"And where have you been?"*

Looking seriously alarmed now, Mom came on into the building.

"Is Scott being accused of something?" he asked.

"Yeah," Gus replied. "Just maybe of murder,"

Mom grew suddenly pale.

"I must ask you to take a seat," the constable said to Mom.

Mom's eyes grew wide. She hurried over to a chair and sat down with the rest of the group. The Wuttkes were holding onto each other for dear life, as if they were about to be attacked by a mugger or something.

Pointing to Mom, the constable turned to London and asked, "Is this one of the two missing people you mentioned?"

"That's right," London said. "This is my mother, Barbara Rose. The other was Scott Raife, another passenger on the *Nachtmusik.*"

She could see that her mother was trembling a bit now.

Nerves? London wondered. *Or fear?*

Mom looked around at everybody, "Would somebody please explain all this?" she said. "Is it true that somebody has been ... ?"

Mom's voice faded.

London explained as calmly as she could, "Since you and Scott ... disappeared, Iver Nilsen fell to his death from up inside the lighthouse tower."

Mom gasped again.

"But surely it was an accident," she said.

Gus growled, "The cop lady doesn't seem to think so. And I've got a pretty good idea who she *ought* to suspect of murder."

For the first time, the constable sounded a bit impatient.

"I have no suspects—not yet," she said. "And I will thank you all for refraining from accusing anybody. Could somebody tell me the nature of the altercation?"

London decided she'd better start explaining things.

"Everybody else aboard the boat was mackerel fishing, but Scott wanted to fish for sea trout. So he used his own rod and reel. He hooked something big—a cod, as it turned out."

Kolberg squinted at London and said, "Fishing for cod is illegal in Oslofjord."

Mardi Wuttke said anxiously, "But Carter and I didn't do any fishing at all."

Carter gently shushed his wife.

Poor Mardi, London thought. *She barely understands what's going on.*

London said, "Well, Scott didn't know that, and the captain never even imagined he might catch a cod, so he never mentioned it. The whole thing came as a real surprise. After Scott reeled the fish in, the captain explained the problem, then unhooked the fish and let it go."

Gus let out an indignant cry, "And that's when Scott and the captain got into a fight."

"Or *almost* got into a fight, anyway," Honey said.

"Tell me about that part," Kolberg said.

116

Trying to make light of it, Mom said, "Oh, it was all very silly—just a bit of a testosterone storm. Scott was angry about letting the fish go. He thought we all should have cooked it and eaten it and just not told anybody about it."

Gus added, "That's when Scott put his hand on the captain's shoulder, and the captain told him he'd better not do that."

"It was just a little scuffle," Honey interrupted.

Kolberg frowned at Honey, who shut up again.

For London's part, she knew that it was more than just "a little scuffle," at least as far as Scott Raife was concerned. The man had been thoroughly humiliated.

Gus snorted and went on, "So the captain grabbed this guy Raife's arm and forced him down against the rail and told him he'd better wise up if he didn't want to wind up swimming."

Mom said, "Well, those weren't the captain's exact words. But he did seem to be on the brink of doing something drastic—maybe almost violent. I thought he was being unnecessarily rough about it. I scolded him about it."

Kolberg peered suspiciously at Mom.

"So you and the missing man *both* had arguments with the captain," she said.

Mom's eyes widened and she said almost in a whisper, "Well, I guess that's one way of putting it, but ..."

Jotting down some notes, Kolberg said, "And then the two of you disappeared completely. Could you explain that, please?"

Mom forced a slight laugh.

"Oh, it was all perfectly innocent, I assure you," she said. "By the time we arrived at the island, Scott was feeling depressed and unhappy and embarrassed about the whole business with the fish. So I decided maybe a walk would cheer him up."

London couldn't help but wince.

A little walk! she thought.

Once again, Mom had found an excuse to blow off London's desire for the two of them to talk.

Mom continued, "We didn't get very far before a man we hadn't seen before came ashore in a rowboat. A really funny-looking boat. Its prow and stern were both curved in the same way."

Sander Nilsen's eyes widened with sudden interest.

"You mean like a Viking ship?" he asked in English.

London remembered the odd boat she'd seen out in the fjord.

117

"Yes, only much tinier, of course," Mom said. "A *færing*, the man said it was called."

Carter Wuttke said, "Mardi and I noticed a boat like that too. But it didn't come ashore when we saw it."

Mom continued, "The man in the boat offered us a boat ride, and we thought that would be a nice change, so we got in and he rowed us out into the fjord. It was fun for a while, a nice change after riding in a noisy motorboat. But eventually things got ... a little strange."

"How so?" Kolberg asked.

Mom shrugged and said, "Well, the man with the boat just got angrier, complaining all about what was happening to the fjord, the pollution and trash and overfishing and all, and then he seemed to get angry about Americans and how they always ruined everything, and how they should just stay home and not come to Norway. Tourists were no good to anybody, he said, and that included us."

Sander's interest seemed to be rising by the second.

"Did he say what his name was?" he asked.

Mom scratched her chin and said, "I think so. It was Tobias somebody ..."

"Tobias Skare?" Sander asked.

"Yes, I think that's what it was," Mom said.

Sander jumped out of his chair and shouted at the constable in Norwegian. London was able to make out what he said.

"It was him! Tobias Skare! He killed my father! If he was anywhere near here, it had to be him!"

"Why do you say that?" Kolberg asked.

"He has hated my father for years," Sander said. "He ran his own rival tour with that ridiculous *færing* of his, and he always resented my father for getting more clients aboard a real fishing boat. Besides, he is simply out of his mind. I always warned Father that Tobias was going to harm him someday. Father never listened."

Jotting down the name, Kolberg said to Sander in Norwegian, "We will find Herr Skare and talk to him," she said to Sander in Norwegian. "And I will need to ask you more questions about him in good time."

Then she added to the others in English, "I am still interested in what happened to Scott Raife. Where is he now?"

Mom shrugged and said, "I really don't have the slightest idea."

"What do you mean?" the constable asked.

"Well, like I said, Herr Skare started behaving pretty weirdly toward us, and I didn't exactly feel comfortable out in a boat with him,

118

so I asked him to row me back here to the island, and I paid him what he thought I owed him. But Scott didn't want to come back here, so he sailed away with Skare again."

"And you do not know where they went?" Kolberg asked.

"No, I really don't."

"Perhaps those two are working together," Sander growled tearfully. Under the constable's glare, he grew silent again.

Kolberg silently jotted down some notes for a moment. Then she glanced at each of the people seated in the room and said, "I do not think there is any point in detaining you on the island, nor in taking you to headquarters for questioning—at least not yet. But I insist that you Americans stay put here in Oslo until you are notified otherwise. And I expect to be able to contact you immediately."

Mardi Wuttke protested, "But Carter and I are scheduled to travel to Bergen tomorrow."

"You will have to cancel that trip," Kolberg said.

Patting his wife's hand, Carter said, "It will be all right, darling."

Honey asked Kolberg, "But how are Gus and London and Barbara and Sir Reggie and I supposed to get back to our ship?"

Kolberg turned toward Sander and asked in him Norwegian, "Do you feel up to the task of taking these people back ashore?"

Sander wiped his eyes and nodded, looking calmer than he had been before.

"Good," Kolberg said, then added to the others in English, "You may prepare for your departure."

As everybody got up and began to move around, Kolberg tugged on London's sleeve.

"I need to speak to you privately," she said.

CHAPTER TWENTY FOUR

London felt a tingle of apprehension as she watched her mother, the Jarretts, the Wuttkes, and Sander Nilsen file out of the lighthouse. At the doorway, Mom turned and gave her a brief smile, and then they were all gone.

Only she and Sir Reggie remained standing there in the room with *Politiførstebetjent* Kolberg.

What does she want to talk to me about? London wondered. *And why me?*

Kolberg said to London, "Because of your, eh, past experience in such matters, I feel that maybe you and I should discuss the case alone. My team photographed the rung that broke under the victim's weight, and when they blew up the pictures, they found some saw marks there."

So that's what the policeman had showed Kolberg on his cellphone a few minutes ago, London realized. *A photo of the broken rung.*

Kolberg continued, "The rungs were already dangerous. But it was obvious that someone had sawed into that one, sabotaging it so that it would surely break under a person's weight and send them falling to their death. And I believe you mentioned that the captain warned the rest of you not to climb up there, and that the captain alone did not heed his own advice."

"That's right," London said. "Which makes it likely that whoever sawed into the rung specifically targeted the captain for murder. The killer must have known that nobody else ever climbed up there."

"That seems like a reasonable conclusion," Kolberg said with a nod. "The case is liable to be a difficult one."

"How so?" London asked. "You've got a pretty closed circle of suspects—just the people who were here on the island."

"Yes, but how many people might that include? The damage to the rung need not have been done during the last few hours. For all we know, somebody sabotaged that rung yesterday, or the day before that, or the day before that."

London nodded, grasping the constable's meaning.

"And this is a small, isolated island that's usually uninhabited," London added. "The captain even said that this building is never locked. A murderer could have come and gone without anyone noticing."

"Especially at night," Kolberg said.

"I don't envy you your job," London said.

Kolberg tilted her head. The expression on her features looked rather ominous as she told London, "I do not exactly envy your situation, either."

London shuddered slightly at those words.

"What do you mean?" she asked slowly, although she already had an idea what might be coming.

Kolberg took a long, slow breath, then said, "I am sure you understand that I must include all the people who came here today as potential suspects ..."

Here it is, London realized. Her heart pounded harder.

Kolberg continued, "That includes the Wuttkes, of course. And the Jarretts. And the rather elusive Scott Raife. And ..."

Kolberg's voice faded.

"And my mother," London said, finishing her thought.

Kolberg nodded, "Yes, her peculiar jaunt with Scott Raife is rather, eh, problematic."

London's throat tightened as she said, "You're about to say that I'm a potential suspect too."

Kolberg nodded silently.

London felt a flicker of anger.

She'd been in this situation several times before, and it seemed cruelly unfair. And until these last few moments, she had thought Kolberg was different from some of the pigheaded male law enforcement officials she'd had to deal with in other cities.

In a hoarse voice London objected, "With all due respect, neither my mother nor myself nor anybody else in our group even knew Captain Nilsen until today. And you said yourself, the rung might have been sabotaged at any time. Surely you don't seriously believe that my mother ... or I ..."

The constable interrupted sharply, "In my work, I have learned never to rule anything or anyone out. Besides, what I believe or do not believe is immaterial. You of all people should understand that. You were the first to find the body. That in itself is sufficient to place you under suspicion."

"But that's not the only reason," London said, sensing that there was more.

"No, it's not," Kolberg said. "As you already know, your reputation precedes you. You have been rather uncannily connected with five different murders all over Europe."

"But I *solved* those murders," London said.

"I know," Kolberg said. "And I am impressed by that. But you have become something of a living legend, and there as many rumors circulating about you as there are facts. Many people in law enforcement—including some of my subordinates *and* superiors—suspect the worst of you. And I have to answer to those people. I have to treat you as a potential suspect—and your mother as well—until you are proven innocent or someone else is proven guilty."

London fell silent as the enormity of her situation sank in. She doubted that she or her mother or anybody else would be convicted of a murder they didn't commit. Surely, she and Mom would be exonerated sooner or later.

Meanwhile, things are liable to be really hard, she thought.

Kolberg added, "All that being said, I think it would be wise to put your considerable detective abilities to work clearing your name. I also need you to help find Herr Raife."

Handing London her card, the constable added, "If you find him before I do, call me and I'll send a car to pick him up. He definitely has more to explain than anyone else at this point."

London asked, "Is there anything else you need me to do?"

Kolberg let out a sigh and said, "Yes, I suppose there is. Stay out of my way. Do not step on my toes. You have a reputation for …"

"Meddling in police business?" London said, completing her thought.

Kolberg nodded and said, "Just keep in mind, my situation is always precarious. I am a woman doing what men tend to think of as a man's job. A lot of my colleagues think that way. My job is never easy, and this case is going to be even harder than most. It is going to take a fair amount of effort for me just to keep you out of jail. Because believe me, there will be plenty of people who want to put you in jail."

Kolberg smiled ironically and added, "Just do not do anything to make me agree with them."

Without another word, *Politiførstebetjent* Kolberg headed out of the lighthouse toward the police boat, where the crew and her team were already aboard and waiting to leave.

London looked down at Reggie, who seemed to have been listening intently.

"Well, Sir Reggie," she said to him. "The constable does have a way of speaking her mind. What do you think of her?"

Sir Reggie just cocked his head as he watched Kolberg climb aboard the police boat.

"I'm not sure what I think of her either," London said. "But I guess we're going to have to stick around here and find out."

As the police boat drew away from the pier, London watched Carter and Mardi Wuttke heading back along the beach toward their own boat at the far end of the island.

London flashed back to how enchanted they'd been with this island just a little while ago, and how they'd wanted to buy it for the International Gaia Engagement Fund. She remembered how disappointed they'd seemed when the captain had told them the island wasn't privately owned.

Even so, the captain seemed to have an idea in mind.

"Let's talk it over after we eat," he'd told them.

Of course, they'd never gotten a chance to do that.

And I bet they'll want to forget they ever came to this island now, London thought.

Then she saw that her fellow passengers were getting ready to board the *Kråkebolle* for the trip back to the mainland.

Sir Reggie let out a nagging whine, as if to remind London of something.

"Yeah, I know, pal," she said to her dog with a sigh. "We'll get on board and go with them. But first, I've got a phone call to make. And it's going to be a tough one."

CHAPTER TWENTY FIVE

Before punching a number into her cell phone, London hesitated.

It was not the first time that she'd had to pass on bad news. The question was, who should she be calling?

For a moment, she wavered between calling Captain Hays or Mr. Lapham. Despite the captain's authoritative manner, London knew that he was a sensitive soul who took bad news hard. So, for that matter, was Mr. Lapham. Even so, London felt that the CEO was likely to handle the news …

Well, more philosophically than the captain, I guess, she decided.

London punched in the number, and Mr. Lapham's voice sounded perky and excited when he took the call.

"London! How has your fishing outing gone? My group caught a ton of mackerel, and we had a delightful cookout on Bleikøya Island. Did you get a good catch? What perfect weather to visit the islands, eh? I believe you were headed for Trollskog, then to some other island. Did you perhaps get to Lindøya? I hear it's lovely. Is that where you are right now?"

London gulped hard.

"No, Mr. Lapham, we didn't get to visit Lindøya. You see …"

Her voice faded.

"Oh, dear," Mr. Lapham said. "You're not calling with good news, are you?"

"I'm afraid not."

"Did your boat sink?"

"No."

"Did somebody get eaten by a shark?"

"No, not that either."

"Did you get caught in some sort of space-time singularity?"

"I, uh, don't think so," she said.

London heard Mr. Lapham let out a long, discouraged sigh.

"Well, that *does* narrow down the possibilities, doesn't it? About the only thing left is another murder."

"I'm afraid that's what it was, Mr. Lapham," London said.

"And just when I'd dared to hope our fortunes had changed for the better! Was the victim any of our *Nachtmusik* people?"

"No," London said. "It was the captain of our fishing boat."

"How dreadful! And you're certain this death was not an accident?"

"The police have already checked the site. They're the ones who discovered that it was a murder."

"Who is going to bring you back here?" the CEO asked.

London glanced over at young Sander, who was helping the passengers into the *Kråkebolle* and also their life jackets. She and Sir Reggie needed to join them quickly.

"We have that taken care of," London replied to Mr. Lapham's question. "I've got to go now. I'll tell you and Captain Hays all about it when I get back to the *Nachtmusik.*"

"Please do so. And I'm dreadfully sorry … well for the déjà vu you must be feeling right now."

They ended the call, and London and Sir Reggie climbed into the boat. A few minutes later, Sander was piloting the *Kråkebolle* away from Trollskog Island with London, Mom, Sir Reggie, and Gus and Honey Jarrett aboard.

Gus and Honey sat on the port side of the boat, and London sat opposite them with Sir Reggie in her lap with Mom at her side. Although it was still daylight, it was getting late in the day. The day seemed unusually long, to say nothing of calamitous. London reminded herself that the sun set later this far north.

Everyone aboard the boat was tired from their ordeal, including London herself. Honey fell asleep with her head on Gus's shoulder, and Gus let his own head drop back as his mouth opened into a snore.

London and her mother didn't speak for a while. London didn't know where to begin, and apparently Mom didn't either. All London knew was that she had some serious questions to ask her mother and she had to hold in check the anger she felt building up inside.

Finally, Mom broke the silence, patting London's hand.

"You poor dear," she said. "This must be especially shocking for you."

"What do you mean?" London asked.

"Well, you were the first of us to see the body. Have you ever seen a dead body before? If not, that would make it even worse for you. Surely you're traumatized. Is there anything I can do to make things better? You might need counseling, you know."

London's eyes widened with surprise.

"Mom, what are you saying?" she said. "I've been seeing dead

125

bodies all over Europe. I thought you'd been keeping track of me. Didn't you know that?"

Mom's chin dropped, and she stammered, "Well, I—I knew the *Nachtmusik* had encountered some deaths along the way, but I didn't know that you were personally …"

Mom's voice faded and London continued, "I found a woman who'd been killed by poison in a cathedral in Hungary. I found a man who'd been thrown off a balcony in Salzburg. In Bamberg, I saw a man who'd been drowned in a vat of beer. In Amsterdam, Sir Reggie and I found a dead art restorer in a canal boat. In Copenhagen, I saw a pastry cook's dead body in an alley. And now … there's this."

"I had no idea," Mom said.

"No, and I suppose you didn't have any idea that I had to turn detective and *solve* all those cases. And right now, it looks like I'm going to have to do that again. And you running off like that won't make it any easier."

Mom was quiet for a moment.

Then she shrugged a little and said, "Well, like I said—counseling might not be such a bad idea."

London let out a groan of despair.

"Mom, why did you go running off, anyway?" she asked. "Why did you leave the island?"

Mom shrugged again and said, "Well, it's like I told everybody, including the constable—"

"No, Mom," London interrupted. "Don't tell me you were just trying to cheer up Scott Raife after his fishing humiliation. There was more to it than that."

"I don't know what you mean," Mom said.

"Oh, I think you do," London said. "You and I were just getting ready to take a nice walk and talk about all the things we've been putting off talking about. But you panicked, didn't you? You ran away from talking about it—*literally* ran away. You were so anxious to get away from me, you actually caught a boat piloted by a complete stranger to take you away from the island."

"That's not a very nice thing to say," Mom said, crossing her arms.

"But it's true, isn't it?"

Mom didn't reply.

Of course, it's true, London thought.

Finally, Mom said in a meek voice, "Maybe we should talk about all that now. Right here."

London felt a swell of frustration at the idea of trying to discuss their lost decades sitting here among other people—even if those people didn't seem particularly attentive.

"We've got other things to talk about," London said sharply.

"Such as?"

London inhaled and exhaled slowly, trying to bring her emotions under control.

Finally, she said, "Mom, were you telling the constable the truth about what you and Scott did after you left the lighthouse? The whole truth, I mean?"

"Why does that even matter?" Mom asked.

London blurted, "Because Scott Raife is a murder suspect, Mom. And as a matter of fact, so are you."

"Me?" Mom gasped.

"Yeah, and so am I," London said more quietly.

"You?"

"That's right."

Mom scoffed and said, "But that's downright crazy. Next you'll be telling me that Sir Reggie is also a suspect."

"This is nothing to joke about, Mom," London said.

"Who said I was joking? None of this makes any sense."

"It makes all kinds of sense—to *Politiførstebetjent* Kolberg, anyway. Scott had a physical altercation with Captain Nilsen before the murder. He's actually got a motive of sorts. And you and Scott were both AWOL at the time of the captain's death. And I was the one who found his body."

Mom tilted her head and said, "Well, dear, I'm positively sure *you* didn't kill him."

"That's nice to hear," London grumbled sarcastically.

"Surely you don't think *I* killed him."

London almost said no, she certainly didn't suspect Mom.

But then she thought, *What do I know about what really happened?*

After all, she didn't even know what her own mother had been doing for the last 20 years.

"Let's just put it this way," London said. "I'm *most* suspicious of Scott, and so is the constable. And I don't like the idea that you were hanging around with him at that particular time. Did he say or do anything suspicious?"

"Not that I remember," Mom said.

"What about when you came ashore after riding around in that boat, and he just stayed and sailed off again? Didn't he say why? Did he tell you anything at all about where he was going next?"

"No, he didn't," Mom said. "I'm sure he didn't."

London flashed back to something the constable had said.

"I also need for you to help find Herr Raife."

How am I supposed to do that? London wondered.

A tense silence fell between London and her mother.

She saw that both Jarretts seemed to be fast asleep, and Sander was occupied with operating the boat. Maybe Mom was right, and the two of them could have their much-needed conversation right now. But London just didn't think she could deal with the added emotional trauma of delving into family secrets.

Maybe I'll never find out why Mom left and where she's been all this time.

Then a new thought struck her.

And maybe I just don't want to know.

London and Mom didn't say a word until they neared the pier where the *Nachtmusik* was moored. Just as Sander started docking the boat, Mom gasped and pointed with surprise.

"Oh, London! Look!"

CHAPTER TWENTY SIX

Mom was pointing at a man standing on the pier between the *Nachtmusik* and a larger ship. He was holding a fishing pole with its line hanging in the water below.

"Scott Raife," London muttered.

Even though Raife had argued with the murdered man and had left the tour group to take off in a different boat, he obviously was not in hiding.

As Sander pulled nearer the pier, London thought, *I guess I should tell him to call the constable.*

But then she remembered *Politiførstebetjent* Kolberg's words.

"If you find him before I do, call me and I'll send a car to pick him up."

She found the card Kolberg had given her and dialed her direct number.

When she got the constable on the line she said, "I've found Scott Raife."

"Where is he?" Kolberg replied with a note of surprise.

"Standing on the pier in front of Akershus Fortress next to where the *Nachtmusik* is docked, the prow end of the ship."

"Try to keep him there until I can send a vehicle to pick him up," Kolberg said, then ended the call.

By then Sander had pulled up to the pier and was helping the group out of the boat. The ever-alert Honey also noticed the man with the fishing pole. She nudged her husband and pointed toward where Scott was standing.

"Hey, Gus, look who's over there," she said.

"Yeah, I see him," Gus said wearily.

"Where do you think he went when he took off like that?"

"I don't know," Gus said. "And I'm too tired to care. Besides, we've got an early flight back to the States tomorrow. Let's get back aboard the ship, OK?"

Honey turned to London, "Don't you just wonder …?"

"I'll talk to him," London told her. "You and Gus just go ahead on board."

Looking pretty tired herself, Honey nodded and followed her husband up the gangway. London felt relieved. She didn't want the Jarretts around when she tried to deal with Scott Raife.

With Sir Reggie trotting between them, London and Mom headed straight over to where Scott was standing on the pier.

London said to Mom, "We're supposed to keep him here for the police. So be careful what you say."

"Aren't I always?" Mom replied pertly.

London almost gagged at the absurdity of those words and thought better of what she'd just said.

"Scratch that," she said to Mom. "Just don't say anything at all. Leave the talking to me."

"Well, if you're going to be like that about it ..."

As they approached Scott Raife, London could see that he was slumped and sad looking, silently staring at his fishing line.

She tried to sound cheerful as she called out, "Hey, Scott. What are you doing?"

He turned toward them and scowled angrily.

"Be quiet," he complained. "You'll scare the fish."

Under different circumstances, London would have laughed. The harbor was abuzz with activity, both on the shore and on the water, with motorboats skimming the water, ship whistles, and all sorts of other noise.

Three people chatting on the pier weren't going to scare any fish. There probably wasn't a fish worth catching within a mile of this place.

When London, Mom, and Sir Reggie reached Scott, he paid no attention to them at all. London wasn't sure what to do next.

"Try to keep him there," the constable had said.

But, she wondered, *what if he just decides to leave?*

Was London supposed to try to stop him by force? She wasn't sure she dared. After all, Scott was the constable's choice suspect in the murder of Captain Nilsen. Could he be dangerous?

Sir Reggie trotted up and stood beside Scott, staring curiously at where the fishing line met the water. That made London feel a little nervous, because she knew that her little Yorkie wouldn't be intimidated if trouble arose. Her dog had forcibly thwarted more than one killer. But she didn't want Sir Reggie to risk his life again, so she hoped things wouldn't come to that.

She thought maybe she should try to engage Scott in some kind of conversation. But about what? They had never been exactly on friendly terms.

At least she figured she shouldn't mention the captain's murder. If Scott knew about it, that probably meant he was the killer. And if he didn't know about it, this was no time to tell him. Even if he was innocent, he still might panic and try to get away.

To London's alarm, Mom spoke right up.

"What are you using for bait?"

London shot Mom a glowering look to try to silence her. But Mom didn't seem to notice—or at least to care.

"What do you think I'm using for bait?" Scott growled back at Mom.

"Well, I'm just asking," Mom said, sounding hurt. "You don't have to bite my head off about it."

"I'm using the same bait I used on the boat," Scott said.

"You mean artificial lures?" Mom said.

Scott silently nodded his head. London sensed that his thoughts were elsewhere.

On having killed a man, maybe? she wondered.

He didn't seem to genuinely care about catching any fish—or even going about it in a remotely plausible way.

To London's surprise, she realized that Mom seemed to be saying the right things. She could keep Scott's attention until the police vehicle arrived. And after all, London herself didn't have any better ideas.

Mom shook her head critically.

"Oh, I'm not sure artificial lures will work, not with your line just hanging in the water like this. What you need is live bait—shrimp, maybe."

"Don't tell me what to do, lady," Scott said in a dull, apathetic voice.

"Well, it's just a thought, but here's what I'd do ..." Mom began.

As Mom kept making suggestions and criticisms, London was glad to have escaped the responsibility of keeping the man occupied. She found herself simply pondering the question of whether Scott Raife could possibly have murdered Captain Nilsen.

She flashed back to the two men's quarrels aboard the *Kråkebolle,* which had culminated in the unexpected catch and release of a big cod and a physical altercation that came perilously close to sending Scott into the drink.

She also remembered Scott's palpable, smoldering, humiliated fury.

It sure seems like a motive, she thought.

And it wasn't as though Scott and Captain Nilsen had tried to make peace when they got to the island. She remembered how the captain had displayed his big, formidable knife and mockingly compared it to the little Swiss Army knife Scott was using to cut his roasted mackerel.

"Now this *is the kind of knife you can really get some use out of,"* the captain had said.

London also remembered Scott's face reddening with renewed humiliation at that moment.

But then another remark snapped into her mind—what *Politiførstebetjent* Kolberg had told her about how the ladder rung had been sabotaged.

"My team photographed the rung that broke under the victim's weight ... they found some saw marks there."

London felt a sharp tingle.

Is it possible ... ?

Meanwhile, Mom was prodding Scott to tell her all about his prowess and courage when he'd run with the bulls in Pamplona. And Scott was starting to get a kick out of bragging about it.

"It was a peak experience, let me tell you," he said.

"Oh, I'd be so scared to run with those bulls!" Mom said with that feigned feminine meekness London was starting to find really offensive. "Did you really do the whole event?"

"Yeah, I did the whole thing, from beginning to end."

"Oooh, how brave of you!" Mom cooed. "Did you even take part in the horn-sharpening ceremony? That's the most dangerous part."

"You bet I did. I'd never have missed that."

London gently interrupted, "Scott, I really liked the looks of that Swiss Army knife of yours. Could let me handle it?"

"Absolutely," Scott said, his chest swelling with renewed machismo.

He took out the small, red knife with the white cross on it. London opened it up and found a corkscrew, a tiny pair of scissors, a can opener, and also the attachment she'd expected to find.

A saw.

It was a tiny saw, of course. But might it be sufficient to have made enough of a cut in that ladder rung that was big enough to sabotage it?

Maybe, London thought.

The blade certainly seemed sharp enough to cut wood. On the other hand, the saw sparkled with a sheen that made London wonder if it had ever been used.

Is it even possible … ?

Before London could decide what to think, she heard an approaching siren.

A small car painted yellow, white, and black with flashing lights came pulling up, and a couple of black-uniformed policemen got out. They walked straight toward Scott.

One of them called out to him in heavily accented English, "Are you Scott Raife?"

Scott turned and stared at the police with a befuddled expression.

"Yeah," he said. "Why?"

The policemen approached Scott and said, "We'd like you to come with us to headquarters."

The other policeman added, also in accented English, "We have some questions to ask you."

"About what?" Scott asked.

"About the death of Iver Nilsen."

Scott stared at the policemen blankly.

"You mean *Captain* Nilsen?" he asked. "He's *dead?*"

"You can talk all about it at headquarters," the first policeman said.

"Please come with us," the other said.

Scott put up no resistance as one of the policemen led him toward the car.

London caught the other policeman's attention and held out the Swiss Army knife to him.

"Excuse me, officer," she said in the best Norwegian she could muster. "This belongs to Herr Raife. You should probably take it with you as …"

As what? London wondered as her voice faded.

London couldn't think of an appropriate word, either in English or in Norwegian.

"As evidence?" the policeman asked in English.

"I, uh, suppose so," London said. "Be sure that *Politiførstebetjent* Kolberg sees it."

The policeman nodded and took the knife, then got into the car and drove away.

London stood staring as the car disappeared into the streets of Oslo. She frantically replayed in her mind what had just happened during the last few moments. Scott had seemed more numb than surprised.

Did that mean he'd guiltily expected the police to come and pick him up?

Or did it mean that he'd really had no idea that the captain was even dead until just a few seconds ago?

London had come to trust her instincts about such questions. But right now, her instincts weren't kicking in at all. She had no idea what to think.

London picked up Sir Reggie and said to Mom, "I wish I knew whether Scott killed Captain Nilsen or not."

Mom scoffed and said, "Oh, I can answer that question."

CHAPTER TWENTY SEVEN

London was stunned by the certainty in Mom's voice.

"What do you mean?" she asked skeptically.

After all, how could Mom state so casually that she could solve a mystery that the local police were just beginning to investigate? London certainly hadn't come to any firm conclusion about the man in question.

"What I mean is—Scott did not kill Captain Nilsen," Mom replied with utter confidence.

"How can you be so sure about that?" London asked, still carrying Sir Reggie in her arms as they walked toward the *Nachtmusik*.

"London, read my lips," Mom said with a pronounced roll of her eyes. "That man never killed anybody. I doubt that he ever even killed a mouse."

"How do you know?"

"Weren't you listening when he and I were talking about the running of the bulls just now? I asked if he'd taken part in the horn-sharpening ceremony. He said that he had."

"So?" London demanded.

Mom laughed aloud.

She said, "Well, London, I *have* run with the bulls in Pamplona. And I can assure you there's no such thing as a horn-sharpening ceremony. I made it up on the spot, and he fell for it. He's never run with the bulls. I'll bet he's never even been to Pamplona."

Mom laughed more softly and continued, "And I'm sure he's never gone rock climbing in the Rockies or done any sky diving either. He's what people sometimes call—how can I put this euphemistically?—an artist who paints with the excrement of a certain large male bovine."

It took London a moment to translate this into a blunter, coarser colloquialism.

Then she squinted with confusion.

"How does that prove he didn't kill anybody?" she asked.

Mom patted London on the shoulder and said, "Ah, the infinite obliviousness of the young! You've still got a lot to learn about men, sweetie. When it comes to the male of the species, there is an inverse

135

relationship between bluster and courage. A team of anthropologists—all of them women, of course—actually studied this phenomenon statistically. In 99.9 percent of documented cases, a male braggart is also a born coward."

London was pretty sure there had never been such a study. And anyway, she found herself oddly unconvinced. At least, she was certain that the killers she was aware of represented a wide variety of personalities.

"I'm sure that some murderers are cowards," she said.

"Oh, I'm sure of that too. But not in this case. Scott Raife is a classic phony. And believe me, I know plenty about that type even without any academic research to back me up."

Then Mom changed the subject, "Tell me—why did you want to see Scott's Swiss Army knife just now?"

London hesitated. *Politiførstebetjent* Kolberg had talked to her in private about exactly how the murder had been committed. London wasn't sure how much of that information she should share with Mom.

"OK, so don't tell me," Mom finally said. "I've already got it all figured out. The police discovered that the broken rung had been sawed to sabotage it. Those neat little saws on Swiss Army knives are small, but perfectly functional. You wanted to look at Scott's knife to see if he might have used the saw attachment to damage that rung. It sure didn't look to me like Scott's saw had been used at all. And besides ..."

Mom shrugged.

"He'd have to have climbed—what?—some 25 feet or so up the ladder to sabotage that rung. And I'm telling you Scott couldn't do that. The very idea of such a climb would have made the poor man faint dead away."

London made no comment. She couldn't deny there was certain logic to what Mom was saying—and even some pretty clever deduction.

Maybe this sleuthing thing of mine is genetic, she thought wryly.

Even so, what Mom was saying with such authority still sounded pretty speculative to London.

Meanwhile, as they approached the *Nachtmusik's* gangway, passengers were leaving with all their baggage. London had almost forgotten that Oslo was the *Nachtmusik's* last destination, and some passengers were already dispersing for their next destinations.

Her throat ached a little at the sight. Of course, the *Nachtmusik's* voyage had been fraught with danger and calamity, but was she really ready for it to end?

She stifled a sigh and thought, *Well, it is ending, whether I'm ready or not.*

At the top of the gangway, Captain Hays was saying farewell to his departing passengers and wishing them happy travels elsewhere. As soon as he caught sight of London, Mom, and Sir Reggie, the captain pulled them aside and spoke to them privately.

"Oh, I'm so relieved that you're back!" he said. "Please assure me that you've survived your ordeal quite safe and sound."

"Yes, we're OK," London said. "But I think you and I had better talk things over with Mr. Lapham."

Captain Hays nodded so vigorously that his walrus mustache shook.

"Yes, yes, of course, absolutely," he said. "I just came from our CEO's suite. He's expecting to talk to you."

London set Sir Reggie down. As she and her dog started to follow the captain to the passageway, Mom tagged along as well.

This is going to be awkward, London thought.

"Uh, Mom," she said, "I think I'd better go take care of this on my own."

Mom's brow twisted into a wounded expression.

"You mean—without me?" she said.

"I'm afraid so," London said.

The captain said nothing, but she sensed that he agreed with her.

"But what am I supposed to do in the meantime?" Mom asked.

"Mom, you've already made all kinds of friends on this ship," London said. "This might be the last chance you get to talk to them."

"Well, *that's* a pretty lame suggestion," Mom said, crossing her arms. "It sure doesn't seem fair to me. Why even the dog gets to take part in all the interesting stuff. Why can't I—?"

Sir Reggie interrupted her with a cheerful yap and rubbed himself against her ankle.

London smiled and said, "It looks like Sir Reggie will be happy to keep you company."

Smiling herself now, Mom picked up Sir Reggie.

"Well, then," she said. "That makes everything much better. Come on, Sir Reggie. Let's go say goodbye to some of our friends."

Mom and Sir Reggie headed off on their own while London and the captain continued into the passageway toward Mr. Lapham's grand suite. London's pulse quickened as her anxiety rose. Of course, Mr. Lapham wanted to talk to her about the murder, which was going to be difficult. But there was at least one other topic that he was likely to bring up which she wasn't ready to discuss with him yet.

The captain rapped on the door, and London heard a familiar voice calling from inside, "Come in."

Captain Hays and London stepped into the room, where they found Mr. Lapham in his customary, stylishly casual attire, seated in his throne-like armchair with his enormous, incredibly fluffy black-and-white cat Siegfried stretched out on his lap. Mr. Lapham was petting Siegfried with his long, slender fingers.

The light from the balcony windows behind him highlighted the CEO's imposing figure. London marveled at how intimidating this man could be, even in such an apparently relaxed attitude.

"Sit down," Mr. Lapham said to London and the captain.

London found herself unnerved even by his calm voice and friendly smile.

I've got some explaining to do, she thought.

CHAPTER TWENTY EIGHT

London sputtered nervously as she and the captain sat down in nearby armchairs.

"Mr. Lapham, I—I don't know where to start—"

"No need to explain everything from scratch, my dear," Mr. Lapham assured her, interrupting with a wave of his hand. "Captain Hays and I were on the phone a few minutes ago with the *Politiførstebetjent*—Monica somebody."

"Monica Kolberg," London said.

"Yes, that's right," Mr. Lapham said. "She told us everything she saw fit for us to know about this awful business."

London felt a twinge of relief not to have to relate the whole misadventure herself.

Mr. Lapham continued, "The constable also told us she would want to interview one of our passengers ..."

"Scott Raife," London said, filling in the name for him.

"Yes, she said he'd made rather a peculiar disappearance," Mr. Lapham said.

The captain added, "We've asked the receptionist to let us know if he comes back aboard."

"Um, that won't be necessary," London said. "The police picked him up a few minutes ago nearby, on the pier."

The captain's bushy eyebrows leaped up.

"Picked him up, did they?" he said. "Do you mean they *arrested* him?"

"No, he hasn't been charged with anything—yet. It's just that his behavior was rather suspicious. Right now, the police just want to ask him some questions."

Captain Hays shook his head.

"I'll have to call the U.S. embassy and tell them one of our citizens might be in a spot of trouble," he said. "I'll do that as soon as we finish this little conference."

"Tell me, my dear," Mr. Lapham said to London, leaning forward and folding his hands. "Do you think it's possible that Mr. Raife is the murderer?"

For a moment, words failed London.

She flashed back to what Mom had said about Scott Raife just now.

"That man never killed anybody. I doubt that he ever even killed a mouse."

London almost said, *"My mom doesn't think so."*

But Mr. Lapham wasn't asking Mom. He was asking London. And the truth was, she still didn't know what to think about Scott's guilt or innocence. And besides, there was another problem that Mr. Lapham and Captain Hays hadn't been told about yet.

"I don't know, sir, but ..."

She hesitated, then said, "I'm afraid my mother and I are also under ... some suspicion."

Captain Hays and Mr. Lapham both let out gasps of dismayed surprise.

"You and your mother!" the captain exclaimed.

"Why, the very idea!" Mr. Lapham said. He bristled angrily, as though he might leap up from his chair and go confront the police himself. Then he controlled his indignation and spoke quite seriously.

Mr. Lapham said, "London, please assure me as emphatically as possible that you did *not* kill anybody."

"No, absolutely not," London said.

"And of course, neither did your mother," Mr. Lapham said.

"No."

London almost added, *I don't think so.*

She was virtually certain Mom hadn't committed any murder. But Mom's disappearance with Scott was a complicating factor, as the constable had pointed out. But thinking about their unscheduled ride in a rowboat reminded London of something.

She continued, "There may be another suspect. His name is Tobias Skare, and he takes people for rides out on the fjord in a rowboat shaped like a Viking ship."

Mr. Lapham tilted his head.

"A *færing,* I believe it's called," he said.

"That's right. He was near the island around the time of the murder. And the victim's son said there was some bad blood between Skare and his father."

The captain stroked his chin and said, "Well, let's just hope the killer is caught soon, and that none of our passengers are involved—neither Scott Raife nor anyone else. I'd hate to end this voyage on that kind of note."

Mr. Lapham nodded, then he added, "I suppose I'd better get in touch with our security expert, Bob Turner, and put him to work on this matter. He can check in with the police tomorrow and offer his help. He's certainly proven his prowess in solving murders during this troublesome voyage. I'm sure he can clear this up before it inconveniences any of our people."

London exchanged looks with Captain Hays, who winked slyly at her. London managed not to giggle. Neither she nor the captain had tried to disabuse Mr. Lapham of his high opinion of Bob Turner's sleuthing abilities. The truth was that Bob Turner was more than a bit of a bumbler, although he could be handy in a physical altercation.

But London and the captain had agreed between themselves, it would be just as well for Mr. Lapham never to find out the truth—that London herself had been the ship's real crime solver, at occasional risk of life and limb. Mr. Lapham was so fatherly and protective of London; he tended to fly into a panic at the very idea of her facing danger.

What he doesn't know won't hurt him, London thought.

Although I suppose it might hurt me *if I'm not careful.*

The captain asked the CEO, "Does that conclude our business for now?"

"I suppose it does," Mr. Lapham grumbled. "But I must say, my astrologer has yet to offer me an explanation for this dreadful business. When we left Denmark, Alex assured me that our passengers' goodwill was enough to counteract any adverse celestial influences. 'You will have smooth sailing from now on,' he told me. I based my decision to continue our voyage on his assessment of the situation. And look where it's gotten us!"

Mr. Lapham added with a grunt of irritation, "Well, I wrote him an email about it, and he wrote back simply, 'There was a change of plans.' Now what on earth is that supposed to even mean? Does the universe change its mind on a whim? Unfortunately, people can die when such mistakes are made."

Captain Hays let out an uncharacteristically scornful scoff.

"Come now, Jeremy. Surely you're not going to go making poor Alex out to be some sort of unwitting accessory. That would be carrying this astrology business a bit too far, I think."

Looking a bit chastened, Mr. Lapham said, "Well, maybe I was letting my anger get the best of me …"

London was a bit startled by this exchange between the two men— particularly the way Captain Hays had called the CEO "Jeremy."

Suddenly it occurred to her that these two interesting men had known each other for many years—perhaps since long before either of them had become the authority figures they now were.

Captain Hays got up from his chair.

"Well then, I'd better go contact the embassy. We will further discuss these matters anon—hopefully after we've received some better news."

London started to get up from her chair as the captain headed for the door.

"London, stay for a moment," Mr. Lapham said. "We have something else to discuss."

London's heart sank.

She didn't feel ready to have this conversation.

After the captain had left, Mr. Lapham lifted Siegfried from his lap and set him on the floor. As the CEO stood up, the huge cat protested loudly, stomped off into the bedroom side of the grand suite, and curled up on the bed.

With a fond smile at the affronted animal, Mr. Lapham turned and went to his balcony window. For a long moment he just stared pensively at the view outside. Then he turned back toward London and spoke in a gentle, apologetic tone.

"I'm sorry to have to trouble you any further at a time like this ..."

Her pulse quickened and she felt a bit lightheaded.

She knew what must be coming next, and she wasn't actually ready to discuss this question.

CHAPTER TWENTY NINE

With so much going on and so many things on her mind, London had completely avoided one very important decision. And yet, of course, the CEO had every right to ask...

"It's all right, I understand," London told him. "You want to know whether I'm going to accept your offer to work aboard the *Galene.*"

Mr. Lapham nodded.

London's throat tightened.

She said, "Mr. Lapham, this might sound ridiculous, but ..."

Her voice faded, and Mr. Lapham finished her thought.

"But you still haven't made up your mind."

London nodded. Mr. Lapham let out a sigh and shook his head.

"London, I think you know that I am patience personified," he said. "And, 'had we but world enough and time,' as the poet put it, I'd be glad to wait a good while longer for your decision. But I am a businessman. And you promised to make a decision before the day was over. And a decision is what I need from you right now."

London was a bit taken aback by those words, *"before the day was over."*

Surely there's still time, she thought.

The sky outside was still fairly light—not even dusk quite yet. Then London reminded herself that that sunset came a lot later in Oslo at this time of year, and sunrise came a lot earlier. Soon it would be time to go to bed—although London doubted that she'd be able to sleep.

Sitting down and facing her again, Mr. Lapham said, "London, what about our esteemed friend Bryce Yeaton? Has he accepted the offer from Aeolus Adventures to serve as head chef aboard the *Danae?"*

"I don't know," London admitted.

Mr. Lapham's eyes widened with disbelief.

"What do you mean, you don't know?" he said. "Haven't you talked with him about it yet?"

London shook her head no.

"Will, good gracious, child, what on earth are you waiting for ... ?"

But then Mr. Lapham caught himself and sighed again.

"Of course, of course," he said. "You've had your hands full. In addition to your routine duties, you've been finding a dead body and dealing with the police and trying to clear your name of a possible murder charge—and to clear a couple of other names as well. My apologies. How absurd of me to expect otherwise."

Then he looked at his watch and said, "But it is rather late. With so many passengers leaving, I imagine business in the Habsburg Restaurant has slowed to a trickle, and its kitchen isn't too busy, and maybe a certain chef has a few extra minutes on his hands, and you might have a little free time right now as well."

He winked at London and said, "If you catch my drift."

London chuckled a little.

"I believe I do," she said. "Thanks for the suggestion."

Mr. Lapham shook his head and grinned.

"I do declare, London Rose, sometimes I'd just like to knock your two heads together!"

"I hope that won't be necessary," London said, rising again from her chair.

Mr. Lapham looked at his watch again and said, "You kids had better work things out quickly, though. I *do* need a decision before midnight. And the clock seems to be ticking a bit faster than usual."

"I understand, sir," London said.

He called out to her again as she headed toward the door.

"Oh, by the way. If you don't mind my asking …"

London was surprised to see the CEO blush.

"No, never mind," he said. "It would be presumptuous of me to ask. Get along now. Sort out this silly business of how you're going to spend the rest of your life and be quick about it!"

As London left the suite, she heard Mr. Lapham calling out to his cat, "All right Mr. Siegfried, I have some special treats that should put you in a better mood."

As the door closed behind her, London found herself smiling at the very human side that the rich and powerful CEO frequently demonstrated. She thought she even had some idea of what he'd wanted to know just a moment ago.

Something about Mom, probably, she thought. *But then he was too shy or embarrassed to ask.*

Mr. Lapham was obviously attracted to Mom, and Mom had told London pretty plainly that she felt the same about him. But London figured that maybe it was just as well that he hadn't been able to ask his question.

What would I tell him? she wondered.

Mom still seemed as much a mystery to London as she must be to Mr. Lapham. She really had no idea whether it would be a good thing for them to get together or not.

Meanwhile, she had something else to attend to. As she walked down the passageway, she took out her cellphone and called Bryce.

When he answered, London said, "I wonder if you might be free for a little nightcap in the Amadeus Lounge."

"I'd like that," Bryce said. "I've still got a few things to take care of here, but I can be up there shortly. And we *do* have a lot to talk about, don't we?"

London felt her heart flutter anxiously.

"Yes, we do," she said. "I'll see you soon."

When London continued into the Amadeus Lounge, she was relieved to find it almost empty. She realized that the whole ship was at least partially deserted now. She'd had an opportunity to say goodbye to some of the passengers, but there were others she hoped to speak with personally before they all left.

She was glad to see the bleached blond who gave her a wave from behind the bar. The chief bartender was her best friend, Elsie Sloan. Here in Oslo, London had been so occupied off the ship that they'd had no time to chat.

By the time London reached the bar, Elsie was already preparing her favorite drink, a Manhattan made from her own special recipe.

"Hey, kid, it's good to see you," Elsie said. "How are things?"

"Things could be a lot better," London replied.

Elsie laughed heartily. "Just don't tell me there's been another murder," she said.

London cringed visibly at her friend's innocent but poorly timed joke.

Elsie's eyes widened.

"Oh, no!" she gasped. "There *has* been another murder!"

London nodded silently.

Elsie shook her head and said, "How stupid of me to say something like that. I should have known better."

"Don't be ridiculous. How could you have known? It's not exactly common knowledge. And with some luck, it will stay that way. Most of the people who are leaving the *Nachtmusik* don't need to even find out about it."

Elsie said, "Well, I won't ask you for any details. As your bartender, my sole duty is to serve you a truly proper drink. And, also, to listen, but only if you want to talk."

London smiled gratefully as Elsie set the dark amber colored drink in front of her.

"Thanks, this is exactly what I need," she said.

London lifted the cocktail glass to her lips and savored a small sip of the delicious and lively blend of rye, vermouth, and bitters. She wasn't sure what Elsie's secret was, but her friend made the best Manhattans she had ever tasted.

"Oh, by the way," London said. "I need you to make a Tom Collins."

Elsie smiled and said, "So you're expecting someone, eh?"

London smiled and nodded. She knew she didn't need to say who she was expecting. The mention of a Tom Collins was enough for Elsie to know that it was Bryce Yeaton.

As Elsie poured gin and lemon juice into a glass, she said, "So what kinds of plans are the two of you making for the future?"

"That's what we've got to talk about," London replied.

"You mean you're just getting around to that?" Elsie said with surprise. "You're cutting it right down the wire don't you think? I mean, the future is practically here."

London sighed and said, "Don't start in on me. I'm getting enough pressure from Mr. Lapham as it is. He expects me to make a job decision by midnight. He wants me to work aboard the *Galene.*"

"The Seine cruise, eh?" Elsie said, stirring Bryce's drink. "Mr. Lapham offered me a bartending gig on that same ship."

London squinted with curiosity.

"So are you taking the job?" London said.

"Naw," Elsie said, finishing up the drink.

"Why not? It's a good one."

Elsie's fell quiet for a moment, and she gazed toward the window and out into the late northern daylight.

"I dunno, London," Elsie finally said, finishing Bryce's drink. "Fear of getting bored, I guess. I can't stand too much of the same-old, same-old. Sometimes I like to unmoor myself and go drifting with the current, see where it takes me. You know how I get."

London nodded.

I do, indeed, she thought wistfully.

She sometimes envied her friend's adventurous nature.

Elsie continued, "It's the nice part of having no attachments—no boyfriend or husband, no kids, no pets, not even a house or an apartment to go home to. I'm not responsible to anybody except myself. I don't have anybody to worry about."

As London listened attentively, she wondered, *Do I hear a note of sadness in her voice?*

She couldn't be sure one way or the other.

Elsie added, "Sometimes I just blindfold myself and stick a thumbtack into a map. If I don't hit Antarctica or the Mariana Trench or the cone of Mt. Vesuvius or someplace else uninhabitable, that's where I go. After that ..."

She shrugged and said, "Well, I just go wherever my urges take me."

London took another sip of her Manhattan and let Elsie's words sink in.

Then Elsie looked away from the window toward the lounge entrance.

"But here comes another customer," she said, pushing the Tom Collins across the bar.

London turned and saw Bryce walking into the lounge, still wearing his chef's uniform and looking tired after a long day's work. He smiled at the sight of London at the bar and headed toward her.

London got a sinking feeling in her stomach.

The time to talk is now, she realized.

But she had no idea what they were going to say to each other.

CHAPTER THIRTY

London thought she detected a flicker of apprehension in Bryce's gray eyes.

Maybe he's as nervous as I am, she thought.

But if he was also concerned about this conversation, was that a good thing or a bad thing?

Bryce stepped up to the bar and looked at the drink Elsie had just prepared.

"What's this I see?" he said with mock surprise, raising the drink to his lips and sniffing it. "Why, I do believe it's a Tom Collins."

"Yeah, I made it for another customer," Elsie joked with an impish grin. "He kept flirting with London until she told him to get lost because she had a boyfriend already. Then he got grouchy and left without touching his drink. It's yours if you want it."

"Don't mind if I do," Bryce said, taking a sip.

Elsie leaned across the bar toward London and said, "Are you going to tell him today's news, or do you want me to?"

"I'd probably better," London said.

"What?" Bryce asked. "What are you two talking about?"

"Somebody else was murdered," London said. "It happened out on one of the islands while a bunch of us were visiting there."

"No!" Bryce exclaimed. "It wasn't one of the passengers, I hope."

London shook her head no.

"What about suspects?" Bryce said.

London swallowed hard. The last thing she wanted to do right now was tell Bryce everything about the murder—including the fact that she and her mother were under at least some suspicion. That would take too much time—and she had Mr. Lapham's deadline to consider.

She said, "I'd really rather not talk about it, if you want to know the truth."

When Bryce stared at her with surprise, London added, "It's not actually a problem—not for us, I mean. Nothing to worry about. Just something for the police to take care of."

London was shocked to hear herself say something so far from the truth. But as she glanced at her watch, she saw that she was running out of time.

"Well ... OK," Bryce said.

Starting to wipe down the bar with a rag, Elsie said, "Yeah, you two have got more urgent things to talk about. Now you'd better go find a quiet spot out of earshot of a certain nosy, gossipy bartender."

London and Bryce both laughed a bit shyly. Then they carried their drinks over to an isolated table and sat down together.

Then they just smiled at each other nervously.

"So," Bryce said, "which of us is going first?"

London stifled a sigh.

"I guess it had better be me," she said. "Mr. Lapham offered me a job aboard the *Galene.*"

Bryce tilted his head with interest.

"You mean the cruise along the Seine?" he said.

"That's right."

Bryce stammered, "That's—a good opportunity."

London shrugged slightly and said, "Yeah, well, not nearly as good as head chef aboard the *Danae.* Have you decided whether you'll accept that position?"

Bryce shook his head sadly.

"London, I just don't know what to do," he said. "If we're working on those two ships, our paths won't cross."

London nodded sadly. She knew that the huge, seagoing *Danae* would be off in the eastern Mediterranean, sailing along the coasts of Italy and Greece. On the *Galene,* she would be traveling in France.

"Well, we don't have a lot of time to make up our minds," she said. "Mr. Lapham wants my decision before midnight."

"That definitely puts on some real pressure," Bryce said.

He drummed his fingers on the table.

Then he said, "What we *could* do is just turn down both offers and take off together."

London's eyes widened with surprise.

"Take off where?"

Bryce smiled and shrugged.

"Maybe the together part is all that matters," he said. "All I really want is to be with you every day, London. How is that supposed to happen if we're thousands of miles away from each other on separate tour boats? There's no job awaiting me aboard the *Galene,* and no job awaiting you aboard the *Danae.*"

London struggled to take in what Bryce was suggesting. Just a few moments ago, Elsie had told her, *"Sometimes I just blindfold myself and stick a thumbtack into a map."*

Was Bryce suggesting something like that?

She fell silent. Her head began to buzz with other memories—especially her childhood fear and grief when Mom had disappeared all those years ago.

It occurred to London that Mom must have faced—or failed to face—a lot of very practical questions about how she and Dad would live, and how they would raise their children. Mom had seemed to be content when she played the stay-at-home mother while Dad kept going wherever his job took him—*"gallivanting around the world,"* as Mom had put it.

Something had gone very wrong with that arrangement.

And I still don't know exactly what it was, London thought.

And maybe she never would—not if she and Mom never really talked it through.

Meanwhile, she was desperately afraid of the past somehow repeating itself.

"It's not that simple, Bryce," London said, her throat catching painfully. "I know that from personal experience. A commitment is a commitment. And if there are children, that changes everything. If one or both of us can't keep complicated long-term commitments …"

Her voice faded, and Bryce finished her thought.

"People will get hurt," he said.

London nodded silently.

Bryce sat fingering the rim of his drink.

"Maybe I've got more confidence than you do," he said. "Confidence in *us,* I mean. You and me. And especially *you.*"

He reached across the table and took London's hand.

"I've watched you deal with all kinds of crazy stuff just since I've known you," he said in an affectionate voice. "You are no ordinary woman, London Rose. I've never known anyone who can roll with the punches and think on your feet as well as you can …"

Then he added with a mischievous twinkle in his eye.

"Unless it's maybe me. Don't underestimate me, London. I can play life by ear as well anybody can. I'm pretty resilient—but also very good at keeping commitments."

London heaved a sad sigh.

"But what sorts of commitments are we talking about?" she asked.

"Just to each other, that's all. And to dealing with life as we meet it—together."

London's heart ached at what a beautiful thought that was.

If only I could believe in it, she thought.

"I … just don't know what to do," London said.

Bryce's smile turned sad, and so did his sparkling gray eyes.

"You mean you don't know what you *want* to do," he said.

London fell quiet as she tried to grasp the distinction he was making.

It sounds so simple, she thought.

If so, why did it seem so hard to make up her mind?

What do I want *to do?*

Bryce didn't say anything either as they finished their drinks. Finally, he got up from his chair and walked over to London and kissed her lightly on the lips.

"I think you should take that job aboard the *Galene,"* he said.

"Why?" London asked, her pulse quickening.

"Because …"

Bryce's voice faded. London heard a catch in his throat when he finished his thought.

"Because I'm going to take the job aboard the *Danae."*

He gave London's hand one final squeeze, then turned and walked out of the lounge. London tried to think of something to say as she watched him leave, but nothing came to her. Then she sat staring at her empty glass for a few moments.

It's over, she thought. *Whatever was going on between Bryce and me—it's over.*

She felt her eyes stinging and an ache in her chest.

Soon Elsie came over to the table, ostensibly to pick up the empty drink glasses. Of course, London knew that Elsie had sensed what had just happened and was checking up on her.

"Do you want to talk about it?" Elsie asked as she put the glasses on a tray.

London shook her head.

"If I try to talk about it, I'll start crying,"

Elsie bent over her and hugged her for a few moments, then walked back over to the bar.

London sat there in silence trying to process what had just happened, and what it meant.

It's over between Bryce and me, she thought.

But whose decision had it been? She couldn't help thinking Bryce had presented her with a choice that she simply couldn't accept. Did he really think she would jump at the chance to plunge blindly into the unknown with him? Was he even ready to make the same kind of plunge with her? Maybe he really didn't want them to be together at all. Perhaps it was he who had really ended her relationship …

No, now I'm just rationalizing, she realized.

It was her decision, and now she would have to accept it and live with it. For a few moments, London felt numb all over. When she felt sensation returning, she got out of her chair and left the Amadeus Lounge.

While she was in the elevator, she felt a wave of sadness rising up inside her.

Go ahead and cry, she thought.

It'll do you good.

But her throat yielded only a single sob, and a single tear fell from her eye—and that was all. As she wiped her eye, she thought about all that had happened during the last couple of days. It was hard to believe she'd only been reunited—if that was the right word—with Mom since yesterday morning. And today there had been another murder.

Small wonder I'm too tired to cry, she thought as she got out of the elevator.

She walked down the passageway to her stateroom. When she went inside, she found that Sir Reggie was already fast asleep on the bed. As she sat down on the bed, she found it odd to see her little dog conked out like this, since she could still see some light through her window. But of course, she knew that was because they were so far north.

Indeed, London glanced at her watch and saw that it was a few minutes before midnight. Time was definitely running out, and she had to tell Mr. Lapham her decision right away.

She wavered for a moment as to how to go about it. Should she go back up to his suite and knock on his door? It seemed awfully late to pay him another visit. Still, he *was* waiting for her answer. Should she call him on her phone?

If I try to talk about it, I'll just fall apart, she thought.

Instead, she decided to send Mr. Lapham a text message.

Her message began:

Mr. Lapham, I am deeply honored by your job offer.

She hesitated, then added:

I accept.

She sat staring at her cellphone for a moment, not knowing whether to expect a reply.

But then Mr. Lapham's reply came:

I thought you would.

London's sadness gave way to a flash of perplexity.

What does he mean by that? she wondered.

How could Mr. Lapham have already known what she was going to decide?

She let out a long, weary sigh. It seemed like just one more thing she didn't understand.

Besides, she thought as she went to the bathroom and began to get ready for bed, *I've still got to clear myself of suspicion of murder.*

And Mom too.

CHAPTER THIRTY ONE

London's eyes snapped open at the sound of her cellphone ringing.

She felt a flutter of panic when she saw that light was streaming through her window.

Had she overslept? Was someone calling to tell her she was running late?

Then she remembered …

I don't have a job to be late for now.

Not aboard the Nachtmusik, *anyway.*

Her next thought made her heart ache.

I don't have a boyfriend who would be calling me, either.

But the ringing continued. Still asleep at her side, Sir Reggie grumbled a little at the sound.

London fumbled around for her cellphone on her side table. When she took the call, she heard a low, sinister voice speaking with a heavy Norwegian accent.

"Is this London Rose?"

"Yes."

"I would like to talk to you. In person."

"Who is this?" London demanded.

The caller simply ignored the question.

"Do you know where the Viking Ship Museum is?" he asked instead.

"Yes," London replied.

"How soon can you meet me there?"

London looked at her watch and thought about the morning ahead. She saw that it wasn't very late, after all. Sunrise was much earlier here in Oslo than she was used to. And besides, for the first time since the *Nachtmusik* had set sail back in Hungary, she didn't have any actual duties to attend to.

Not that it's any of this guy's business, she thought.

"Who is this?" she asked again.

"I think you should visit the Viking Ship Museum," the man insisted. "Everybody who comes to Oslo should visit the Viking Ship Museum. I promise, you would find it very interesting."

"I'm going to hang up now," she said.

"When can you meet me at the Viking Ship Museum?"

London was feeling goosebumps now. Somehow, she couldn't bring herself to simply end the call. In spite of herself, she wanted to know who this persistent caller was and what he really wanted.

London swallowed hard.

Am I really going to do this? she wondered.

She told him, "In a couple of hours, I think."

"I will be there," the caller said, then ended the call.

London sat staring at the phone for a moment, wondering whether she was dreaming. But no, she was suddenly quite wide awake. And for some reason, she'd just agreed to meet a total stranger at the Viking Ship Museum.

Why did I do that? she wondered.

It wasn't the first weird phone call she'd ever gotten in her life. Normally she had the good sense to simply ignore them. But somehow, this one seemed different.

He knew my name, for one thing, she thought.

Not that that was necessarily surprising. Anyone wanting to find her phone number simply had to look at Epoch World Cruise Lines staff list on the company's website, where it could be found along with her email address.

Nevertheless, the timing seemed extremely strange, coming so soon after yesterday's death in the lighthouse. Did the caller know something about the murder? Might he even be the murderer himself?

Steady, London told herself. *Don't let your imagination run away with you.*

And now that she could think a bit more clearly, she reminded herself that she wasn't under any obligation to keep that "appointment" at the Viking Ship Museum. The man who had called her might not even be there if she *did* show up. And if she simply didn't go, he probably wouldn't even bother her again. In any case, she would soon be off to …

She wasn't sure exactly where she would be off to, or how soon. She hadn't yet been told whether she would be required to report directly to her next location in France. Perhaps she'd have time to visit her sister back in the states as she often did between jobs. Or perhaps she and Mom would finally have that long overdue conversation before they both moved on to whatever came next.

I'll just forget all about that call, she told herself.

Meanwhile, Sir Reggie was still grumbling, half-asleep.

London gave him a playful shake.

"Wake up, lazybones," she said. "You'll miss breakfast."

Sir Reggie perked up at the mention of food. London got up and fixed him his morning meal.

As she got ready to face her day, it felt strange not to be putting on her uniform as usual, or to be preparing herself for any occasion in particular. Looking at the clothes lined up in her closet, London didn't feel up to any of the brighter colors hanging there. She certainly wasn't going to wear that blue polka-dotted dress she'd had on back in Vienna that night when she'd first danced with Bryce.

She chose black slacks and a gray long-sleeved tunic from her mix-and-match outfits. She also put on comfortable flat-heeled walking shoes.

As she pulled a brush through her short auburn hair, she studied her sad face carefully in the mirror.

Do I really look like a murderer? she asked herself.

This wasn't the first time during the *Nachtmusik's* voyage that she'd been suspected of such a foul deed. Why did she seem to attract murder and mayhem wherever she went?

It probably has nothing to do with me, she thought.

And maybe it didn't have anything to do with those omens and celestial influences that so obsessed Mr. Lapham. Probably, she figured, it was all just dumb bad luck. But even so, she still had to clear Mom and herself from suspicion.

Suddenly, that black and gray outfit she had on just didn't look right to London.

She left the bathroom and searched around in her closet until she found a multicolored sash that she wrapped around her slender waist. Checking the mirror again, she decided that it looked fine.

"That's all the cheerfulness I'm up to today, Sir Reggie," she said.

There was no response. She looked around the stateroom and realized that her Yorkie wasn't there. It wasn't really unusual. He often used his doggie door to go out and roam around on his own. Maybe he and Siegfried the cat had already gotten together to go looking for excitement.

Do they know this might be their last day to hang out together? she wondered.

They were both exceptionally smart animals, which of course was why they enjoyed each other's company. She hoped they were going to have a good time together today.

Even so, London felt a surge of loneliness as she stood there in her stateroom. She found herself staring silently at the empty table over by the windows. Normally right about how, she'd be expecting a knock on the door announcing that her breakfast was being delivered—a delicious plate of Eggs Benedict, specially prepared for her by the head chef himself.

She said, sadly, aloud to herself, "There probably won't be a knock on the door this morning."

But sure enough, at that very second, she heard that very sound—a knock on the door.

She hurried over and eagerly opened it. But no steward pushing a steel cart laden with breakfast was waiting outside.

Mom was standing there with an eager smile on her face.

"You look quite … um … civilian this morning," Mom commented cheerfully. "Are you ready to head up to the Habsburg Restaurant for breakfast?"

London managed to stifle a sigh of disappointment.

"Sure," she said. "Let's go."

Of course, she thought, *Bryce might be there in the restaurant, serving the last of the ship's passengers.*

Then she had to wonder what difference it would make if he was. Would they still have anything to talk about?

Probably not, she told herself. *What more is there to say?*

As she and Mom arrived at the *Romanze* deck and stepped into the restaurant, London was startled by how empty the place was. There wasn't waiter in sight and the kitchen itself was locked up and shuttered. A simple smorgasbord had been set up for any stragglers who might want breakfast.

"Oh, my," Mom said. "Where is your boyfriend?"

Gone, London thought despondently.

Bryce must be on his way to experience the rest of his life.

And it won't include me.

Just then, a familiar male voice spoke from behind them.

"Good morning, ladies. I don't guess you expected to see me here."

CHAPTER THIRTY TWO

London was indeed startled to see the man who had walked up behind her and Mom as they surveyed the smorgasbord that had been set up for breakfast.

"You do look surprised to see me," Scott Raife repeated with a sly smile.

London stammered, "Well, it-it's just that ..."

Mom interrupted, "The last time we saw you, you were getting hauled away by the local cops."

"Oh, that," Scott said with a forced-looking shrug of indifference. "What did you think, they were going to charge me with murder?"

London and Mom exchanged a look that silently said, *"Well, maybe."*

"We ... Mom was ... sure you're innocent," London told him. "But we thought they might charge you anyhow."

Scott continued in his usual blustery manner.

"Well, I told the cops what they could do with their stupid suspicions. I told them I was no killer, and if they didn't believe me, that was going to be their problem. And it was going to be a *big* problem—a real international incident."

He puffed out his chest and added, "Well, they soon figured out that they were messing with the wrong foreigner. So they apologized for the whole misunderstanding and I got sprung. They said I could leave Oslo any time I liked. They won't make a mistake like *that* again, I bet. And I for one am anxious to get out of this city as soon as possible."

With that final word, he turned and strutted on out of the restaurant.

London's mom gave her a nudge.

"What do you bet the police came to the same conclusion as I did?" Mom said.

London silently agreed. Scott's buffoonish bellicosity had probably freed him of suspicion. It seemed likely that the police—especially *Politiførstebetjent* Kolberg—had figured out pretty quickly that this guy just didn't have the makings of a murderer.

"Let's see what's for breakfast," London suggested.

As they approached the smorgasbord Mom gazed all around.

158

"This is odd—I expected Bryce to be here to greet us," she said.

London couldn't hold back a melancholy sigh.

"Oh, dear," Mom said. "You and Bryce had a little tiff, didn't you?"

London's jaw clenched as she perused the traditional Scandinavian breakfast items.

It wasn't a "tiff," she wanted to say.

She was annoyed by the way Mom was making her and Bryce sound like a pair of infatuated teenagers.

"Do you want to talk about it?" Mom said.

London silently shook her head as she put together her own breakfast plate, choosing a pumpernickel roll, some cheese, a little dish of sour cream, and another dish with a couple of smoked herrings.

"Are you sure you don't want talk?" Mom said, gathering pretty much the same items for her own plate.

"I'm sure," London replied.

And please don't ask me again, she thought.

London didn't want to get all emotional right now.

She and Mom poured themselves cups of coffee and glasses of orange juice and carried their trays over to a table, where they sat down. They cut the hard bread and made little sandwiches with the sour cream and the smoked herring.

As London took a bite of her sandwich, she remembered the pickled herring bites she'd eaten the day before yesterday back on the island of Skittmon off the coast of Sweden. Those pickled herring had been oniony and sweet at the same time, while this smoked herring was more robust and salty. London liked the flavor and wished she were in a better mood to enjoy it.

As they began to eat, Mom asked, "So what's the status of the murder investigation?"

"I don't know," London said. "I haven't heard anything from the police."

Mom giggled and said, "I've got to say, it's a bit of a rush being ever-so-slightly suspected of murder. This is a first for me. It gets the old adrenalin going, doesn't it? Trying to clear one's own name, I mean."

Mom took a small piece of paper out of her pocket.

"By the way, I've already gotten to work on that," Mom said, handing London the paper, which had a phone number and an address on it.

"What's this?" London asked.

"It's the location and contact information for *Nilsen Fyord Krudstogter*—Nilsen's Fjord Cruises. Remember, Iver Nilsen told us he lived over on Lindøya. That's also where he runs his business. I thought it would be a good place to start gathering information. What do you say to giving the office a call, and see if anybody is there?"

London sat looking at the information for a moment.

Maybe this isn't such a bad idea, she thought.

Again, she wondered whether a talent for sleuthing might be a family trait.

London took out her cellphone, put it on speakerphone so both she and Mom could listen, and punched in the number.

Then they heard a recording of a woman's voice. The recording was poor, and the woman spoke fast, so London had trouble picking up what she was saying in Norwegian. But she did pick out the words *Nilsen Fyord Krudstogter,* so she definitely had the right number.

The voice sounded chipper and cheerful, so London knew the recording must have been made before Captain Nilsen's murder. London figured the business might be completely closed down now. Nevertheless, she heard a beep prompting her to leave a message.

London found herself struggling to make herself understood in Norwegian.

"Hello … my name is London Rose … and I was at Trollskog Island yesterday when …"

London balked at finishing the sentence, *"When Herr Nilsen was killed."*

It didn't seem like a good thing to leave on an answering service. Instead, she stammered, "Could—could you please give me a call?"

She recited her cellphone number and ended the call.

Mom shook her head disapprovingly as she took a sip of her orange juice.

"Oh, London. You could have done much better than that. Of course, your Norwegian isn't all that great, but even so …"

London felt her irritation rise.

"What was I supposed to say?" she asked.

Mom shrugged and said, "Well, you could have been more assertive. Suggested a time when you could pay the office a visit. Insisted on making an appointment. It's easy to get to Lindøya."

She tapped on her head with a wink and added, "I've got the ferry schedule memorized."

London's patience was evaporating.

"Mom, I don't even know if I want to go to Lindøya," she said.

"Of course you do," Mom said, swallowing a bite of her breakfast. "It's the best possible place to start looking for clues. And you'd better get cracking, don't you think? As far as we know, we're both still murder suspects. The cops could decide to scoop us up at any moment. What if there's some kind of awful miscarriage of justice, and we wind up facing the death penalty?"

"There's no death penalty in Norway," London said.

"Well, I'm sure you don't just get a slap on the wrist for it, anyway. Going to prison is one of the few experiences I've never had, and I'd like to keep it that way, if you don't mind."

Mom held out her hand and added, "Give me that phone. Let me leave a message. I'll be sure to get it right this time."

"No, I don't think so," London said, tucking the phone straight into her purse.

"Why not?"

London didn't know what to say. But she felt more and more sure by the very second that Mom's pushiness was a ruse, another way of avoiding an inevitable conversation. The two of them fell quiet as they finished eating their breakfasts. Finally, London decided to get right to the point.

"Mom, don't you think it's time we really talked?"

"What about?"

"You know perfectly well what about," London snapped. Then she swallowed hard and said, "Mom, you have no idea how much I missed you. And how much Tia missed you. And Dad too. We didn't even know if you were still alive. For all we knew, you'd been murdered or something awful like that. We never stopped worrying."

Mom lowered her head silently.

London continued, "Did you know I've been looking for you ever since I came to Europe to work on the *Nachtmusik?* In just about every city, I've tried to find some clue as to whether you'd been there or not. All this time I've been chasing after you into one blind alley after another, feeling like a fool for always turning out to be wrong."

Mom stared at her for a moment, then said, "I know you think I'm just avoiding telling you why ..."

She sighed and started again.

"The problem is, whenever I think about explaining, I realize that I don't understand it all myself. But I do want you to know I've changed.

161

Whatever drove me back then, that really isn't me now. You see, 20 years ago I really did intend to just take a short vacation by myself. I really did need to get away. What happened next was completely unplanned."

London's phone rang. She decided to ignore it and listen to Mom.

"Be patient, London," Mom said. "I will tell you in my own good time. And I won't run away before I do. I promise."

Before London could reply, the phone buzzed again.

"I guess I'd better take that," she sighed

When she took the call, she heard Amy's voice. The concierge sounded quite agitated.

"London, I need you to come down to the *Allegro* deck right away."

"What's the problem?" London asked.

Amy grunted with exasperation.

"Oh, I think you know what the problem is," she said.

London was on the verge of saying, *"No, I don't know what the problem is."*

But before she could open her mouth, Amy said, "Please get down here right away."

Then she ended the call.

"I've got to go," she said, getting up from her chair.

"What's the problem?" Mom asked.

"That's what I've got to find out," London said.

"I'll come with you," Mom said, wiping her mouth with her napkin and rising from her chair.

There's no point in arguing, London decided as she and Mom headed out of the restaurant.

CHAPTER THIRTY THREE

When London and Mom reached the *Allegro* deck, everything was completely quiet for moment. Then they heard a loud knocking followed by Amy's voice.

"Open up! I know you're in there."

London and Mom followed the voice and the knocking into the passageway where most of the officers' quarters were located. Amy was standing outside the door to Emil's stateroom, staring at it and tapping her foot.

"Amy!" Mom said. "What on earth are you doing?"

Amy turned and glared at Mom.

"I hadn't expected you to show up, Barbara." Amy said. "This is your fault, you know."

"What's my fault?" Mom said. "I don't understand."

Amy crossed her arms and walked toward Mom.

"It's your fault Emil won't come out of his stateroom," she said. "He's been locked up in there for a solid 24 hours now. He hasn't come out since yesterday morning, when he told us he'd quit his job. I keep coming around and knocking until my knuckles are raw. I can't get him to come out."

"But how is that my fault?" Mom asked.

Amy scoffed indignantly and said, "Don't you remember? You corrected him *twice* yesterday morning during his lecture when we were sailing into Oslofjord. And the night before that, you made him feel like a fool during your cabaret act when he goofed up about who wrote the song 'Stardust.'"

London didn't see much point in finding fault.

She said to Amy, "I don't understand why you called me just now. What do you expect me to do about this?"

Amy rolled her eyes and shook her head.

"I just want you to help me figure out what to do, I guess," she said. "And to keep me from doing something really crazy. I was about to set off the fire alarm. I figured somebody would get him out of there then."

London was suddenly relieved that Amy had called her before she'd done that.

"That would be a really bad idea, Amy," she said. "Besides, are you sure he's still in there? Maybe he sneaked away earlier."

"Oh, he's in there, all right. He's been ordering his food to be delivered—not that he'll be able to do that anymore, now that the kitchen is closed."

Amy knocked on the door again.

"You can't stay in there forever, Emil," Amy yelled. "You're liable to starve to death. And anyway, the *Nachtmusik's* going to sail away for who knows where pretty soon, and you've got no idea where you might wind up, and you don't even have a job. How's that going to work out?"

Another silence fell.

London could see that Amy was trembling with anxiety. She actually looked disheveled, with her usually smooth helmet of hair sticking up in odd directions.

Mom said to Amy, "I'm sorry you've got this problem. But I still don't understand why you think it's all my fault. How was I to know he had such a delicate ego? I only met the man for the first time the day before yesterday."

Amy let out a long, sad sigh.

"You're right, Barbara," she said. "I shouldn't take it out on you. The truth is, I really feel guilty myself. This is as much my fault as yours. I couldn't help rubbing it in about that song goof. I made him feel even worse about it. I ought to have known better. I should have been more thoughtful."

Indeed, London remembered how Amy had gloated over Emil's humiliation yesterday morning.

"Don't you agree that 'Stardust'—by Hoagy Carmichael—*is one of the loveliest songs ever?"*

London didn't think that had been very nice of Amy.

Meanwhile, Amy stepped back from the door and almost shouted, "Emil, you're pushing me to take extreme measures. Don't forget, I've got a master key to every room on this whole ship. If you don't open up, I'll just let myself right in."

Suddenly London heard Emil's voice yell from inside.

"Don't you dare!"

I guess he's in there, all right, London thought.

"Who's going to stop me?" Amy said, crossing her arms.

"Just leave me alone," Emil called back. "That is all I want from anybody."

164

Amy started to pace in front of the door.

"Emil, this is ridiculous," she said. "I can't wait around here forever. I've got a plane to catch."

"Where are you flying to?" Emil barked through the door.

Amy stopped pacing and fell silent.

"Well, I—I haven't decided yet," she sputtered. "But I *will* have a plane to catch. And sometime soon. This morning. Probably in just a little while. I've got to get going."

"Who is stopping you?" Emil said.

Amy looked really stumped. London watched her expression change from cranky and indignant to sad and hurt.

In a pleading, almost tearful voice, Amy said, "Emil, can't I come in and see you? Just one last time, I mean? Don't you want to at least … say goodbye?"

Amy waited in vain for a reply. She took her master keycard out of her purse and looked at closely. She held it toward the door latch as if to use it.

London said, "Amy, I'm not sure that's such a good idea."

"Why not?" Amy asked.

"It might only make things worse."

Indeed, London was afraid Emil might fly into a rage if Amy came in without permission.

Meanwhile, Mom seemed to have decided to intervene. She stepped forward and called through the door.

"Herr Waldmüller, it's Barbara Rose."

A silence fell.

"I've come to make an apology."

A longer silence fell.

Then door swung open, and Emil stood there with a forbidding expression. London was a bit apprehensive at how small her mother looked next to this stern academic.

"I should never have interrupted your lecture," Mom said. "I should never have questioned you in public about the song at the cabaret. I hope you will accept my heartfelt apology for my terrible manners."

Everything was quiet for a moment.

"Apology accepted," Emil finally said.

Then he turned toward Amy and his glare softened.

"My dear, you and I do need to talk," he said, gesturing for her to pass into the room.

In the next moment, Amy disappeared into Emil's room and the door closed behind them. London and Mom stood alone in the hallway.

Mom brushed her hands with satisfaction.

"Well," she said, "I believe we were able to be of some help, after all."

"*You* were able to help," London said, giving Mom's hand a squeeze.

The truth was, she was genuinely impressed by the graciousness of Mom's apology and the effect it had had on the situation.

At that moment they heard a noisy yap, and Sir Reggie came running toward them with his leash in his mouth.

"Now what do you suppose *he* wants?" Mom said in an amused voice.

Chuckling as she put on Sir Reggie's leash, London said, "Maybe he came to remind us about a certain unsolved murder case. We've still got our innocence to prove. What do you say the three of us get to work?"

"Right-o!" Mom chuckled with a salute. "The game's afoot!"

CHAPTER THIRTY FOUR

As London and her mother and her Yorkshire Terrier hurried down the ship's gangway, Mom commented, "This is a first for me."

"What?" London asked. "You've been to Oslo before."

"Investigating a murder," Mom replied. "Hunting a killer. I've done some crazy things in my life, but I have never ever been on a murder case before."

"I wish it was a first for me," London replied.

"Oh, but it's so exciting. And look at Sir Reggie."

The Yorkie was pulling on his leash as he charged ahead them.

"He's really into the hunt," Mom said with a laugh. "He acts like he's already caught the killer's scent."

"If he knows who we're looking for, he hasn't told me," London replied with a grin. "But I'm glad he's so eager to find out."

As they reached the pier, London began to look at public transportation schedules on her cellphone.

Mom said, "So I guess we start our investigation over on Lindøya Island, huh?"

London glanced at her with surprise.

"Why would we do that?" she asked.

"Well, why *wouldn't* we do that?" Mom scoffed. "I found the address for Iver Nilsen's business there. We need to check it out."

"But we didn't reach anybody when we tried to call there."

"So?"

"So for all we know, we won't find anything, just a closed-up empty office."

"How will we know unless we go there?"

London stifled a sigh of frustration.

"Mom, we can't just go dashing around without anything more to go on than an address."

"It's not very far," Mom said. "And it's a lovely ferry ride."

"Even so, we don't have that kind of time to waste."

"So where *are* we going?" Mom asked, a bit sharply.

London hesitated to answer. She wasn't used to being questioned about every step she made when she got involved in a search like this.

167

She knew that not everything she did would make sense to anyone else. It didn't always make sense to her, either. Besides, she wasn't entirely sure that the destination she had in mind was any more promising than Lindøya might be. In fact, until just now, she'd dismissed the whole idea altogether. She wasn't even sure why she'd changed her mind.

Just a gut feeling, I guess, she thought.

She saw that they had arrived at a tram stop just in time for the blue, two-car vehicle to come rolling silently and sleekly along the tracks to a stop.

"I'll tell you on the way," London told Mom as the tram doors folded open.

She picked up Sir Reggie, and they climbed into the vehicle. After paying 58 Norwegian Krones each for tickets, they took their seats with London holding Sir Reggie on her lap.

Mom said, "OK, *now* tell me where we're going."

"The Viking Ship Museum."

"Why on earth are we going there?" Mom asked with disbelief.

"I got a strange phone call earlier this morning," London said. "I had decided to ignore it, but after thinking it over, I think I'd better follow up."

"A phone call?" Mom asked. "Who from?"

"I don't know," London admitted. "But he said he wanted to meet me at the Viking Museum shortly. I actually told him I would be there in a couple of hours."

"That's it?" Mom snorted. "Some total stranger wants to meet you at the Viking Museum? It sounds like some random crank call to me."

London didn't reply for a moment. The truth was, she still had her own doubts about the call.

Finally, she began, "It just seems like too much of a coincidence—"

Mom interrupted, "Than what? That you got a crank call the day after you became a murder suspect? That's just some of the usual random goofiness life throws at everybody. Probably a guy just punching in numbers."

"No," London said. "It wasn't random. He knew my name."

"Then maybe a stalker?" Mom asked, thoughtfully. "Did he say why he wanted you to meet him?"

"He just said he wanted to talk with me in person," London replied.

"Well, that could be anything," Mom said decisively. "It sounds creepy to me. And it probably has nothing to do with the case at hand."

London fell silent. For all she knew, Mom might well be right.

Maybe we should be on our way to Lindøya after all.

But they were on the tram now and on their way.

Mom crossed her arms and said, "OK, you're the one who's had experience at this murder stuff. I'll let you call the shots. But let the record show that I consider this to be a waste of valuable time."

"Objection noted," London grumbled.

Meanwhile, the tram was rolling past parts of Oslo that London hadn't seen yesterday, but which she might have had a chance to visit …

If someone hadn't gotten murdered … again.

Not surprisingly, Mom relished the opportunity to play tour guide.

"Look over there," she said, pointing. "See that handsome neoclassical building with the columns in front and the equestrian statue at the top of the steps? That's the Royal Palace. King Harald V lives there. He caused a bit of a stir by marrying a commoner, but it worked out, and she's Queen Sonja now, and they've had a daughter and a son …"

London's attention faded as Mom chattered on about the sights they passed by.

I guess we could *be talking about the last 20 years right now,* she kept thinking.

But now hardly seemed the best time or place.

"Be patient, London," Mom had promised. *"I will tell you in my own good time."*

For some reason, London felt as though she could take Mom at her word.

The tram soon turned south onto Bygdøy peninsula, a luxurious-looking Oslo neighborhood filled with fine, large homes and spacious parks and wooded areas.

Mom said with a sigh of enjoyment, "Oh, I do love Bygdøy! Whenever I come here, I always fantasize about living here myself someday."

"How do you plan to get rich enough to live in this kind of neighborhood?" London said.

Mom gave London a sharp poke in the ribs.

"I *don't* plan to get that rich," she said. "Didn't I just say it was a *fantasy?* Don't you know how fantasies work? It's not supposed to really happen."

Mom sighed and added, "How many things do I need to teach you from scratch?"

"You don't have to teach me anything," London said, sorry she'd asked the question.

"Well, I can if you need me to," Mom said. "I've gotten really good at this fantasy thing over the years. Maybe you'd be happier if you had a richer fantasy life. I get the feeling you're much too realistic ... too practical ... about things in general. That can be a real drag on your mental well-being."

"My mental well-being is fine," London replied stiffly.

"OK, if you say so," Mom said, looking rather pleased with herself. "I'll just have to take your word for it."

Soon the tram stopped within sight of an austere white building with a sharply sloping roof. It was their destination, the Viking Ship Museum. When they walked inside, the ticket seller smiled down at Sir Reggie and said in English, "Little dogs and children are allowed in for free." London and Mom each paid 120 Krones for their adult tickets.

London picked up Sir Reggie, and they all proceeded past the concessions counter into a cavernous, tunnel-shaped room with large windows. Most of the space was taken up by an enormous wooden ship that had elegantly crafted spirals topping off the curved prow and stern.

In spite of that huge and impressive craft on display, the corridor seemed to be empty of other visitors.

London glanced around and said, "I don't see anyone else here."

She was startled to hear her own voice echoing through the building.

At that, Sir Reggie let out a soft woof. He wiggled in her arms and looked all around as his own woof also echoed around them.

"It's pretty early in the day," Mom said, speaking softly. "We might be the only visitors. I sure don't see any sign of your caller."

London looked at her watch. She had told him about two hours, but she had taken a little longer than that to arrive.

I guess he didn't wait, London thought. *Or he was never here. Anyway, it must not have been all that important after all.*

She felt disappointed, and oddly worried that she might have missed an important source of information.

Then Mom peered closely at London and said in a playfully spooky voice, "That doesn't mean we're all alone in here. If you listen very closely, you can hear two women whispering."

London rolled her eyes.

"Oh, Mom, not another ghost story, please!" she said.

Then a man's voice echoed through the corridor.

"She is right, London Rose. Listen closely and you too can hear them."

CHAPTER THIRTY FIVE

London gasped aloud at the sound of the seemingly disembodied voice that had just spoken to her in Norwegian-accented English. Even Sir Reggie was alarmed, and almost jumped out of her arms. With a frown on her face, Mom kept turning all around, searching to see where the sound came from.

Then a man stepped into view from a nearby stairwell.

He was tall and gaunt with receding silvery hair, a tall forehead, an aquiline nose, a sharp chin, and an icy, forbidding expression. But in a flash his expression turned to one of startled surprise.

He and Mom said a single word in near unison.

"You!"

Mom and the man stood staring at each other in stunned silence, and London looked back and forth at both of them.

"Would somebody please tell me what's going on?" she said.

Mom said in a hushed near whisper. "London, I believe we have found your caller."

The man's eyes narrowed as he looked at Mom.

"Madam, I hadn't expected to see *you* here," he said.

"The feeling is very mutual," Mom replied sharply. Then she turned toward London and said, "I guess I should introduce you to Tobias Skare."

It took London a moment to bring that name to mind.

"Oh, yes," London said. "The owner of the little Viking rowboat."

"The very same," Skare said, with a slight bow.

Mom said to the man, "I'm this young woman's mother."

"Ah, I had not made that connection," Skare said.

Mom crossed her arms and tapped her feet, which clicked noisily through the corridor.

"I think you owe my daughter an explanation," she said.

"I think so too," London said. "Why did you call me?"

The man's narrow lips twisted into a smirk.

"I just wanted to meet the woman who reported me to the police," he said. "I got a rather annoying visit from them this morning. I cannot say I much enjoy being a murder suspect. While it is true that I will not

172

shed many tears over Iver Nilsen, I certainly did not kill him."

"London had nothing to do with reporting you," Mom snapped.

"No?" Skare asked.

"No," Mom said. "I'm the one who told the constable about your rude, off-putting behavior. But it was actually the victim's son—Sander—who told the constable that he thought you were the killer. And for all we know, he was absolutely right."

London almost hushed Mom for speaking so sharply. The truth was, she felt as though she, Mom, and Sir Reggie were at this man's mercy all alone here in this cavernous museum without so much as a security guard in sight.

Had Skare given her this location because he thought that he could confront her alone here?

I'm being irrational, of course, she tried to convince herself.

The man looked at London with a curious expression.

"If this is true, I beg your pardon for my mistake," he said to her. "After I returned your rather quarrelsome mother to Trollskog Island …"

"Now look here!" Mom interjected angrily.

But the man just continued, "… I rowed the other passenger—the equally annoying gentlemen with the fishing rod—to the pier where your cruise ship was docked. On the way, he happened to mention that the leader of your little outing's name was London—a distinctive and unusual name."

London didn't need him to spell out how he'd then found her phone number. Just as she'd guessed this morning, he'd easily gotten it off the Epoch World Cruise Lines staff list. After all, there weren't any other "Londons" working for the company.

Skare said to her, "Alas, I jumped to the conclusion that you were responsible for my trouble with the police. For that, I now sincerely apologize."

London wasn't sure what that apology might be worth. She still didn't know whether this man might be Iver Nilsen's murderer.

She remembered too clearly what Sander said about him at the lighthouse.

"He has hated my father for years."

However, another question still nagged at her.

"Why did you want to meet me in this museum?" she asked Skare.

"Well, why not here?" Skare said with a slight shrug. "I believe all foreigners should visit this place. And your mother was quite right—if you listen closely, you *can* hear two women's voices speaking here. Just be quiet and pay attention."

The group fell silent. London could hear a slight whoosh of a draft glide past her ears. And even now that the three of them weren't talking, there was still a low, echoey rumble in the air, like the sound she had heard conch shells make when she'd held them to her ear.

And yet London didn't hear any women's voices …

Or at least I don't think so.

Nevertheless, she found herself slipping under the spell of this corridor with its ancient wooden ship. The man's voice was even rather hypnotizing.

He said, "This vessel is known as the Oseberg Ship, so-called after where it was found. In its day it was a sleek, mighty craft with 15 pairs of oars and a sail of some 1000 square feet. We may never know what the men who built and sailed her called her—although perhaps someday the whispering women will tell us."

Mom gasped audibly. For a moment, she seemed thoroughly intimidated and maybe even a little afraid.

Nevertheless, she explained, "This ship was excavated from a Viking burial mound around the year 1905. It was probably buried there around the year 800 AD. The skeletons of two women were found in the ship. No one knows who they were, but they were apparently very important, because they were surrounded by luxurious 'grave goods'—offerings to accompany the dead into the next world, including silk garments and tapestries."

Skare nodded approvingly at Mom's knowledge.

"And you, too, think you might hear their voices?"

Mom swallowed hard again.

"I—I suppose I do," she stammered

"What do you think they want to say?" Skare asked.

"I can't really make out their words … but I guess … I would like to think … they want to tell us all about themselves, about who they really were, and what their lives were like."

Skare squinted, and his smile darkened.

"Either that," he said, "or they are saying you are not welcome here—you foreign gawkers who have no respect for this country's glorious Viking past."

London shuddered, feeling as though a cold chill had suddenly blown through the museum. Even Sir Reggie shivered in her arms. London remembered what Mom had told her about this man's behavior

174

aboard his *færing,* the little rowboat that was shaped somewhat like this massive ship—how he'd complained angrily about pollution, trash, and overfishing in the fjord.

And, also, about Americans, she remembered.

As if sensing London and Mom's discomfort, Skare's smile brightened somewhat.

"But pardon me—now I am being rude," he said. "Despite our differences, I really was very sorry to hear of Iver's death."

Skare fell silent for a moment, and London struggled to read his expression.

Is he really sorry Iver is dead? she wondered.

She didn't sense any real grief about him. In fact, she had no particular reason to think she and Mom weren't in the presence of the captain's murderer.

Skare continued, "We were once friends, and I always held out hope that someday we could make up ... and he would tell me the secret."

London shuddered again at how he emphasized those two words—"the secret."

"What secret?" Mom asked, apparently also struck by the words.

"The secret of Trollskog Island," Skare said. "When we were still friends, Iver told me he knew a secret about the island—something that nobody else knew. He teased me about it, said he would maybe tell me about someday, but then we quarreled, and he never did."

Mom and London exchanged glances.

Mom asked, "What do you think the secret was?"

"I wish I knew," Skare said. "But I think it may have had something to do with a troll. The name 'Trollskog' means 'troll woods.' Maybe Iver knew of a troll who lived on the island. Maybe he had even befriended the troll. I hope it is true, and I hope to meet that troll myself someday. In fact, I go that island often, hoping to find the troll."

This keeps getting spookier, London thought.

She wondered whether Skare might actually be making some of this stuff up. Was he trying to spin the conversation away from whatever grievance he'd had against Captain Nilsen.

Before Skare could continue, London's phone rang. Her heart quickened as she saw that the call was from the number she'd tried to reach over breakfast.

"I've got to take this," she said to Mom and Skare.

She stepped away from them and set Sir Reggie down on the floor and took the call. She heard a woman speaking in English with a thick Norwegian accent.

"Hello, is this London Rose?"

"It is," London said, trying to keep her voice quiet in the echoey corridor.

"My name is Mette Gaarder, and I am the office manager for Nilsen Fyord Krydstogter. I just arrived a minute ago and heard your message. How may I help you?"

London scratched her chin, trying to remember exactly why she had made the call in the first place.

It was Mom's idea, she recalled.

The truth was, she wasn't sure what she'd hoped the call would accomplish.

London said in a fumbling voice, "Uh, first I ... I just want to say how sorry I am about what happened to your employer, Iver Nilsen."

The woman sighed sadly.

"Yes, it was a terrible shock. Did you know Iver personally?"

London said, "Not very well, but he seemed like a nice man. You see, I ..."

London hesitated.

What should I tell her? she wondered.

How much *should I tell her?*

She began, "I'm the social director aboard a cruise ship called the *Nachtmusik,* and I—"

Mette Gaarder interrupted in a cheerful voice.

"Oh, yes, now I remember! You booked the *Kråkebolle* for a fishing cruise yesterday. And you must have been on Trollskog Island when ..."

London heard the woman gasp.

"Oh, my! You must have been there when poor Iver was killed!"

"That's right," London said.

How much more she should say about the murder? Should she mention that she was the person who found the body? Surely, London figured, it wouldn't be a good idea to admit that she herself was something of a murder suspect.

Mette Gaarder said, "Where are you right now?"

"I'm in Bygdøy, at the Viking Museum."

"That is just a short ferry ride from here. Perhaps you would like to come here, and we can talk."

"I—I'd like that," London stammered.

"You are also a short walk from the Dronnigen dock. There are ferries leaving there for Lindøya every half hour. You can get here very soon. I look forward to seeing you."

"Yes, I—I look forward to see you too," London said.

They ended the call, and London picked up Sir Reggie again and walked back over toward Mom and Skare. The man was holding Mom's rapt attention with whatever he was saying to her.

London felt torn about cutting the meeting short. She still hadn't had a chance to ask Skare just what the nature of his quarrel with Captain Nilsen had been. On the other hand, she felt pretty sure he would never give her a straight answer.

Besides, I'm a little scared of this guy, she told herself.

"Mom, we've got to go," London said.

"Where to?" Mom asked, as if snapping out of a revery.

Then Mom's eyes widened with realization.

"Oh! You heard back from Lindøya Island, didn't you?"

London scowled at Mom, far from pleased that she had blabbed away their next destination to this sinister man.

"Lindøya!" Skare exclaimed. "Why, of course! You are going to pay a visit to Iver's business there. Would you like me to row you over in my *færing?* It is docked nearby, and Lindøya is not very far, and I can get you there pretty quickly."

"Thank you, but no," Mom said emphatically. "Thank you for your time."

"It was my pleasure," Skare said, although something in his voice told London that he hadn't considered it much of a pleasure at all.

As London, Mom, and Sir Reggie left the museum, Mom exhaled sharply as if she'd been holding her breath for a long time.

"What a relief to get away from that weird man!" Mom exclaimed. "What do you suppose he was thinking, offering us a ride in that rickety little rowboat? Why, the man pretty much came out and said he hated our guts! What did he plan to do, throw us overboard?"

London really had no idea. But as she and Mom and Sir Reggie headed toward the Dronnigen dock, a new question took shape in her mind.

What is the secret of Trollskog Island?

CHAPTER THIRTY SIX

London felt a flash of irritation as she and Mom and Sir Reggie walked toward the Dronnigen dock.

"Why did you have to tell him where we were going?" she asked Mom rather crossly.

"Huh? I didn't tell him anything."

"You did so. You said the name Lindøya Island loud and clear."

"Did I?" Mom said. "The truth is, I'm still so rattled, I can't remember what I said or didn't say. I guess I just wasn't thinking. Well, surely he isn't going to follow us there."

When London didn't reply, Mom added nervously, "Or is he?"

"I don't know what he's going to do," London said. "But we do know he can really get around Oslofjord in that little *færing* of his. What did he say to you when I was on the phone?"

"It was a lot of growling about how bad things are nowadays, and how things haven't been the same since the Viking Age came to an end about a thousand years ago. He's really nostalgic about all that plundering and pillaging and conquering. He said he was born in the wrong time."

Mom shuddered and added, "I for one wish he *had* been born in a different time. I'd be just as happy never to have met him. He really gives me the creeps, and I'll admit that he got under my skin, like he's some kind of a mesmerist or something."

"Did he say anything more about the secret of Trollskog Island?" London asked.

"No. Anyhow, what's that got to do with our investigation?"

That's what I'd like to find out, London thought.

She didn't know why, but she had a strong gut feeling that the so-called "secret" mattered a lot.

When London, Mom, and Sir Reggie arrived at the dock, a large, stout ferryboat was ready for boarding. They hurried to buy their tickets for 58 Krones each, then climbed aboard the ship.

As the ferryboat pulled away from the dock, they climbed to the upper level, an open deck just behind a four-sided glass bridge that was riddled with antennae. They stood at the railing overlooking the water,

178

and Mom picked up Sir Reggie so he could get a good look at the squawking, diving seagulls that followed the boat.

"You'd love to fly off after them, wouldn't you?" Mom giggled when the little dog woofed at the gulls.

Meanwhile, London knew she had another call to make. She took out the card *Politiførstebetjent* Kolberg had given her and dialed her number.

When she got the constable on the phone, London said, "I thought I should let you know that I had an encounter with Tobias Skare just now."

She heard a slight gasp of surprise.

"Where?" Kolberg asked. "What happened?"

London said, "He called me early this morning without even telling me who he was. He told me he wanted to meet me at the Viking Ship Museum. I thought it might be some kind of tip on the case, so I went there with my mother. Then I found out who he was."

"What did he say?"

"He said he'd been paid a visit by the police this morning, and that he seemed to be a suspect in Iver Nilsen's murder. He thought I had been his accuser, and he wanted to confront me, I guess. You obviously didn't arrest him. Does that mean he's cleared of suspicion?"

"Not exactly," Kolberg said. "What I mean to say is, we do not have sufficient evidence to hold him. He's a strange man, certainly, and a far from pleasant one. And he did admit that there had been considerable animosity between himself and Nilsen. But given the nature of the crime, I'm not sure that animosity alone seems like a plausible motive. The more I think about it, I believe somebody had a very specific reason for murdering Nilsen."

London fought down a scoff of annoyance.

"Do you think *I* had a specific reason?" she said. "Or my mother?"

"I do not know of any such reasons—yet," Kolberg said.

London fell silent for as she remembered what Kolberg had said yesterday.

"I think it would be wise to put your considerable detective abilities to work clearing your name."

Finally, London said, "So it's still up to me to prove my own innocence. And my mother's as well."

"That would be very helpful," Kolberg said.

London shook her head with frustration.

Then she said, "Well, I just thought I should tell you what

happened."

"I appreciate that. Please keep me informed."

"I'll do that."

They ended the call, and Mom turned toward London and asked, "I take it that was the constable you just called."

London nodded.

"What did she say?" Mom asked.

"Let's put it this way," London said with a sigh. "At the moment, she seems to consider you and me to be as viable as suspects as she does Tobias Skare."

Mom's eyes widened with amazement.

"What?" she said. "That's crazy!"

Not so crazy, London admitted to herself. *She's just doing her job.*

Instead, she said, "All the more reason to solve this case ourselves. I hope we turn up something while we're on Lindøya Island. I for one am getting tired of being suspected of murder."

Mom shook her head and said, "Yes, I must admit, the thrill does go out of it after a while. I'm sure it gets pretty tedious after several times."

The ferry was already approaching the heavily wooded island of Lindøya. Although the island was quite small, it was nevertheless larger than Trollskog. And unlike Trollskog, Lindøya was obviously inhabited, with red, yellow, and green cottages and docked boats all along the shore.

Mom scratched Sir Reggie's head and said, "Oh, how delightful to see Lindøya again. You'll like it here, Sir Reggie."

Then she looked at London and added, "Did I happen to mention that I once spent a few days here? It's an enchanting resort in the summer, with walking trails and swimming spots and a botanical garden."

Mom pointed and said, "You can't see it from here, but over on the southeastern shore there's even a nudist beach."

London was just as happy that the nudist beach wasn't in view. She also didn't feel like asking Mom just how familiar she was with the beach. But the fact that the beach even existed was quite striking.

A nudist beach—in Norway! London thought.

It was a reminder of just how warm and pleasant summers could be here in Oslofjord, even this far north. And today was certainly a beautiful, sunny day.

The ferryboat docked at a large pier, where it unloaded its cars and passengers while others waited to come aboard. Mom set Sir Reggie down on the pier, and he walked between London and Mom as they looked for the address Mom had found for Nilsen's business.

They knew they were headed in the right direction when the *Kråkebolle* itself came into view. Nilsen's fishing boat was moored to a wooden dock just ahead. Then a sign came into view that read *Nilsen Fyord Krudstogter*—Nilsen's Fjord Cruises. The sign was perched in front of an inviting two-story cottage with yellow clapboard siding.

Mom pointed toward the tiny yard in front of the house.

"London, look," she said.

Sure enough, a small lemon tree was planted in a wooden barrel, where it basked in the sunlight. There were ripe, bright yellow lemons on almost every branch. London remembered Iver Nilsen telling her and Mom about the lemon tree he had at home.

"I guess his home and his business are the same place," London said to Mom.

The two of them walked up to the front door, which stood open behind a screen door, and London knocked shyly.

"Come on in!" a woman's voice called out in accented English— the same voice London had heard over the phone a little while ago.

London and Mom and Sir Reggie went on inside, where a short, stout, cheerful woman wearing brightly colored clothes stood up behind a desk. A pair of horn-rimmed reading glasses hung by a chain around her neck.

"You must be Frøken Rose, the American woman I spoke to on the phone," she said.

"Please, call me London."

"Very well, then—London. Please call me Mette."

London shook her hand and said, "And this is my mother, Barbara Rose."

"Very pleased to meet you, Barbara Rose."

Mette stooped down and smiled at Sir Reggie.

"Would you care to introduce yourself, sir?" she said.

Sir Reggie let out a lively bark. Laughing, Mom said, "I believe he just said that his name is Sir Reggie."

"Very pleased to meet you, Sir Reggie," Mette said. Then she said to London and Mom, "Have a seat, make yourselves comfortable. Would you like some tea?"

"That would be nice," London said.

"Yes, I'd like that," Mom said.

Mette had a carafe of already-heated water on a hotplate. She put teabags in three cups and poured water into them, then offered two of the cups to Mom and London and kept one for herself as she sat back down at her desk.

She glanced back and forth between Mom and London and asked, "Do you have any news about the … ? Oh, I can't even say it."

"We were hoping you could tell us something," Mom said.

Mette shrugged and said, "Well, the police have been here, of course. They came last night, including the *Politiførstebetjent* herself. They had many questions, but no answers."

London asked, "Do you have any ideas about who might have wanted to kill him?"

"No, I really don't think so," Mette said.

London flashed back to his altercation with Scott yesterday, and how she herself had felt compelled to intervene.

"I noticed that he had a bit of a temper," London said to Mette.

"Oh, yes, but he never stayed angry for long. Not long enough for anybody to get really angry back."

London and Mom and Mette fell silent as they sipped their tea. London couldn't shake off the feeling that this was going to be a pointless errand after all.

What did we expect Mette to tell us that we don't already know? she wondered.

"It is all so strange," Mette said with a shudder. "It is a help, I suppose, to have people here who … were there at the time. It makes the whole the whole thing seem less—unreal."

Another silence fell.

Then Mette said in a broken voice, "Poor Iver!"

London immediately sensed that Mette had been very close to Iver Nilsen.

"We're very sorry for your loss," London said to her.

"Thank you," Mette said. "I have been wandering around in here alone all morning, not sure what to do. Of course, I had to cancel all the boat tours for the time being. But what am I supposed to do next? I really have no idea."

Indicating some family pictures and personal items on her desk, "Maybe I should just take my things and leave. The truth is, I do not know whether I still have a job here or not. But it would be hard to go. I have worked here for decades. I wore—how do you say it in English?—*many hats* here. I was the housekeeper as well as the business manager."

London was about to ask Mette more about her history with Iver Nilsen when she heard a man speak sharply behind her.

"I did not expect to see *you* here."

CHAPTER THIRTY SEVEN

London was sure that she knew that voice, and Sir Reggie seemed to recognize it too. The little dog jumped up into London's lap and peered over her shoulder at the speaker. When she swiveled around, London saw just the person she had expected. The victim's son, Sander Nilsen, was opening the screen door and coming into the cottage.

She thought that the young man looked even more pale and frail than she remembered—a striking contrast to his robust, muscular, vigorous father.

Mette spoke to Sander in English so London and Mom could understand.

"Sander, these two kind women have come to find out what they can about what happened to your father."

Sander scoffed and said to Mom and London in his clumsier English, "That *is* kind of them. I wish the police would be so kind."

He continued speaking to Mette in Norwegian. Although she still had trouble speaking the language, London found that she could understand it better than she could speak it, which was often the case.

"Have you heard anything more from theP*politiførstebetjent?*" Sander asked.

"Not a thing," Mette replied in English.

"Do you think the police are even serious about finding Father's killer?"

"Of course they are," Mette said. "You just have to be patient."

"Patient?" Sander snapped. "My father has been murdered. How can I be patient until his killer is brought to justice?"

"It might take some time," Mette said.

"It should not take any time," Sander said. "I told the *Politiførstebetjent* yesterday who the killer is. It is certainly Tobias Skare. He's the only person in the world who hated Father enough to kill him."

London and Mom glanced at each other at the mention of Skare's name.

Mom said in near-perfect Norwegian, "I believe the *Politiførstebetjent* are already considering Herr Skare. In fact, when we talked to him a little while ago—"

London tried to hush Mom, but she was too late.

"You talked to him?" Sander interrupted. "Where did that happen? How?"

London had no idea how to begin explaining what had happened, especially not in Norwegian. And she certainly didn't want to get into the strange encounter with Skare with this distraught young man.

Mom looked embarrassed at her blunder. But there was no way for her to break off the story now.

"At the Viking Ship Museum," she said. "He told us he had been visited by the police. He seemed to be upset about that, which was why he contacted us and asked us to meet with him at the museum. He wanted to know if we knew what the police had on him. Of course, we do not know anything about that. But the police do have their eye on him. If they get enough evidence, I am sure they will arrest him."

London was relieved that Mom had managed some sort of explanation.

Sander shook his head and sat wearily down. London sensed that the young man hadn't gotten any sleep to speak of last night.

Small wonder, she thought.

Then Sander said to Mette in Norwegian, "Why did you phone me a while ago?"

"I told you," Mette said. "I wanted you to come around to the office."

"But why?"

Mette patted a thick ledger on her desk.

"Because I think you ought to start learning about the business end of things, now that your father is gone."

Sander shook his head with despair

"I do not want to learn about the business end of things," he said. "I want my father back. And nothing can bring him back."

"This business belongs to you now," Mette gently insisted.

"I do not want it. It should go to someone else. It should go to Henrik Lokken. He is the one who deserves it. I cannot do anything right. I can just barely pilot a boat, nothing else. I cannot fish, and I certainly do not have a head for business. I wish things were different, but that is the way things are."

"Your father was sure you could learn," Mette said.

"I cannot learn. I can write songs, and I can play the guitar, and I can sing. That is all I am good at. And it is what I had better stick to."

Then Sander added in an almost inaudible whisper, "I always hoped I could make Father understand. Every single day I hoped for that. But now ..."

A tense silence fell over the room.

Then Sander got up from his chair and spoke to London and Mom in polite, stilted English.

"I am sorry to have intruded. Please forgive me. I will go now."

Mette called out gently, "Sander ..."

But Sander walked out the door and was gone.

Mette let out a long sigh and said to London and Mom in English, "I am sorry that had to happen while you were here. As you can tell, the boy is very distraught—all the more so because he feels so very guilty. He loved his father very dearly, and his father loved him in return, and he even liked to hear Sander sing and play the guitar and wished him well with his music, but ..."

Mette shrugged slightly.

"He still couldn't fulfill his father's hopes," Mom said.

"No, he could not, although he tried his best," Mette said. "Sander seems to find it hard to be successful at anything. Not that it should matter for a boy that young. He ought to be able to take his time, find his own way. I feel very sorry for him."

Reggie had fallen asleep in London's lap, but now his ears perked up at a noise outside. London listened closely and realized it was coming from the dock—the *Kråkebolle's* engine. Then she heard the boat head away from the dock out into the fjord.

Hearing the same sounds, Mom asked, "Where is he going?"

Mette explained, "Sander takes the boat out whenever he is feeling depressed. I wish he would not, and his father did not like him to do that either. He is an adequate pilot, but he needs supervision, and he might get himself hurt or even drowned. Especially now, when he is feeling so sad and guilty."

London sensed the depth of Mette's sympathy. She, too, felt sad for the grieving young man.

"I hope he will return safely and soon," she commented

Mom said to Mette, "He mentioned someone's name—Henrik something."

Mette nodded and said, "Henrik Lokken. He was Iver's mate until about a month ago. They were also business partners."

London and Mom exchanged looks of interest. Was this a new name to add to their investigation list?

London said, "Sander mentioned that he thought Lokken ought to get the business."

"Yes, I know," Mette said. "That was what Iver wanted too, during the years when he and Henrik worked together. Henrik was like a son to Iver, and a truly excellent sailor. In Iver's original will, he left the *Kråkebolle* and the entire business to Henrik."

Mette paused reflectively, then said, "But about a month ago, Iver started feeling guilty toward his son. He did not think it was fair to leave the *Kråkebolle* to someone else. And he never gave up hope that he could teach Sander to become a good sailor and fisherman. He thought maybe knowing he was going to inherit the business would inspire the boy to do better."

Mette sighed again and said, "Sadly, it did not work out that way. Sander kept telling his father that he appreciated the gesture, but that he really did not want the boat or the business."

"How did Henrik feel about the change?" Mom asked.

"He was angry at first," Mette said. "That's why he quit working as Iver's mate. But he just could not stay angry for long. He loved Iver too much to harbor any bad feelings toward him, or toward Sander, either. Like I said, he was like a son to Iver. And he and Sander were like brothers."

Mom said, "Couldn't Sander just ... well, turn the business over to Henrik anyway?"

"Oh, Henrik would never accept anything that would go against Iver's wishes.
I suppose Henrik, too, hoped that maybe Sander would learn to live up to his inheritance."

London and Mom exchanged glances again.

This time Mom mouthed silently to London, *"Are you thinking what I'm thinking?"*

London nodded in agreement.

Henrik Lokken might still be angrier than Mette or anybody else knew.

In fact, she thought, *he just might be Iver Nilsen's killer.*

187

CHAPTER THIRTY EIGHT

London felt a tingle all over as she considered what Mette had just told them.

Henrik Lokken had expected to inherit a boat and a business, only to have it all snatched away from him when Iver Nilsen changed his will.

That certainly seemed to her like a possible motive for murder.

She saw by Mom's expression that also she felt intrigued. Even Sir Reggie seemed suddenly very attentive.

London asked Mette, "Could you tell us where we might find Henrik Lokken?"

For the first time during their visit, Mette hesitated and squinted skeptically at London, then at Mom.

"Why would you want to talk to him?" Mette asked.

London and Mom exchanged yet another look, as if to ask each other, *"What should we tell her?"*

So far, Mette had apparently welcomed the opportunity to talk to anybody who might know something about her employer's death. She hadn't seemed very concerned about just *why* London and Mom were asking all these questions. But now the office manager was obviously starting to wonder, and London couldn't blame her.

While London tried to think of what she should say, Mette pushed back against their request.

"Henrik is grieving as much as any of us," she said. "I am not sure what good could come of disturbing him. And the truth is, I do not know why you should *want* to disturb him. "

Mom looked on the verge of saying something, but London silenced her with a subtle wave of her hand. One thing she'd learned about Mom during the couple of days they'd spent together was that she sometimes had an unfortunate way of saying the wrong thing.

London took a long, deep breath.

She said, "Mette, my mother and I have strong personal reasons to …"

She hesitated before she said, "… to find out what happened to Iver Nilsen."

188

Mette's eyes widened worriedly.

London swallowed hard and said, "I was the first person to find Herr Nilsen's body. And consequently ..."

Mette gasped aloud as London's voice faded.

"Do you mean that you are a suspect?" she asked.

Mom nodded and added, "And I'm afraid I'm a suspect as well."

Mette sat staring for a moment, trying to absorb what she'd just heard.

Finally, she stammered, "But ... but surely you would never ... I mean, what possible *reason* could you have had to ... ?"

London leaned forward in her chair and said, "Mette, I absolutely promise you that we did not kill Herr Nilsen. I don't think the *Politiførstebetjent* seriously believes that we did. But because of the circumstances, she can't completely eliminate us as suspects. It's her job to not to ignore any possibilities."

Mom added, "So you see, my daughter and I have a lot at stake in bringing Herr Nilsen's killer to justice. We need to clear our own names of suspicion."

Mette nodded slowly.

"I—I am starting to understand, I think," she said. "But I cannot believe it's possible that Henrik Lokken would ever have done any harm to Iver. It is just not in his nature."

London was touched by the strength of Mette's trust in Iver's longtime mate and friend. She could understand how the woman felt. At the same time, she couldn't ignore the possibility—maybe even the likelihood—that Mette's affection for Henrik Lokken was blinding her to some awful truth about him.

But now was no time to try to explain that possibility to her.

Instead. London said, "Henrik might know something important—something that might help us. All we want is to ask him a few questions."

Mette fell silent for a long moment, apparently struggling with her feelings. Finally, she jotted something down on a slip of paper.

"This is his address." she said. "As you walk along the road to your left, look for a red cottage. It is just beyond the largest pier near here, where the shore juts out. But please show some consideration toward Henrik. This is very hard for all of us who knew and cared about Iver."

London and Mom thanked Mette; then they and Sir Reggie left the house and headed toward the address she had given them.

As they walked past various boats and docks and cottages, Mom

"What do you think are the chances … ?"

London knew what Mom meant to ask, but she didn't know what to say for a moment. But she did flash back to what *Politiførstebetjent* Kolberg had said about Tobias Skare a little while ago.

"I'm not sure that animosity alone seems like a plausible motive."

The constable had believed that Nilsen's killer had acted for *"a very specific reason."*

The fact that Henrik Lokken had been cut out of his inheritance in favor of Iver's rather inept son certainly seemed like a very specific reason to London—and very personal.

And also pretty obvious, London thought.

Surely, she and Mom weren't the first people to consider it.

"I don't know," London said in reply to her mother's question. "But I think we can be pretty sure that Henrik Lokken has already shown up on the constable's radar. If she hasn't arrested him already, it may be because she's already eliminated him as a suspect."

"Maybe," Mom said. "Or maybe she's just looking for some last bit of evidence."

We'll just have to see, London thought.

A short distance past a rocky outcrop with a large pier extending from it, the house they were looking for came into view. The red cottage was not much larger than the little ramshackle shed that had been built right next to it.

In the small yard in front of the cottage, an athletic, shirtless man with large, powerful hands and a thick mane of blond hair was building what looked like a sailboat. The construction was clearly in the early stages. The craft was upside-down, and the hull consisted of little yet, except a line of well-shaped ribs. The man was intently sanding one of the ribs.

London almost called out to him, but quickly thought better of it. For all she knew, he spoke no English at all.

London gave Mom a nudge and whispered, "Your Norwegian is better than mine. Go ahead."

She hoped she could trust Mom to say the right things and ask the right questions just this once.

Mom called out to the man in Norwegian, "Excuse me, but are you Henrik Lokken?"

The man looked up from his work with a curious expression.

"Who is asking?" he replied in Norwegian.

Mom swallowed nervously, then said, "My name is Barbara Rose, and this is my daughter London, and ..."

Mom's voice faded as she struggled to decide what to tell him.

Then Lokken said in English, "Are you Americans?"

London and Mom both nodded.

Lokken smiled and said, "And your dog is American too?"

Reggie let out an affirmative yap.

"His name is Sir Reggie," Mom said.

"That sounds rather British," Lokken said in a pleasant voice, "But that is fine, too. I speak English pretty well. Most people on Lindøya do. We see a lot of Americans here, even American dogs."

Then with a chuckle, he resumed sanding and added, "But if you are looking for a ride in my boat, you have arrived a little early, as you can see. I doubt if I will finish building it before winter. Perhaps you should come back about this time next year."

London was relieved that he spoke English, and also that she wasn't going to have to rely too much on her mother's tact.

"Herr Lokken, this is kind of hard to explain, but ... my mother and I were on Trollskog Island when ..."

Lokken stopped sanding and stared at her.

"When Iver was killed?" he said.

"That's right," London said.

Lokken shrugged, looking markedly less friendly now as he resumed his sanding yet again.

"That must have been very unpleasant for you," he said.

London figured this time she'd better get right to the point.

"Herr Lokken, my mother and I are in a very delicate position. I was the one who found Iver's body. So the police are naturally ... well, suspicious of me. And they think they have reasons to suspect my mother too."

Lokken let out another, darker-sounding chuckle.

"Well," he said, "I believe the English phrase is, 'join the club.' The *Politiførstebetjent* herself paid me a visit this morning. And it was not an altogether friendly visit."

London detected a tightening in Lokken's muscles as he kept sanding in a rather unconvincingly nonchalant manner.

Is this the killer? she wondered.

While it seemed like a distinct possibility, London reminded herself that *Politiførstebetjent* Kolberg apparently hadn't taken him into custody. Had Lokken managed to clear himself of suspicion? If so,

191

were London and her mother wasting their time talking to him? Or were they about to beat the police to the truth about Iver's murder?

She asked cautiously, "Is it true that ... you and Iver Nilsen were at odds recently?"

Lokken stopped sanding and stared at her.

"'At odds?'" he said in a tight voice. "That's one way of putting it, I suppose."

"How would you put it?" London said.

"Well, how much of the story do you already know?" Lokken asked.

London said, "We know that Iver decided to leave his boat and his business to his son instead of to you."

"That is right."

"And you didn't take it well," Mom added.

Lokken leaned back on his work stool and crossed his arms.

"No I did not take it very well, but not for the reasons you might think," he said. "I did not care about inheriting anything from Iver. The man had done so much for me over the years; he did not owe me anything. But leaving the boat and the business to Sander was a mistake. The old man meant well, but it was a mistake."

Lokken fingered the wood that he'd been sanding.

"What kind of mistake?" Mom asked.

"A business mistake, for sure," Lokken grumbled. "But most of all it was a mistake that is still going to hurt poor Sander," he said. "I love the boy like a little brother, but he just does not have what it takes to handle that kind of responsibility. Of course, he will try his best, but he will certainly fail. And to realize he had let his father down even in death ... well, that will ruin his life forever."

As he kept examining his handiwork, Lokken admitted, "So, yes, I was angry with Iver. And I said some things that I should not have said, and that I wish with all my heart I could take back. And I am not even surprised that the police consider me a suspect. But I would never have hurt the man, much less actually kill him."

Mom and London looked at each, as if to silently ask, *"Is he telling the truth?"*

Lokken sounded perfectly sincere to London. But was that just an act? Then he started sanding again.

"Now if you do not have any more questions," he said, "I would very much prefer—"

But before he could tell London and Mom that he wanted them to leave him alone, he was interrupted by the roar of an approaching engine.

London, Mom, Lokken, and Sir Reggie all turned toward the noise. They saw a large boat with a glass-enclosed cabin and the word *POLITI* on its side—the same police boat that had arrived at Trollskog Island yesterday. It pulled up to the large pier at the end of the rocky outcrop, and *Politiførstebetjent* Kolberg and two police officers jumped out and came striding toward Lokken's home.

Lokken called out to Kolberg in Norwegian as she approached.

"I should have known you would be back today. What do you want from me now?"

Kolberg waved a piece of paper at him, then handed it to him.

"I have a warrant to search your tool shed," she said.

"What for?" Lokken asked, sounding genuinely surprised.

Kolberg didn't reply, just stood staring at him while the two officers continued on into the shed. The officers soon came out again, one of them brandishing a small, slender handsaw.

"We found it exactly where we were told to look for it," the officer said to Kolberg, handing the object to Kolberg.

Kolberg looked at the saw closely. London noticed that her attention was drawn to several damaged teeth along the sawblade.

Handing the saw back to the officer, Kolberg said to Lokken, "Henrik Lokken, I am placing you under arrest for the murder of Iver Nilsen."

Lokken's eyes widened with alarm, and he stood up from his stool. London, too, let out a gasp of surprise and disbelief.

"Now wait a minute," Lokken said. "You are making a mistake."

"I do not think so," Kolberg said as the officers put Lokken into handcuffs.

As they led him away, Lokken kept protesting with what sounded like genuine bewilderment.

"This is a mistake … You have got the wrong man … I did not kill Iver … I would never even think of it …"

He continued protesting as the officers put him in the boat.

London felt stunned and confused. A moment ago, she hadn't known whether to think Lokken was innocent or guilty.

But now …

Meanwhile, Kolberg looked back and forth at London and Mom and smiled.

"I suppose I should tell you why this is happening," she said in

English.

CHAPTER THIRTY NINE

London stared at the slightly damaged saw in *Politiførstebetjent* Kolberg's hand.

Then she looked the constable in the eye and said, "Yes, I think you ought to explain all this."

Sir Reggie sat down and looked back and forth from one person to another, as though he was also waiting for an explanation.

Kolberg nodded and said to Mom and London, "I take it that the two of you found out that we already had some suspicion of Henrik Lokken, and that is why you came here to talk to him. Indeed, we paid him a visit this morning, but did not have sufficient evidence to make an arrest."

She fingered the saw blade and added, "But this saw changes all that. You see, we received two important phone tips during the course of the day. The first was from a neighbor of Iver Nilsen's—Sigurd Helgeland is his name. Herr Helgeland said that he overheard a fierce argument between Nilsen and Lokken, and that Lokken had threatened to kill Nilsen."

London flashed back to something Lokken had just told them.

"I said some things that I should not have said, and that I wish with all my heart I could take back."

So far, London thought, the constable hadn't said anything to contradict what Lokken had just said to her and her mother.

Kolberg continued, "Then we got another call—an anonymous call from someone who said he was close friends with Lokken."

"Anonymous?" Mom asked.

"Yes, he said he was afraid for his life if Lokken found out he had called—and I for one cannot blame him. He said that Lokken bragged to him about killing Nilsen. He even showed him how he'd done it— with this little saw. A keyhole saw, it is called."

Kolberg brandished the tool again, fingering the broken teeth on the blade.

"It is a small saw," she commented, "but strong enough to cut through the rung of a wooden ladder."

The constable continued, "The witness said that Lokken described

195

how he had sawed the ladder rung just enough to for it to break under Nilsen's weight. Lokken also told him that he ran into a nail while he was sawing, and that the saw's teeth got damaged—and you can see that damage here. The witness actually saw where Lokken hid the saw, underneath the workbench in his toolshed. And that is where my officers found it just now."

London and Mom looked at each other. London could tell they were thinking the same thing—that the evidence against Lokken was very strong.

Kolberg smiled again and said to London and Mom, "Anyway, you may now consider yourselves free from suspicion. You may come and go as you like. May I offer you a ride back to your ship?"

London and Mom looked at each as they considered the offer. Again, London sensed they were thinking the same thing—that a ride back to the *Nachtmusik* in a police boat with a murder suspect aboard didn't sound especially appealing right now.

Mom said to Kolberg, "Thanks, but I think we'll stay here on Lindøya for a little while."

London said, "It's such a lovely island, and we haven't had a chance to look around."

"We can catch a ferry back," Mom added.

"I do not blame you," Kolberg said. "I would not mind spending the day here myself. Alas, duty calls, and I have a murderer to take into custody. Enjoy the rest of your time in Oslo."

The constable turned and headed back to the boat. She got on board, and the engine roared again as the boat pulled away from the dock and cruised on its way.

"Well," Mom said with a shrug, "I guess that's that."

"I guess so too," London said.

But the whole thing seemed strangely anticlimactic. Sir Reggie let out a little whine as if to suggest he wasn't entirely convinced the case was truly closed. And the truth was, London couldn't shake off her own doubts.

She and Mom and the dog began to stroll along the shore.

"So what do you think?" Mom asked. "Did you get the feeling Herr Lokken had the makings of a killer?"

London scoffed slightly and said, "You're the one who brags about having such insights into male behavior. What do *you* think?"

"I didn't get much of a feeling from him one way or the other," Mom admitted. "He seemed perfectly sincere, but some people are really good at faking that."

Sir Reggie let out a dissatisfied growl, as if his own canine intuitions hadn't kicked in as to whether Lokken was the killer or not.

Before London could raise any further questions, Mom pointed toward the fjord.

"London, look who's here!" she exclaimed.

Tobias Skare's Viking-style rowboat was approaching the shore, coming right toward them with Tobias himself at the oars.

"What on earth is he doing here?" Mom asked.

London didn't reply, but she remembered too well how Mom had blurted out their next destination to Skare before they'd left the Viking Ship Museum.

The tall, silver-haired man pulled his boat up onto the sandy shore. He stepped out with a wide smile on his gaunt face, but London thought that his good cheer was only a little less forbidding than the cold expression he had shown them earlier.

"Hello again, ladies," he said in accented English. "How surprising to find you here!"

London crossed her arms and said, "Surprising for us, anyway. Why do I get the feeling you followed us here?"

Skare smiled that vaguely sardonic smile of his.

"Well, what if I did?" he said. "I am not saying I did, or I did not. Either way, I am free to go where I like on the fjord, and if our paths intersect, what is the harm? As it happens, I am on my way over to Trollskog Island. Maybe this time I will find the island's secret." Then he laughed and added, "I have hopes that it will turn out to be an actual troll. Would you care to join me?"

London looked at Mom and whispered, "Does he think we're going to get in that boat with him?"

But she saw that Mom had a pensive expression on her face. "Well, the murderer has been caught," Mom replied quietly. "Maybe I misjudged this guy after all."

"Seriously?" London asked.

"He's a bit obsessive about pollution and overfishing and the lost glories of the Viking age, but really he's just an eccentric. I've known a lot of them, and I should have recognized right away that he's not actually dangerous. Besides, eccentrics are frequently quite entertaining to be around."

London didn't feel at all sure about that, but before she could voice her disagreement, Sir Reggie went into action. The little dog took off running so fast that his leash flew out of London's hand.

London called out, "Sir Reggie, come back here!"

But in an instant, her dog had scrambled up the side of the *færing*. He climbed onto one of the boat's benches and sat there and let out a defiant yap.

Skare chuckled as he got back into his boat and took the oars in his hands.

"Well, Sir Reggie is eager to join me in the adventure," he said with another laugh. "Won't you ladies join us after all?"

London certainly wasn't going to let Skare just row away with her dog.

"Come on," she called to Mom as she hurried toward the boat. "It looks like we're going looking for the secret of Trollskog Island."

CHAPTER FORTY

A few moments later, London was sitting on a bench in the peculiar rowboat that was shaped like an ancient Viking ship. Sir Reggie was in her lap and Mom at her side as Tobias Skare rowed away from Lindøya Island.

London hadn't been in a rowboat for a long time. She'd forgotten how peaceful it was to be out on the water without an engine roaring all the time and how spellbinding the repetitious movements of oars could be. Their progress across the water wasn't fast, but it was certainly pleasant.

Stay alert, she told herself. *Don't get lulled.*

Then she grumbled quietly in her dog's year, "I sure hope you know what you're getting us into."

Sir Reggie didn't reply, but he certainly looked pleased with himself.

Why did he insist on taking this ride? she wondered.

Had some kind of canine instincts kicked in, or was he just bored? Or had her dog taken a liking to the odd man who had seemed determined to take them along?

She saw that Mom was watching Skare's arm movements with silent approval. Gaunt though the man was, he was also well-muscled, with arms and shoulders that were proportionately large and powerful in comparison to the rest of his frame due to years of rowing. The boat moved along smoothly, and Trollskog Island soon came into view.

Skare eyed the water traffic around them and shook his head bitterly.

"I can remember this fjord in better days," he said. "Before it was so full of plastic and garbage, and when schools of cod still swam here. Of course, it has been going downhill since long before my time. Steam power was the first disaster, with smokestacks coughing soot into the air, and then the internal combustion engine with its toxic fumes and gases."

He tilted his head as if in reflection.

"That was why Iver Nilsen and I first quarreled, I believe," he said. "We were both little more than boys at the time. When he bought his first motorboat, I was furious about it. I told him I would never turn my back on sails and oars. And I never have, not in all the years since."

He rowed on in silence for a few moments. Then he said, "Too bad we fell out like that. Maybe he would have told me the secret of Trollskog Island. I have always been curious ..."

His voice faced, and he seemed lost in thoughts and memories.

Mom interrupted his reverie with a question, "So you said we're looking for a troll on the island?"

Skare snapped back to attention and grinned wryly.

"So we are, so we are," he said. "I had almost forgotten."

Mom asked, "Are they all stumpy and hairy and ugly?"

"In their original form, usually," Skare said in a sage-like tone that reminded London a bit of Emil. "These days they do a lot of shape-shifting. They might appear as a fox, a hare, a gull, or an eagle. They can also appear in human form once in a while."

He heaved a sigh and added, "I fell in love once with a troll who took the shape of a beautiful woman. When I kissed her, she turned into a horrible troll again. It was very traumatic. I have been a bachelor ever since, and I will die a bachelor."

London and Mom glanced at each other.

This man might be a little crazier than Mom realized, London thought.

It came as a relief when the boat pulled up onto the shore of the island. The three people and the dog all climbed out, and Skare pulled his boat securely onto the sand.

Then Skare brushed off his hands and said, "Now we must break up and go in separate directions and look for trolls."

"How do we know when we've found a troll?" Mom asked.

"Especially if it appears in some other form?" London added, playing along with Skare's story.

"Oh, you will know," Skare said. "Your hair will stand on end and your skin will tingle all over. There is no mistaking a troll when you come upon one."

"But what do we do then?" Mom asked.

Skare shrugged and said, "Well, you have cellphones, do you not?"

London and Mom both nodded.

"Then snap his picture before he gets away." Skare said. "We will need photographic evidence. But do not give chase! They are not usually armed, but they can be very dangerous!"

He turned and began walking along the beach. With a glance back at London, Mom, and Sir Reggie, he told them, "Now I will go this way, and the three of you should break up and go in different directions. The more of the island we can cover, the sooner we can find a troll."

For a moment, London, Mom, and Sir Reggie just stood watching him walk away.

Finally, Mom crossed her arms and grumbled to London, "I can't believe I let you talk me into this stupid outing."

"Me!" London exclaimed. "You were the one who said it would be OK. You said you thought we'd misjudged him. You said it might be entertaining to go with him."

"I guess I did at that," Mom said.

Then she wagged her finger at Sir Reggie and said, "But this is your fault mostly. If you hadn't jumped into that stupid *færing,* we'd never have joined you."

Sir Reggie just kept wagging his tail unapologetically.

"So what do you make of all this troll-hunting business?" London asked Mom.

"Oh, it's the oldest practical joke in the world," Mom said, rolling her eyes. "It happened to me once when I went out with some friends on a camping trip. Only then it was called a 'snipe hunt.'"

London vaguely remembered Mom telling her about the snipe hunt many years ago.

London said, "But there are no such things as snipes, right?"

"Right, but the poor dupe on the butt end of the joke doesn't know that. In my case, my so-called friends told me to stand by a hollow log with a burlap bag waiting for a snipe to come out. Then they went away and left me out there all alone for a whole hour in the middle of the night."

Mom shuddered at the memory.

"It was just awful," she said. "I couldn't have been more traumatized if I'd kissed a troll myself. And I'm absolutely sure this guy is up to something a lot like that. As soon as we're off on our own, he'll jump in his boat and go rowing away, leaving us stranded."

London chuckled and said, "That doesn't sound so bad to me. I'd rather be stranded on this interesting island for a while than jump in the boat with that guy again. Who knows where we might end up?"

"Right," Mom said. "We can always call for a water taxi whenever we're ready to leave. Anyhow, you said you wanted to look for the island's secret."

"I wouldn't know where to begin with that," London replied. "But the murder is solved, the killer is in custody, and a weird Viking environmentalist is about to take off without us. Maybe we should start thinking of this trip as a vacation rather than an investigation."

She reached down and unsnapped the leash from Sir Reggie's collar. She thought she might as well give her dog some freedom for a while.

Sir Reggie began to poke around the nearby bushes and relieved himself against a clump of weeds. Then he trotted ahead of London and her mother for a while as they strolled along a path at the bottom of the single hill that rose in the middle of Trollskog Island.

"The lighthouse is just on the other side of this hill," London said. "We can get a water taxi to come into that pier to pick us up."

"Let's take our time," Mom said. "This is such a lovely area with wildflowers blooming all around us."

As they continued strolling along, London was also impressed by the beauty of the island. For a moment, she imagined taking this pleasant walk with Bryce, perhaps near the end of a romantic day, but …

That's never going to happen, she reminded herself.

In fact, Bryce might well be far away from Oslo by now.

Mom and London hadn't gotten very far before Sir Reggie perked up his ears and then turned onto another path that led up the hill. When London called him, he looked back at her for a moment, then again seemed to be listening to something far away.

Before London could give her dog a firmer command, Sir Reggie turned and charged on up the path and out of sight.

"Oh well," London said, "we should head for the lighthouse anyhow."

London turned into the uphill path to follow her dog, but Mom groaned and rolled her eyes.

"You go ahead," she said. "I don't feel much like climbing that hill, but I'll get over there eventually. You go get your dog and I'll take my time."

London saw no point in arguing. Leaving Mom at the bottom of the hill, she started up the twisted, scrubby trail toward the top.

"Sir Reggie!" she called out.

But her dog didn't come running back to her. She was starting to worry about him. And although she knew better than to believe all this talk about trolls, she realized it was having an effect on her imagination.

So was all of the talk about the "secret of the island."

She had a strange feeling that Skare wasn't kidding about that.

She remembered his wistfulness and regret when he'd talked about his falling-out with Iver Nilsen, and what might have happened if they'd remained friends.

"Maybe he would have told me the secret of Trollskog Island."

Yes, Skare was sincere about that, London felt sure of it.

But if there is a secret, it sure isn't trolls, she reminded herself.

When she reached the rocky crest of the hill, there was Sir Reggie, waiting for her. He wagged his tail and yapped enthusiastically at her arrival.

"Sir Reggie!" London scolded, wagging her finger at him. "Why didn't you come when I called?"

Then she realized what might have attracted her dog's attention. She could see the lighthouse at the end of the pier below.

But that wasn't all that was visible down there.

The thing she saw near the lighthouse wasn't a troll, and it didn't look like any island secret ...

But it's certainly interesting, London thought.

CHAPTER FORTY ONE

A fishing boat was tied up at the pier below, just where their boat had docked on the day that she first came to Trollskog Island. And it was the very same boat—Iver Nilsen's *Kråkebolle.*

Only it's Sander's boat now, London reminded herself.

She remembered hearing that engine's roar as the despairing young man sailed away from Lindøya Island, and how worried Mette had been about him taking the boat out when he was so depressed.

"He is not an especially good pilot, and he might get himself hurt or even drowned."

Well, at least he got here safely, London thought.

But this seemed to her to be a strange place for Sander to visit right now. After all, this island actually belonged to the Oslo municipal government, and the lighthouse itself must be depressing for Sander so soon after his father had been killed here. She had to wonder what had driven the young man back.

In any case, she wasn't unhappy to see Sander's boat, especially now that she and Mom and Sir Reggie were almost certain to need a ride back to Oslo.

Looking all around from her hilltop, London could see Tobias Skare's *færing* still resting on the sandy beach where they had landed. Skare himself was leaning casually against his eccentric Viking-style rowboat.

He's sure not searching for trolls, London thought wryly.

He was probably just getting a bit of rest before he rowed away, leaving London and Mom and Sir Reggie alone on the island …

Or so he thinks.

Peering more directly downward, she spotted Mom sitting on a rock just a short way up the hillside, gazing out over the Fjord.

London waved and shouted, "Yoo-hoo, Mom!"

Mom turned and looked up at her.

"Sander is here!" London shouted.

She could barely hear Mom call back, "Sander?"

"Yes, come and meet me at the lighthouse!" London yelled.

Mom waved back and got to her feet, apparently understanding.

Then London and Sir Reggie made their way down the path that led to the pier and the lighthouse. As they walked along the pier, she didn't see any sign of Sander anywhere.

He must be inside the lighthouse, she thought. *It's probably not a good place for him to be alone.*

But when London and Sir Reggie walked into the main room, she still saw no sign of anyone else there.

She called out in Norwegian.

"Sander! Are you here?"

There was no reply.

London felt a strange tingle all over.

Something seems awfully wrong here, she thought.

She also noticed that Sir Reggie was becoming distinctly uneasy. The little dog was leaning against her ankle as if seeking protection.

"What's the matter with you, Sir Reggie?" London asked.

He whined worriedly.

"Don't be silly," she told him.

Looking around the room, she saw that everything looked much as it had when they'd come here for that marvelous dinner that had been followed by such tragedy. She remembered that Captain Nilsen himself had washed those dishes just a short time before he had died.

Her attention turned to something else that she had noticed when they first arrived at the lighthouse—the large pegboard spread out over one wall. Yesterday she'd been struck by how neatly and carefully the tools had been arranged, with every space occupied with its proper tool.

But today something seemed different.

She stood and surveyed the whole pegboard. She soon realized there was a space among the tools that hadn't been there yesterday. It wasn't a large space, but she was sure that it hadn't been empty when she first looked at those tools.

Something is missing.

With Sir Reggie still cowering against her, London took a few steps toward the pegboard to get a closer look. On the right of the space hung a set of saws. Farthest right was a large crosscut saw, then a smaller bow cut saw, then a still smaller coping saw, and next … that empty place.

Where a smaller saw ought to be, she thought.

She blinked, and suddenly she caught an almost photographic flash of how this pegboard had looked yesterday, including the missing saw.

A keyhole saw, she realized with a shudder.

The same kind of saw that was found in Henrik Lokken's tool shed.

When had it gone missing from here? She didn't know. Of course, she wouldn't have noticed such a subtle change after the captain had been found dead and everyone was focused on the horror of that moment.

Then she heard a familiar voice speaking behind her in heavily accented English.

"What are you doing here?"

She spun around, almost kicking poor Sir Reggie who was still huddled against her. London gasped aloud as she found herself face to face with young Sander Nilsen.

Sander asked again, "What are you doing here?"

I could ask you the same thing, London thought.

She realized that he must have been in the lighthouse tower when she came in. But why hadn't he answered when she called his name? And why was his expression so hostile? Did he think that London had come here for some sinister reason—to snoop or steal, perhaps?

London found herself utterly speechless, on the verge of saying something ridiculous about coming here with Tobias Skare and her mother to hunt trolls or look for the secret of the island.

Then the truth started to creep up inside her.

She felt eerily lucid—and also eerily calm.

"It was you," she said quietly to Sander in English. "You sawed the rung in the ladder."

Sander stared back at her silently.

"Then you planted the saw in Henrik Lokken's tool shed," she said.

Sander's eyes narrowed, and he still made no reply.

"But why?" London asked. "Why would you kill your own father?"

Sander's face reddened with fury. The normally baby-faced young man looked quite menacing. Without replying, he reached behind him and pulled a knife out of his belt—the same big knife his father had used yesterday to gut the mackerel.

London took a step back and her dog whimpered.

Now I know why Sir Reggie's so scared, she thought.

I should have been paying more attention. We've got to get out of here.

She reached down to grab Sir Reggie, but Sander moved faster. He shoved her aside and then snatched Sir Reggie up by the scruff of his neck.

Gripping the dog in the crook of his arm, Sander held the knife to

206

Sir Reggie's side.

London's heart jumped up into her throat.

"You are going to cooperate," he told London. "You are going to come with me and get into my boat."

London nodded mutely. She really had no choice but to obey him.

"Now go on ahead," Sander ordered her.

London walked toward the lighthouse entrance with Sander close behind her, still holding Sir Reggie in his threatening grip.

"Why did you do it?" she asked as they stepped out into the sunlight.

"Why do you think?" Sander said.

London's mind clicked frantically away as she tried to make some sense of everything that was happening. Then a phrase echoed through her mind.

"... the secret of the island ..."

What was that secret?

What did she even know about the island, except that it was owned by the Oslo municipal government, and the Wuttkes had wanted it to buy to give away to International Gaia Engagement Fund, and ... ?

London felt a vital piece of the puzzle start falling into place.

She remembered how Iver Nilsen had offered to help the Wuttkes buy the island from the city.

"You might be surprised what kind of a deal you might get," he'd said.

She also remembered how agitated Sander had gotten to hear Iver say that.

"It is not your decision to make," Sander had told him in Norwegian.

Suddenly something became horribly clear in London's mind.

"Your father owned this island, didn't he?" she said to Sander in Norwegian.

"It has been in our family for more generations than I can count," Sander replied in Norwegian, still walking behind London. "Nobody knew; it was a family secret. And my father was determined to keep it that way. If the truth got out, he knew he would be nagged by and pestered by people who would want to buy the island and turn it into ... something he would not like it to become. The truth was, he often told me he was more than ready to *give* it away to the right people ..."

"To people like the Wuttkes," London said. "And organizations like the IGEF."

207

"I could not let him do that," Sander said. "I could not let my own father rob me of my inheritance."

London now found herself at the edge of the pier looking down into the boat. She felt a sharp shove from behind, and she tumbled off the edge of the pier all the way into the boat. She was dazed for a moment as she lay there in a heap, but she quickly realized that no bones were broken.

Now she knew perfectly well what Sander had in mind. Neither she nor Sir Reggie would survive this boat ride. Somewhere far out in the fjord he would push them out of the boat, and they would drown.

But what could she do to stop him?

Meanwhile, still holding Sir Reggie in the crook of his arm, Sander untied the boat with his free hand. Then he climbed down the stone stairs alongside the boat and got into it. Sir Reggie was starting to wriggle now, and London was more worried than ever about his safety.

Clumsily gripping the little dog with one arm, Sander went to the controls. He managed to start the engine with one hand, then pulled away from the pier and headed for open water.

Suddenly Sir Reggie let out a ferocious bark and then Sander yelped with pain.

Sir Reggie had sunk his teeth into his captor's hand.

Sander let go of the dog, who came running over to where London was still crouched on the floor of the moving boat.

London knew she had no time to think.

She grabbed Sir Reggie in both arms, scrambled to her feet, and jumped with him over the side into the fjord. The water was cold enough to stun her for a moment, and she choked on a mouthful of water. She was underwater, but she regained her bearings and kicked off her shoes and swam to the surface.

To her relief, she saw that Sir Reggie was paddling around. He swam to London and tugged on her clothing, doing his diminutive best to keep her head above water.

London caught her breath, got herself oriented, and started swimming toward shore. Sir Reggie paddled along beside her.

We can make it, she thought.

Then London heard a roar of an engine, and she looked back. She saw that Sander had turned *Kråkebolle* around and was driving straight toward her. She and Sir Reggie would never reach the shore before the killer caught up and overran them.

She knew they were only seconds away from certain death.

CHAPTER FORTY TWO

As London flailed hopelessly toward the shore, the roar of the fishing boat grew louder. She looked back again, but now another object obstructed her vision—something large and shadowy.

Then she recognized the dark shape. It was Tobias Skare's Viking-style *færing*. The peculiar boat was moving between her and the approaching *Kråkebolle.*

That realization was followed by the sound of a crash, and pieces of the rowboat came flying through the air, splashing into the water all around her.

The larger powered boat had crashed into the rowboat and smashed it to pieces. When the water settled down, London was relieved to see Skare still floating, clinging to the remnant of a curved Viking bow.

As London treaded water and Sir Reggie paddled around her, she watched the *Kråkebolle* veer aside and careen harmlessly past. Sander had completely lost control. His craft hurtled toward the shore and came to a grinding halt on the rocks and sand.

Looking dazed, Sander climbed out of the crippled vessel and staggered onto the rocky shore.

He's going to get away, London thought.

But a diminutive woman was waiting for him there. Perched on a higher rock, London's mother swung hard and punched the escaping villain in the face.

Sander fell and didn't move.

London and Sir Reggie made their way to the shore and climbed out of the water to find Mom standing triumphantly over the unconscious killer. She was shaking her fist, which must have stung sharply from the blow she'd just delivered.

"There," Mom said pertly. "That ought to take care of things."

*

A short time later, London and Sir Reggie sat on a boulder near the pier, soaked to the skin and huddled together under a dry blanket they'd found aboard the ruined *Kråkebolle.* Mom was sitting next to them, and

209

they all watched as Tobias Skare demonstrated his efficiency with an assortment of clever and skillful sailors' knots.

As he bound Sander Nilsen, hand and foot, Skare explained each of the knots to the dazed young killer.

"You will need to know these if you ever do any serious sailing." He told Sander in Norwegian, "I am surprised your father never taught them to you already."

Mom shook her head and said, "I doubt Sander will have a chance to do much sailing where he's going to wind up soon."

London thought for a moment, then said, "I hadn't guessed Sander to be the killer. Do you remember how he cried like a baby when he saw his father's body? His grief seemed so sincere. Was it only an act?"

Mom scratched her chin thoughtfully.

"No, I actually don't think so," she thought. "I mean, in one sense, it was cold-blooded, premeditated murder. But in another sense ..."

Mom paused to consider that matter.

"His decision to saw that rung may have been impulsive, triggered by his fear of losing this island. Once he'd done it, he might well have hoped that his father would be his usual careful self and not break that rung. I don't doubt that he really loved his father. And his grief may have been genuine—mingled with horror and shock at the terrible thing he knew he had done."

London fell silent as she thought it over.

Yes, that does make sense, she thought.

Whatever else Mom might be, she certainly seemed to have become a shrewd judge of character over the years. And she apparently had picked up some other unusual skills.

Maybe I've got a lot to learn from her.

"Where did you learn to punch like that?" London asked Mom.

"From my boxing days," Mom said. "That's a story for another time."

Shaking her hand, she added, "Alas, my fist is getting kind of soft with age. But of course, I didn't have gloves for this fight."

"Well, you did score a knockout," London said with smile.

"I did at that," Mom said.

Skare had finished tying his knots, so he came over and sat down near them. London offered to include him under the blanket, but he waved it off.

"Those knots should hold him until the police get here," Skare said.

Mom pointed into the distance and said, "And there they come now!"

Sure enough, the familiar large vessel with the word *POLITI* on its side was approaching the island.

"Who actually called the police, anyway?" London asked.

"I did," Mom said. "I followed you up the hill, like I told you I would, and when I got to the top the first thing I did was look back and spot Herr Skare here doing just what we thought he was going to do—rowing away from the island without us. Then I turned and saw Sander forcing you into the boat down on the pier. As I came dashing down the hillside, I took out my cellphone and called the police and told them my daughter was being abducted right before my eyes."

Shaking her hand again, she added, "I got to the beach just in time to deliver the *coup de grâce.*"

Skare said with a grunt, "I admit that my intentions were … mischievous. But as I rowed near the lighthouse, I saw what Sander was about to do with his boat. I knew right then that I had to save a young woman—and maybe more importantly, her dog—even it meant sacrificing my own boat."

London patted the man on the shoulder.

"I'm awfully sorry about what happened to your *færing,* " she said.

"I am at peace with my loss," Skare said in a philosophical tone.

He fell silent for a moment, then said, "The truth is, I am getting a little old for all that rowing. My back isn't what it used to be, and it keeps me awake at nights. It is probably time for me to give up rowing. I am thinking about buying …"

His voice faded.

"Not a motorboat, surely," London said with surprise.

"I have yet to decide," Skare said.

Mom put in, "I hear they've got electric motors for boats these days. No gas or fumes and they're very quiet."

"Is that so?" Skare said.

Then he smiled and chuckled a little.

"Well," he said, "I am sure the Vikings of old would approve."

Meanwhile, the police boat had finished its docking maneuvers at the pier, and *Politiførstebetjent* Kolberg came striding toward them, accompanied by a pair of officers.

She looked over those awaiting her, the two wet adults, the wet dog, and the perfectly dry woman with them; then she stared at the sight of Sander sitting there thoroughly tied up in sailors' knots.

"I believe it is now *you* who owe *me* an explanation, Frøken Rose," she said, glaring at London. "I was told that you had been kidnapped, but now I see …"

"Yes, I was kidnapped," London said. "And nearly murdered. And rescued by this brave Viking and by my own mother." Nodding toward Sander Nilsen, she added, "The short version is that we have caught Iver Nilsen's murderer."

The *Politiførstebetjent*'s frowned sharply.

"But we have already made an arrest in that case," she said.

"I'm afraid you arrested the wrong man," Mom said.

"I believe you will quickly get a confession from this one," Tobias Skare told the constable.

"I really do not understand," Kolberg said.

London explained, "This island was actually owned by Iver Nilsen."

Kolberg's mouth fell open.

"I—I had no idea," she said.

"Almost nobody did," London said. "Sander was afraid his father might give it away for practically nothing and he'd never inherit it. He killed him before that could happen."

"But the saw … ?" Kolberg began.

"Sander used it himself to sabotage the rung," London said. "Then he planted it in Lokken's tool shed in order to frame him."

Kolberg stared again at Sander, who simply lowered his gaze and made no effort to protest the accusation.

"I would never have thought it," she remarked. Then she told her other officers to take Sander into custody, and they picked him up and hauled him away to the police boat.

Kolberg fell silent again, then looked hard at London, Mom, and Sir Reggie, "Tell me, how much longer do the three of you plan to stay in Oslo?"

London smiled as she felt a surge of relief at the case finally being solved.

"We plan to leave as soon as we possibly can," she said.

The constable chuckled slightly and nodded.

"Do not take this the wrong way but … I am glad to hear it. Now come with me to the boat, and we will take you back to the land of the dry."

As London and her companions followed Kolberg toward the police boat, she heard Mom's phone ring. It reminded her that her own phone was well-soaked and probably no longer working.

Mom answered, asked "What? Who?" a couple of times, and then handed the phone to London.

"It's Amy," Mom said. "She insists on talking to you."

When London answered the phone, Amy practically screamed in her ear, "Where are you? I've been trying to reach you for an hour now."

CHAPTER FORTY THREE

Amy's voice on Mom's cellphone sounded excited.

"Wherever you are, you need to get back to the *Nachtmusik* right away," she told London.

"Why?" London asked, stopping in her tracks. "What has happened now?"

In the pause that followed, London tried to picture what kind of drama might have Amy so wired up.

Did the ship sink? Or has Emil locked himself up somewhere again?

Finally, Amy said, "There's someone here to see you."

"Who?"

After another moment of hesitation, Amy said, "I—I don't think I should tell you that. Just get back here right away."

London stifled a discouraged sigh.

Haven't I solved enough mysteries for one day? she wondered.

She said, "Amy, I'm over on Trollskog Island right now, and I'm soaking wet."

"Why are you soaking wet?" Amy asked. "No, don't bother telling me. It doesn't matter. Just get here as fast as you can. I'll keep the, uh, person waiting for you in the Amadeus Lounge."

Amy abruptly ended the call, and London stared at the cellphone for a moment.

"What was that all about?" Mom asked.

"I don't know," London said, handing the cellphone back to Mom. "I guess we'll find out when we get back to the *Nachtmusik*."

"Then we'd better catch up with our ride," Mom said. They both hurried to rejoin *Politiførstebetjent* Kolberg and the others on the way to the police boat.

Maybe it's Bryce, London thought. *Maybe he came back.*

But she didn't quite dare hope for that.

*

When the police boat dropped London, Mom, and Sir Reggie off

214

near where the *Nachtmusik* was moored, they said goodbye to Tobias Skare.

"Do you have any idea what will become of Trollskog Island now?" London asked him.

"I suppose it still belongs to the boy," Skare muttered.

"Well, he's not going to get much use of it in prison," she said. "Perhaps he'll be willing to sell it to the Wuttke family after all. They had decent plans to donate it to an environmental group."

Skare's face brightened, "And maybe they will need some sort of live-in manager. I will certainly look into that."

Mom startled the man with a hug. She said, "Thank you again for saving my daughter. If you need a recommendation for that job or anything else, I can get you letters from some fairly high-level names. The *Politiførstebetjent* can give you my phone number."

The odd and sometimes forbidding Viking environmentalist stepped back onto the police boat with a wide grin on his face.

As London and Mom headed toward the *Nachtmusik*, Mom said, "I'll bet that will work out. And who knows? Maybe he'll even find a troll he can love there."

With London still wrapped up in a blanket and carrying Sir Reggie, they started up the gangway to their ship. Halfway up, they met Bob Turner and Stanley Tedrow who were coming down with all their baggage in tow.

"Hey, ladies!" Bob called out. "I'm glad we caught you before we left!"

Stanley perused London from head to toe.

"Um ... how did you get so wet?"

Bob peered at London through his mirrored sunglasses.

"Yeah, how did *that* happen?" he asked.

"Well, I, uh, sort of almost drowned," London said. "And Sir Reggie too."

Mom added with a laugh, "My daughter just solved a murder case."

London shrugged and said, "Sir Reggie helped, of course. And Mom properly punched out the killer. And we also were helped out by a Viking sailor."

"Well done!" Bob said, clapping his hands. "Mr. Lapham mentioned a murder just this morning, told me to go over to the police station and see if I could help with the investigation. I went there, and it looked like the local cops had everything under control, and besides, everybody was speaking Norwegian, so I came back to the ship."

London was pleased to know Bob didn't seem to have caused the police any annoyance.

"But where are you going now?" Mom asked the two men.

"To New York," Bob said with a note of triumph in his voice. "To meet with Stanley's publisher."

"Publisher?" London asked.

Stanley puffed out his chest and said, "I sold my new novel to a big-time publisher."

"And did he ever get a whopper of a contract," Bob added.

"Yeah, I'll be fixed for life," Stanley said. "And my editor here will do pretty well, too."

"What's the book about?" Mom asked.

"Oh, I can't tell you that," Stanley said with a wink. "Except to say it's a murder mystery. And it has to do with a tour boat."

London tilted her head with curiosity. Had Stanley based his novel on the real-life misadventures of the *Nachtmusik*?

I guess I'll just have to wait until it comes out and read it, she figured.

"Anyway, it was nice knowing you," Bob said. Scratching Sir Reggie under the chin, he added, "Especially you, partner. I'll miss our crime-solving exploits together."

Then he leaned over and whispered rather loudly to the little dog, "I think you'll really like one of the sleuths in the book."

Stanley looked at his watch and said to Bob, "We'd better get going—we've got a plane to catch."

As they started on their way, Bob turned and said, "Oh, by the way, you ought to go to the Amadeus Lounge. Mr. Lapham is holding a little final get-together for the crew and staff."

There sure seems to be a lot going on in the lounge right now, London thought as they boarded the ship.

While Mom went to her stateroom to "freshen up," London walked into her own stateroom and took a long look around. She smiled as she remembered how stunned she'd been by the stateroom's size when Elsie had first shown it to her back at the beginning of the *Nachtmusik's* voyage.

"This is your *room,"* Elsie had insisted. *"Yours and no one else's."*

The room had seemed like a palace then. It seemed perfectly cozy and homey now. London felt sad at the thought that she'd soon leave the room and probably never see it again.

London then took a shower and then rinsed off her little dog. When they were both dry, she looked in her closet for another set of civilian clothes and decided on plain dark slacks and a colorful top.

Mom returned in a figure-hugging floral-print Maxi-dress.

"You look ready for a party," London told her.

"They did say it was a final get-together," Mom said. "I might be saying goodbye, but I don't want to be forgettable."

"Believe me," London replied, "you never will be."

London and Mom and Sir Reggie took the elevator up to the *Menuetto* deck.

As they walked into the Amadeus Lounge, they saw that Bob had been right—most of the staff and crew were here, many of them sitting where a row of tables were lined up together, apparently awaiting the arrival of Jeremy Lapham.

But before London could join them, a sight caught her eye that made her gasp.

There was no mistaking that face with its straight, shoulder-length black hair.

CHAPTER FORTY FOUR

"Tia!" London and Mom exclaimed in unison.

There stood London's sister, who had obviously come all the way from Connecticut for this reunion.

Tia looked at Mom with a shy, awkward smile.

"Hi, Mom," she said. "It's good to see you."

Stunned into silence, London and Mom joined her at the table, and Sir Reggie jumped up into London's lap.

"You've got a cute dog, I see," Tia said.

Mom stammered, "His—his name is Sir Reggie, but ..."

"How did you get here?" London asked her sister.

Tia chuckled and shrugged.

"By plane, of course. After I talked to you on the phone, I called Dad to tell him what was going on. He helped me get over being mad and realize that I just had to do this—to see Mom after all this time. So I got someone to take care of the kids and caught a flight to Oslo."

Mom's eyes widened and her mouth dropped.

"Kids?" she gasped.

"Didn't London tell you?" Tia said. "You've got three grandchildren. Their names are Stella, Margie, and Bret."

Mom had turned pale with shock.

"Of ... of course," she stammered, "I would have expected you'd have a family. London and I just haven't gotten around to talking about much ..."

I can't believe I didn't tell her, London thought.

But then, things had been awfully weird since Mom had reappeared. And Mom had been avoiding any kind of personal conversations.

"I—I guess I've got a lot of catching up to do," Mom said.

"So do all of us," Tia said.

London patted Mom's hand and said, "I think it's definitely time we had that little talk. And please—don't try to tell us you don't remember. You don't have amnesia, not really. We deserve to know the whole truth."

"Yes, yes, you're absolutely right," Mom said.

218

She paused as if to collect her thoughts. London's heart was pounding now, and she realized she was holding her breath.

Small wonder, she thought. *I've been waiting 20 years for this moment.*

Finally, Mom said, "While your father kept working as a flight attendant, I tried to be a good stay-at-home mom for you two girls. I did my very best to settle into that nice little house in that nice quiet neighborhood, and I believe I managed it pretty well. But I had been used to traveling the world, and by the time you were both in your teens, I really needed a break from everyday life. So I came to Europe—just for a week or so, I thought. But I was so emotionally vulnerable. And I didn't count on falling in love."

London and Tia exchanged looks.

She could tell they were thinking the same thing.

Why wouldn't *Mom have fallen in love?*

By then, she'd been single for years.

It didn't seem like something they could fault her for.

Mom continued, "He was a German ballet dancer named Stefan, and he really was a marvelous man, or at least he seemed like one—intelligent and sensitive as well as handsome and talented. Right away I told him I wanted to bring him to the U.S. to meet you two girls and your father. But he said he wasn't ready. He asked me to give him some time."

Mom sighed deeply.

"Well, I *did* give him some time—a month at first, then a couple of months, then a year, then two years, and I knew all the while that every day I spent away from home was making it harder for me to come back into your lives. But I was *so* foolish and deluded."

She fell silent for a moment, then said, "After three years, I knew it was pointless waiting for him to be ready to meet you all. I left him. And I wanted to come home right there and then but ..."

Mom swallowed hard.

"But I was so ashamed. How could I face you after I'd been so selfish and stupid? I kept trying to get up the courage to face you. Meanwhile I sang and tutored and did a short stint as a bullfighter and whatever else I could to support myself in Europe. And I ... I never came back. And I'm sorry. But I'm not the same person who made those stupid mistakes all those years ago. I hope you can believe me."

A tear fell from Mom's eye. London's eyes filled up with tears as well as she saw her sister take one of mom's hands and squeeze it

219

gently. London took the other hand and held it too.

It's going to be a long road to forgiveness, London thought.

Even so, the journey down that road had definitely begun.

And she knew that Tia felt exactly the same way.

Just then, Mr. Lapham himself came sweeping into the lounge.

"Ah, I'm glad to see so many of you here!" he called out. "I have excellent news. Just this morning I sold the *Nachtmusik*. I hope her new owners have better luck with her than we did. And now, before we all go off on our separate ways, let's have some champagne!"

Elsie and her assistants brought three buckets with champagne bottles and poured glasses for everybody, including themselves.

Meanwhile, Mr. Lapham had kept the chair next to his own free. With an appreciative smile at her colorful outfit, he gallantly invited Mom to sit down next to him.

London leaned toward her and said, "Mom, I think you've got something you want to say to Mr. Lapham."

Mom gulped and nodded her head.

"Jeremy, I'm afraid I haven't been altogether honest with you."

"No?" Mr. Lapham said with a look of concern.

"I really never saw the ghostly woman at the Akershus Fortress. I just made that up."

Mr. Lapham chuckled, "Oh, I knew that."

"You did?" Mom asked with an amazed expression.

"Yes. You were obviously exercising your feminine wiles. And quite effectively, I must say. You have me quite wound around your little finger. As a matter of fact, I've been trying to get up the courage to ask you something. I was wondering whether ..."

He paused, and Mom gazed back at him breathlessly.

London could hardly believe her ears.

Is he going to ask her to marry him? she wondered.

Surely it couldn't be something as drastic as that.

Mr. Lapham continued, "I thought I'd make a trip to Paris starting tomorrow, and I wondered if a certain charming and adventurous and very lovely lady would accompany me."

Mom gasped and said, "Oh, Jeremy, I would love to, but I'm afraid I must decline."

"Indeed?" Mr. Lapham said, sounding very disappointed.

"Yes. You see, I have just been reunited with my other daughter Tia."

Mr. Lapham nodded toward Tia and said, "Another daughter? I am pleased to make your acquaintance."

Mom continued, "And I'm long overdue to go back to the United States and—"

Tia laughed and said, "Oh, Mother, there will be plenty of time for that. Meanwhile I've got someone to take care of the kids for a whole week. How would you and this dashing gentleman whose name seems to be Jeremy feel about my tagging along with you to Paris?"

"I'd be delighted to have you along," Mr. Lapham said to Tia with a smile. "That is, if your mother is willing to make the trip."

Mom gave Mr. Lapham a kiss on the cheek and said, "I'll be thrilled to come to Paris with you, Jeremy. And Tia, I'll be even more thrilled for you to join us."

At that moment, Mom's cellphone buzzed.

"Oh, bother," she said, as she reached for the phone.

Her eyes opened wide at what she saw.

"Oh, London!" she exclaimed. "You have a text message from a certain Australian chef! It seems that he's been trying to reach ever since your own phone met such a terrible fate in the waters of Oslofjord."

London grabbed the phone out of Mom's hand and saw the rest of Bryce's message

I turned down the offer to work aboard the Danae.
I'm at the Oslo Airport.
I am about to go wherever my heart takes me.
I hope you will join me here.

London suddenly flashed back to that terrible moment just a little while ago, when she coughed up salt water and saw a large motorboat bearing down on her and she'd known for a virtual fact that she was going to die.

She'd escaped death and was now getting a chance at a fresh start in life. And suddenly, every moment seemed infinitely precious.

Too precious not to take a few chances in life, she thought.

And too precious to let Bryce slip away.

With shaking fingers, she typed as fast as she could.

I will be there.

Bryce quickly replied.

221

Hurry.

London felt ready to explode with happiness and wanted to share the news with everybody. But then something occurred to her …

"Oh, Mr. Lapham," she said. "I'm so sorry, but I won't be accepting the social director job aboard the *Galene* after all."

Mr. Lapham let out a hearty laugh.

"Oh, I knew that all along," he said. "I even knew it when you said you accepted it."

"You—you *knew?* she stammered.

"Yes, you were being perfectly stupid about it, but I knew you'd wind up running away with my cook. You would have been worse than a fool not to. If you hadn't, I'd have packed you up in a big box and mailed you to him. Honestly, sometimes I just wanted to knock your two heads together."

Is there anything this man doesn't know? London wondered.

"But who will you hire to take my place?" she asked.

"Oh, that's already taken care of," Mr. Lapham said, nodding toward Amy. "I've offered the job of social director to my capable concierge, who has graciously accepted it."

Then he nodded toward Emil, who was sitting at the table holding hands with Amy with an uncharacteristically broad smile on his face.

Mr. Lapham added, "And I'm pleased to say that the brilliant historian with whom Amy is romantically involved has agreed to resume his duties aboard the *Galene."*

London felt like her smile was about take wing and go flying around the room.

"You couldn't ask for two better people," she said.

Mr. Lapham added to London, "And don't fret about the future. I'll be glad to hire you and Bryce if you feel inclined to work for me again."

Mr. Lapham waved her away brusquely.

"Off with you, now," he said. "I doubt that you have much time."

London was utterly speechless now. She exchanged grateful and affectionate smiles with Mom, Tia, Mr. Lapham, Amy, and Emil, and Elsie, then picked up Sir Reggie and hurried on her way.

*

A short time later, London rushed into the concourse of Oslo Airport, trailed by a load of luggage and with Sir Reggie dashing ahead of her on his leash. Her heart sank to see how crowded the place was.

"How am I ever going to find Bryce?" she said to Sir Reggie. "How can I even be sure he's still here somewhere?"

As if in reply, Sir Reggie let out a yap and started to drag her through the crowd. The little dog led her straight to a ticket counter where Bryce was standing in line. She almost hyperventilated with relief and excitement.

There he is, she thought. *The man I want to spend the rest of my life with.*

Without a word, she and Bryce fell into each other's arms and shared a long kiss.

Then London asked, "So—where do you want to go?"

"I was getting ready to buy two tickets to Paris," Bryce said.

"Oh, Paris!" London said with a smile. "You know, Mr. Lapham and my mother are going there too."

"Wow," Bryce said. "We might run into them there."

"We might."

"Wouldn't that be nice?"

"Yes, it would."

They stood staring at each other for a moment.

Then London said, "Let's go to Venice instead."

"Yes, let's," Bryce said.

They kissed again and got into a different line.

NOW AVAILABLE!

A MURDER IN PARIS
(A Year in Europe—Book 1)

"When you think that life cannot get better, Blake Pierce comes up with another masterpiece of thriller and mystery! This book is full of twists, and the end brings a surprising revelation. Strongly recommended for the permanent library of any reader who enjoys a very well-written thriller."
--Books and Movie Reviews (re *Almost Gone*)

A MURDER IN PARIS is the debut novel in a charming new cozy mystery series by USA Today bestselling author Blake Pierce, whose #1 bestseller *Once Gone* has received 1,500 five-star reviews.

Diana Hope, 55, is still adjusting to her recent separation when she discovers her ex-husband has just proposed to a woman 30 years younger. Secretly hoping they would reunite, Diana is devastated. She realizes the time has come to reimagine life without him—in fact, to reimagine her life, period.

Devoting the last 30 years of her life to being a dutiful wife and mother and to climbing the corporate ladder, Diana has been relentlessly driven, and has not taken a moment to do anything for herself. Now, the time has come.

Diana never forgot her first boyfriend, who begged her to join him for a year in Europe after college. She had wanted to go so badly, but it had seemed like a wild, romantic idea, and a gap year, she'd thought, would hinder her resume and career. But now, with her daughters grown, her husband gone, and her career no longer fulfilling, Diana realizes it's time for herself—and to take that romantic year in Europe she'd always dreamed of.

Diana prepares to embark on the year of her life, finally turning to her bucket list, hoping to tour the most beautiful sights and sample the most scrumptious cuisines—and maybe, even, to fall in love again. But a year in Europe may have different plans in store for her. Can A-type Diana learn to go with the flow, to be spontaneous, to let down her guard and to learn to truly enjoy life again?

In A MURDER IN PARIS (Book #1), Diana hopes to kick off her journey, and find new love, with an unforgettable night at the Versailles ball. But when the dramatic night takes a harrowing turn she could never expect, Diana realizes she will have to solve the crime—or else have her trip end in disaster.

A YEAR IN EUROPE is a charming and laugh-out-loud cozy mystery series, packed with food and travel, with mysteries that will leave you on the edge of your seat, and with experiences that will leave you with a sense of wonder. As Diana embarks on her quixotic quest for love and meaning, you will find yourself falling in love and rooting for her. You will be in shock at the twists and turns her journey takes as she somehow finds herself at the center of a mystery, and must play amateur sleuth to solve it. Fans of books like *Eat, Pray, Love* and *Under the Tuscan Sun* have finally found the cozy mystery series they've been hoping for!

Book #2-#4 are also available!

Blake Pierce

Blake Pierce is the USA Today bestselling author of the RILEY PAGE mystery series, which includes seventeen books. Blake Pierce is also the author of the MACKENZIE WHITE mystery series, comprising fourteen books; of the AVERY BLACK mystery series, comprising six books; of the KERI LOCKE mystery series, comprising five books; of the MAKING OF RILEY PAIGE mystery series, comprising six books; of the KATE WISE mystery series, comprising seven books; of the CHLOE FINE psychological suspense mystery, comprising six books; of the JESSE HUNT psychological suspense thriller series, comprising nineteen books; of the AU PAIR psychological suspense thriller series, comprising three books; of the ZOE PRIME mystery series, comprising six books; of the ADELE SHARP mystery series, comprising thirteen books, of the EUROPEAN VOYAGE cozy mystery series, comprising four books; of the new LAURA FROST FBI suspense thriller, comprising six books (and counting); of the new ELLA DARK FBI suspense thriller, comprising nine books (and counting); of the A YEAR IN EUROPE cozy mystery series, comprising nine books, of the AVA GOLD mystery series, comprising six books (and counting); and of the RACHEL GIFT mystery series, comprising six books (and counting).

An avid reader and lifelong fan of the mystery and thriller genres, Blake loves to hear from you, so please feel free to visit www.blakepierceauthor.com to learn more and stay in touch.

BOOKS BY BLAKE PIERCE

RACHEL GIFT MYSTERY SERIES
HER LAST WISH (Book #1)
HER LAST CHANCE (Book #2)
HER LAST HOPE (Book #3)
HER LAST FEAR (Book #4)
HER LAST CHOICE (Book #5)
HER LAST BREATH (Book #6)

AVA GOLD MYSTERY SERIES
CITY OF PREY (Book #1)
CITY OF FEAR (Book #2)
CITY OF BONES (Book #3)
CITY OF GHOSTS (Book #4)
CITY OF DEATH (Book #5)
CITY OF VICE (Book #6)

A YEAR IN EUROPE
A MURDER IN PARIS (Book #1)
DEATH IN FLORENCE (Book #2)
VENGEANCE IN VIENNA (Book #3)
A FATALITY IN SPAIN (Book #4)

ELLA DARK FBI SUSPENSE THRILLER
GIRL, ALONE (Book #1)
GIRL, TAKEN (Book #2)
GIRL, HUNTED (Book #3)
GIRL, SILENCED (Book #4)
GIRL, VANISHED (Book 5)
GIRL ERASED (Book #6)
GIRL, FORSAKEN (Book #7)
GIRL, TRAPPED (Book #8)
GIRL, EXPENDABLE (Book #9)

LAURA FROST FBI SUSPENSE THRILLER
ALREADY GONE (Book #1)
ALREADY SEEN (Book #2)
ALREADY TRAPPED (Book #3)

ALREADY MISSING (Book #4)
ALREADY DEAD (Book #5)
ALREADY TAKEN (Book #6)

EUROPEAN VOYAGE COZY MYSTERY SERIES
MURDER (AND BAKLAVA) (Book #1)
DEATH (AND APPLE STRUDEL) (Book #2)
CRIME (AND LAGER) (Book #3)
MISFORTUNE (AND GOUDA) (Book #4)
CALAMITY (AND A DANISH) (Book #5)
MAYHEM (AND HERRING) (Book #6)

ADELE SHARP MYSTERY SERIES
LEFT TO DIE (Book #1)
LEFT TO RUN (Book #2)
LEFT TO HIDE (Book #3)
LEFT TO KILL (Book #4)
LEFT TO MURDER (Book #5)
LEFT TO ENVY (Book #6)
LEFT TO LAPSE (Book #7)
LEFT TO VANISH (Book #8)
LEFT TO HUNT (Book #9)
LEFT TO FEAR (Book #10)
LEFT TO PREY (Book #11)
LEFT TO LURE (Book #12)
LEFT TO CRAVE (Book #13)

THE AU PAIR SERIES
ALMOST GONE (Book#1)
ALMOST LOST (Book #2)
ALMOST DEAD (Book #3)

ZOE PRIME MYSTERY SERIES
FACE OF DEATH (Book#1)
FACE OF MURDER (Book #2)
FACE OF FEAR (Book #3)
FACE OF MADNESS (Book #4)
FACE OF FURY (Book #5)
FACE OF DARKNESS (Book #6)

THE MAKING OF RILEY PAIGE SERIES
WATCHING (Book #1)
WAITING (Book #2)
LURING (Book #3)
TAKING (Book #4)
STALKING (Book #5)
KILLING (Book #6)

RILEY PAIGE MYSTERY SERIES
ONCE GONE (Book #1)
ONCE TAKEN (Book #2)
ONCE CRAVED (Book #3)
ONCE LURED (Book #4)
ONCE HUNTED (Book #5)
ONCE PINED (Book #6)
ONCE FORSAKEN (Book #7)
ONCE COLD (Book #8)
ONCE STALKED (Book #9)
ONCE LOST (Book #10)
ONCE BURIED (Book #11)
ONCE BOUND (Book #12)
ONCE TRAPPED (Book #13)
ONCE DORMANT (Book #14)
ONCE SHUNNED (Book #15)
ONCE MISSED (Book #16)
ONCE CHOSEN (Book #17)

MACKENZIE WHITE MYSTERY SERIES
BEFORE HE KILLS (Book #1)
BEFORE HE SEES (Book #2)
BEFORE HE COVETS (Book #3)
BEFORE HE TAKES (Book #4)
BEFORE HE NEEDS (Book #5)
BEFORE HE FEELS (Book #6)
BEFORE HE SINS (Book #7)
BEFORE HE HUNTS (Book #8)
BEFORE HE PREYS (Book #9)
BEFORE HE LONGS (Book #10)
BEFORE HE LAPSES (Book #11)

Made in United States
Orlando, FL
09 May 2022

17702684R00134